Praise for the
Flower Shop Mysteries

Nightshade on Elm Street

"Abby's warm and caring relationships, especially with Marco, will draw readers back as this cozy series continues to grow." —*Publishers Weekly*

"Pleasant and entertaining, just what a cozy should be.... Colorful characters and a bit of romance add whimsy." —*Romantic Times*

"An engaging cozy.... The investigation contains entertaining red herrings and twists ... a fun lighthearted whodunit." —Genre Go Round Reviews

"A delightful installment.... I can't wait to see what awaits Abby and Marco in marriage." —Fresh Fiction

To Catch a Leaf

"This story is multifaceted and complex and perfectly paced. There are twists and surprises along with the comfort of the characters we have all grown to love.... This story is a must read!" —Dollycas's Thoughts

"Ms. Collins has a devious and creative mind when it comes to each new Flower Shop mystery. Her plots are ingenious [and] Abby and Marco's chemistry is alluring." —Once Upon a Romance

Night of the Living Dandelion

"Great plotting and interesting secondary characters add depth and humor.... Abby and Marco's relationship strengthens and sizzles." —*Romantic Times*

"A heartwarming cozy.... Fans of the series will feel mesmerized by the plot." —Genre Go Round Reviews

continued ...

Dirty Rotten Tendrils

"Each book in this series contains murder, continuous mayhem, a bit of sizzle, and one justice-seeking amateur sleuth." —Once Upon a Romance

"Abby is an excellent heroine who finds herself in some of the most unlikely, entertaining situations."
—The Mystery Reader

Sleeping with Anemone

"A nimble, well-crafted plot with forget-me-not characters." —Laura Childs, author of the Tea Shop Mysteries

"A treat not to be missed."
—Kate Carlisle, *New York Times* bestselling author of the Bibliophile Mysteries

"Foul play fails to daunt a lively heroine who knows her flowers. A clever, fast-moving plot and distinctive characters add up to fun."
—JoAnna Carl, author of the Chocoholic Mysteries

Evil in Carnations

"Collins isn't losing steam in her eighth foray into the world of florist and part-time accidental detective Abby Knight. The fun, family, and romance are still fresh, and the mystery is tidily wrapped up, with just enough suspense to keep readers flipping pages."
—Romantic Times

"Ms. Collins's writing remains above par with quality and consistency: fun and breezy, intriguing and suspenseful, excitement and sizzle." —Once Upon a Romance

Shoots to Kill

"Colorful characters, a sharp and funny heroine, and a sexy hunk boyfriend."
—Maggie Sefton, author of the Knitting Mysteries

"Once again Kate Collins delivers an entertaining, amusing, and deliciously suspenseful mystery."
—Cleo Coyle, author of the Coffeehouse Mysteries

A Rose from the Dead

"The latest Flower Shop Mystery is an amusing graveyard amateur sleuth that will have the audience laughing." —The Best Reviews

Acts of Violets

"A delightful lighthearted cozy." —The Best Reviews

Snipped in the Bud

"Lighthearted and fast-paced, Collins's new book is an entertaining read." —Romantic Times

Dearly Depotted

"Abby is truly a hilarious heroine.... Don't miss this fresh-as-a-daisy read." —Rendezvous

"Ms. Collins's writing style is crisp, her characters fun ... and her stories are well thought out and engaging." —Fresh Fiction

Slay It with Flowers

"What a delight! Ms. Collins has a flair for engaging characters and witty dialogue." —Fresh Fiction

"You can't help but laugh ... an enormously entertaining read." —Rendezvous

Mum's the Word

"Abby Knight [is] rash, brash, and audacious. Move over, Stephanie Plum. Abby Knight has come to town."
—Denise Swanson, author of the Scumble River Mysteries

"A bountiful bouquet of clues, colorful characters, and tantalizing twists....Kate Collins carefully cultivates clues, plants surprising suspects, and harvests a killer in this fresh and frolicsome new Flower Shop Mystery series."
—Ellen Byerrum, author of the Crime of Fashion Mystery series

"As fresh as a daisy, with a bouquet of irresistible characters."
—Elaine Viets, author of the Dead End Job Mysteries

Other Flower Shop Mysteries

Seed No Evil

A Flower Shop Mystery

Kate Collins

AN OBSIDIAN MYSTERY

OBSIDIAN
Published by the Penguin Group
Penguin Group (USA) Inc., 375 Hudson Street,
New York, New York 10014, USA

USA | Canada | UK | Ireland | Australia | New Zealand | India | South Africa | China

Penguin Books Ltd., Registered Offices: 80 Strand, London WC2R 0RL, England
For more information about the Penguin Group visit penguin.com.

First published by Obsidian, an imprint of New American Library,
a division of Penguin Group (USA) Inc.

First Printing, August 2013

ISBN 978-0-451-41549-3

Printed in the United States of America
10 9 8 7 6 5 4 3 2 1

ALWAYS LEARNING   **PEARSON**

To my son, Jason, and my daughter, Julie

"No language can express the power, and beauty, and heroism, and majesty of a mother's love. It shrinks not where man cowers, and grows stronger where man faints, and over wastes of worldly fortunes sends the radiance of its quenchless fidelity like a star."

—Edwin Hubbell Chapin

ACKNOWLEDGMENTS

I would like to thank my friends Karen Monti and Renee Stanzione at City Traditions II and Fran Sackler of Frank Sackler Floral Designs for their assistance with the flowers mentioned in this book. As a "pretend" florist, I always welcome such help. I'd also like to shower appreciation on my Cozy Chick author friends, Deb Baker, Lorraine Bartlett, Julie Hyzy, Maggie Sefton, Leann Sweeney, and J. B. Stanley, for rushing in to help when a crisis hit during the writing of this book. And I couldn't close this paragraph without a ginormous thank-you to my soul sister, Barb Ferrari, who has always been there for me.

CHAPTER ONE

Monday mornings are the bane of most people's existence. I, however, view them as curtains going up on a brand-new play. So when I opened the yellow frame door with its charming beveled glass center and stepped inside my personal theater—that being Bloomers Flower Shop, located in the heart of New Chapel, Indiana's cozy town square—I couldn't wait to find out what the opening scene was going to be.

I entered Bloomers stage right and feasted my eyes on the scenery—a plethora of flowers in various arrangements, a veritable artist's palette of tones, tints, shades, and hues that covered the color spectrum. And then there were the sounds—telephone ringing, bell over the door jingling, and my assistants, Lottie and Grace, coming to greet me with their cheery voices.

"Abby, sweetie," Lottie said, her head of short brassy curls shaking a warning, "we've got a bad situation. Nine orders came in for funeral arrangements, and there's not a single lily in the cooler. I don't know what happened. I thought I ordered them on Thursday, but apparently I forgot. I put in a call to our main supplier, but the truck won't be here until later today."

"Abby, dear," Grace said in her lovely English cadence. "I'm sorry to add to your woes, but disaster has struck the coffee-and-tea parlor. The espresso machine gave up the ghost, and the clotted cream has curdled well beyond the pale. Also, the chap is here to install the security door in the rear of the shop but says the hinges are so rusty on the old one, it'll take him twice as long and require that the door stand open for a length of time. He charges hourly, by the way."

Not exactly the cheerful sounds I'd expected.

"Your cousin Jillian called," Lottie said, reading from a pink memo. "She said to tell you she'll be here tomorrow afternoon to something or other."

"What does that mean?"

"It means she mumbled so I wouldn't be able to understand her. I asked her to spell it and she said—and I quote—*I. T.* And then she snickered and hung up."

"And your mum is in the back," Grace added. "I believe at the moment she's supervising the door installation."

Cue the curtain guy and dim the lights. I want a refund on my ticket.

As every good thespian knows, the show must go on, and so must the floral business, for many reasons, the most important of which is to pay the bills. Besides, what could be so awful that it would take away from the joy of my upcoming marriage to the man of my dreams? Another of my mom's horrific art projects that she expected me to sell at Bloomers? More of Jillian's harping about my ad hoc wedding plans? Not a chance. Nothing could mar my complete and utter happiness.

"Why is Mom here so early?" I asked.

"We'll let her go into it, shall we?" Grace suggested, getting a nod of agreement from Lottie.

Grace, a diminutive sixtysomething-year-old, was wearing a pale gray skirt and a baby blue sweater set with silver earrings and a pearl necklace, all of which set off her short, stylish gray hair. Lottie, in contrast, a big-boned fortysomething Kentuckian, had on her traditional white stretch jeans with a bright pink T-shirt and deep pink Keds. Her choice of color, she claimed, ensured she was always "in the pink," which, as the mother of teenage quadruplet sons, wasn't an easy feat.

"Did Mom bring another art project?" I asked, hoping to mentally prepare myself.

"That's why she's here," Lottie said. "Go talk to her. She's upset."

I walked through the shop, stepped through the purple curtain into my workroom, and breathed in my nirvana. Although the space was windowless, the colorful blossoms and heady fragrances made the area a veritable tropical garden. Vases of all sizes and containers of dried flowers filled shelves above the counters along two walls. A large, slate-covered worktable occupied the middle of the room; two big walk-in coolers took up one side, and a desk holding my computer equipment and telephone filled the other side. Beneath the table were sacks of potting soil, green foam, and a plastic-lined trash can.

Beyond the workroom were a tiny galley kitchen and an even tinier bathroom. At the very back was the exit onto the alley, guarded by a big, rusty iron door that had needed to be replaced since probably sometime around 1970. That was where I found my mother, watching a man from the door store struggling with the hinge pins.

"Abigail!" Mom called, brightening. She stepped around the installer and came toward me, drawing me into a motherly hug, the kind she ended by leaning back to inspect me. "Did you have breakfast today? You look pale."

By pale, she meant my freckles were showing more than usual. Along with being a mere five feet two inches tall and having fiery red hair, I was also blessed—or cursed, depending upon my mood—with freckles, part of my Irish heritage. Erin Go Braugh.

"Lottie makes breakfast for us on Mondays, so I haven't eaten yet," I said. "Why aren't you in school? What's up?"

"I skipped the in-service meeting this morning. Can we sit down?"

Uh-oh. That was a bad sign.

My mother, Maureen "Mad Mo" Knight, had been a kindergarten teacher for almost twenty years and always said that after working with five-year-olds for that long, nothing could ruffle her feathers. Her caramel brown hair was always in a neat chin-length bob, her big brown eyes were a sea of cocoa calm, and her peaches-and-cream complexion glowed with good health. The worry lines in her forehead, however, were new.

I led her back into the workroom and pulled out two wooden stools just as Grace bustled in with cups of coffee and a plate of blueberry scones.

"Here you go, loveys. Lottie will be making breakfast in a bit, Abby, and I'll be off to pick up a new espresso machine. I should be back before ten, but just in case, be sure to keep your eye on the clock."

"Thanks, Grace." I took a sip of coffee and sighed with pleasure. "Delicious, as always. Do I taste a hint of cinnamon?"

She gave me a coy smile and glided out of the room. Grace never divulged her gourmet coffee recipes.

"Okay, Mom, tell me what's going on."

"I'm frozen, Abigail. I have artist's block, and that has never happened to me before. You know I'm usually brimming with ideas for a new project, but this time I haven't been able to come up with a single one that's worth anything. Not one! I sat in front of my pottery wheel for two hours on Saturday and stared at a lump of wet clay. The only idea that came to me was to make a clock in the shape of a giant tick, with tick hands."

"I'm not getting the reference."

"You know, a tick 'n' clock? As in a ticking clock?"

The light finally went on in my attic. "Now I get it."

"But not until I explained it. I'm telling you, Abigail, artist's block is terrible."

Not as terrible as actually making a tick 'n' clock.

Mom prided herself on her creativity. The kind of art she made was subject to change weekly because she was continually moving from one medium to the next, first trying clay, then plaster, followed by vinyl, feathers, beads, mirrored tiles, knitting yarn, felt, and finally back to clay. Mom completed a new piece each weekend, then brought it to my shop on Monday after school so we could put it out with our other gift items . . . if we dared. And because she truly believed she was helping us draw in customers, I never had the heart to discourage her.

"What can I do to help?" I asked, sipping the coffee.

"I was hoping you'd ask. I'd like you to find out what's going on in our local chapter of PAR. There's a rumor spreading among the members that the board of directors is considering changing the policy of their animal shelter from no-kill to kill."

"That's horrible, Mom. They're supposed to protect animal rights."

"Tell me about it," Mom said. "I can't stand the thought of homeless animals being put down. This could ruin PAR's reputation, not to mention all the good work our organization has done for this community."

PAR, which stood for Protecting Animal Rights, was a statewide organization with a large chapter that drew members from New Chapel and the surrounding towns. A few months back, I had helped PAR lead a protest against a proposed dairy farm factory. The megacompany behind it had a reputation for pumping its herds with bovine hormones to make the cows produce more milk. Unfortunately, it caused men who drank their milk to grow breasts. With my help, PAR had stopped the dairy factory in its tracks.

Because my mom grew up on a farm and loved animals, she'd been happy to step into my role at PAR when I got too busy helping Marco, my hunky husband-to-be, with his private investigation business. She'd led a few protest movements and had seemed delighted to be working with a charitable organization that could make such a difference in animal rights.

"Have you heard why the board would want to change the policy?" I asked.

"No, and I don't even know for certain whether the rumor is true. But if so, your father says it has to be about money. I know it's more expensive to run a no-kill shelter, but if this change happens, I can guarantee that our members will be outraged and our chapter may fold. Who'll raise funds to support the animal shelter then? It's in enough financial trouble as it is. Who'll protect the rights of all the innocent creatures that live within our boundaries? What if another megafarm wants to plant roots in New Chapel?

"Abigail, this situation is distracting me to such a degree that I can't create. And when I can't create, I get harried. And when I get harried, your father gets flustered and cranky and we argue all the time. And that distracts me even more. Do you understand why I need you to investigate?"

"I'm not sure how to go about investigating a nonprofit organization, Mom. Marco is the private eye."

"I was hoping he'd help, too. The reason I wanted to come by Bloomers on this particular morning is that the monthly PAR meeting is tonight. The meeting starts at seven o'clock and lasts about an hour . . . or longer if they're arguing, which they seem to be doing a lot of these days.

"There's a social gathering afterward, which would be the perfect opportunity for you to talk with the board members, especially our chairwoman, Dayton Blaine, as well as Bev Powers, our executive director. But you know who they are. I don't need to explain them."

Everyone in New Chapel knew who Dayton Blaine was. Her family owned Blaine Manufacturing, a company started by her great-grandfather, which gave her a lot of clout in town. Bev Powers was a town councilwoman who was in the newspapers constantly because she was always suing someone.

"Please say you'll help, honey. I need to know the

animals will be safely taken care of so I can get back my creative edge."

How could I refuse when she looked at me with those large, imploring eyes? "Will that take away the worry line between your eyebrows?"

"I'm afraid that's going to be a fixture until I see you and Marco happily married."

Seeing us married wasn't something Marco and I had planned to have happen. Dealing with my mom and Marco's mom, not to mention my fashion-plate cousin, Jillian, all of whom had decided how our wedding should proceed, had pushed Marco and me to the point of planning an elopement. This was especially true after our parents had gotten together and chosen a wedding destination cruise to Cozumel for the entire bridal party and guests, with our tickets as their wedding gift. Our honeymoon, as they saw it, would take place on the return trip. Imagine a honeymoon with an entire family present—make that our *crazy* families present. I was still having nightmares.

Fortunately, I had talked to my father in time to stage an intervention, and the cruise tickets were never purchased. Whew. We had compromised by planning an intimate wedding for immediate family only, followed by a private honeymoon, followed by a gigantic reception for all the relatives and friends who would be left out of the wedding ceremony.

"Mom, you don't need to worry about the wedding. My dress is ordered, invitations sent out, flowers chosen, and reservations made for the wedding dinner. That's the beauty of having such a small affair. Two bridesmaids, two groomsmen, and thirty people are super easy to plan for."

SEED NO EVIL   9

"I hope you won't regret having such a small ceremony, honey, but I am abundantly happy that you aren't
eloping. It would have broken my heart if I couldn't see
you and Marco exchange vows. You might be an adult,
but you'll always be my little girl."

The fear of breaking hearts was the main reason why
we'd changed our minds about eloping. Our moms and
my dad would have been crushed, and we just couldn't
do that to them.

Back to the subject at hand. "I'll talk to Marco during
my lunch hour and see if he's free to go with me to the
meeting. Do you want me to pick you up?"

"Thanks for asking, but on Mondays at five o'clock I
volunteer at the animal shelter, and sometimes I'm there
two hours, so I'll just meet you instead."

"It sounds like a plan, Mom."

"I'll feel so much better with you and Marco looking
into this," Mom said, giving me a hug.

"We'll do our best to find out what's going on."

On the minus side, what we would do with that knowledge was beyond me. Every case Marco and I had
worked on since we'd teamed up more than a year ago
had centered around a murder investigation. But being
creative was important to my mom and she was important to me, so we'd figure it out.

On the plus side, with my wedding coming up soon, it
was a *huge* relief to be working on an investigation that
had absolutely nothing—nada, zero, zip—to do with
murder.

CHAPTER TWO

By noon, Lottie and I had managed to fulfill all the funeral orders except the two that had specified lilies, and Grace had installed the new espresso machine and was operating the coffee-and-tea parlor full steam ahead. I'd added the Victorian-inspired parlor when I'd first purchased the shop more than a year and a half ago as a way to draw in more customers, and luckily, it had paid off. For many of the clerks and secretaries at the courthouse across the street, Bloomers was the first stop of the morning to get their cup of java and a scone.

I stepped into the parlor to let Grace know I was leaving and found her making the rounds of customers seated at the white ice-cream parlor tables, with the coffeepot in one hand and teapot in the other, pouring refills and chatting.

"Grace," I said, taking her aside, "I've got a meeting with Marco at the bar about my mom's situation. I've already told Lottie. I'll be back by one o'clock, well ahead of the Monday Afternoon Lady Poets Society get-together."

"I'd wish you luck, but you don't need it," Grace said in a whisper. "That darling man of yours will be delighted to help. Such is the power of love."

I found myself humming the oldie song "The Power of Love" as I stepped out on the sidewalk and headed north. It seemed impossible to think that in less than two weeks I'd be married to the man of my dreams and off on my honeymoon to gorgeous Key West, Florida. I had to pinch myself to believe it was all going to come true.

Feeling on top of the world, I squinted into the sunshine of the warm September day and smiled. I'd also never dreamed that I'd own a shop on the town square, and yet right behind me was a sign that said *Bloomers Flower Shop, Abby Knight, Proprietor.* After having failed to make a go of law school, I wouldn't have given two cents for my future.

I turned around to take a long look at the three-story redbrick building that housed my floral business. Bloomers was the second shop from the south end of Franklin Street, directly across from the big four-story limestone courthouse with its tall clock tower on top. Around the square were local shops, restaurants, banks, and law offices, all thriving even in a tough economy. I was thrilled to be a part of it.

With a happy sigh, I turned again and headed to Marco's establishment, Down the Hatch Bar and Grill.

Down the Hatch was New Chapel's favorite watering hole, a gathering place for the attorneys and judges from the courthouse, as well as college kids from New Chapel University. Marco had purchased the bar just a few weeks before I bought Bloomers, but of course I hadn't known him then. It wasn't until someone backed into my old yellow Corvette that I met Marco. He'd presented himself at Bloomers, offered his services as a private investigator to help me find the hit-and-run driver, and *wowzers!* We'd felt instant chemistry.

I opened the door, stepped into Down the Hatch, and glanced around for my fiancé. The bar had been decorated in a corny fishing theme decades ago, long before Marco became owner. There was a fake carp mounted above the long, dark wood bar, a bright blue plastic anchor on the wall above the row of booths opposite the bar, a big brass bell hanging from a post near the cash register, and a fishing net suspended from the beamed ceiling. I kept urging Marco to give the bar a giant makeover, but so far he was resisting, claiming his clientele would revolt if he changed a thing.

"Where's Marco?" I asked Gert, the petite, gravelly voiced waitress who had been there as long as the fake carp.

"In his office, hon. Last time I checked, he was on the phone dickering with a beer salesman. Want me to tell him you're here?"

"No, thanks. I'll surprise him."

The bar was busy serving lunch, so I stepped around another waitress carrying a big tray of food and headed past the row of booths to the hallway that led to Marco's office. I rapped lightly on the door, then opened it and peeked in.

"'Morning, Buttercup." Marco leaned back to stretch, lacing his fingers behind his dark, wavy hair, putting his hard-muscled torso on display. "Your timing is perfect. I just got off the phone."

He was wearing blue jeans and a formfitting gray T-shirt with DOWN THE HATCH running the length of one sleeve in white lettering. A sexy look, I thought, but then everything Marco wore made him look sexy to me. I gazed at him adoringly. He was ruggedly handsome, had dark, soulful eyes, and sported a light five o'clock shadow most of the day.

Marco had graduated from Indiana University, enlisted in the army and quickly advanced to the Army Rangers Special Ops division, where he served for two years. He returned to New Chapel, became a police officer, and a year later decided such a regimented life was not for him. Now, in addition to the bar, Marco had his own private investigation business, which I was gradually joining.

"Sit down and tell me what's on your mind," Marco said.

"How do you know something's on my mind?" I teased, settling into a black leather director's chair opposite his desk. "Maybe I just want to have lunch with you."

"Lunch with me doesn't cause worry lines between your eyebrows. Or at least it never did before. Should I be worried, too?"

I smoothed out the lines with my index finger. Who knew that worry lines ran in families? "Okay. It's true. Something's on my mind, but that's because something's on my mom's mind, and for once it's not our wedding."

"Shouldn't we be celebrating?"

"You'd think. But Mom is so miserable, Marco, I promised I'd help her, and I'm hoping you'll want to help, too."

He paused. It wasn't a long pause, but it was just enough to make me take notice, and in that split second, I wondered several things: Was he tired of hearing about my problems? Did he have an issue of his own that he wasn't sharing with me? Was it possible the upcoming wedding was weighing heavily on him?

Amazing what the brain can come up with in a nano-second.

"Why don't we talk about it over lunch?" he said, ris-ing. "You have that lean and hungry look."

Marco knew me too well. I wasn't really lean, but I was always up for a meal.

Over bowls of chicken and rice soup, I explained the situation at PAR to Marco, and as Grace had predicted, he agreed to attend the meeting with me, as long as his younger brother, Rafe, would take over for him behind the bar. His willing attitude calmed my former worries to the extent that I convinced myself I'd imagined that pause.

"I'll give Rafe a call right now," Marco said, and pulled out his cell phone. "He's not due to come in until three o'clock."

Rafe, or Raphael Salvare, was a ten-years-younger ver-sion of Marco. He'd come to town from Ohio half a year ago on orders of his mom, who had decided that if Rafe could drop out of college one semester before gradua-tion in order to find himself, she could send him to big brother Marco to help speed up that process. Marco had instantly put him to work, but it had taken several at-tempts at other kinds of employment before Rafe had decided he not only enjoyed the bar atmosphere but could actually tolerate working for his brother.

The plan was for Rafe to manage Down the Hatch once we were married, giving Marco time to focus on his PI business and, more important, time to spend with me. We'd come up with the plan because with my floral business, which occupied my day, Marco's bar business, which occupied his evenings, and his PI business, which could occupy any given hour of the day, we simply weren't seeing each other, and I knew that had to change to make our marriage work.

With a little encouragement from me, Marco had decided that the best solution was for him to keep ownership of the bar but let someone else manage it. Rafe had seemed like a good candidate for the job.

Marco ended his call and put away his phone, one corner of his mouth lifting in a half smile. "Rafe says hi and, yes, he'll cover for me."

The meeting was held at the old town hall, a redbrick building with black trim and shutters that had been built in the early nineteen hundreds. We entered the first-floor meeting room through big double doors at the rear and looked for my mom but didn't see her, so we took seats in back so she could find us. The meeting wasn't well attended, with only about fifty people in the room. Clusters of people sat in rows on folding chairs that faced a raised platform, the murmur of their voices filling the high-ceilinged room.

At the front was a table at which sat four women, with a podium to their right. I recognized one of the women as Chairman of the Board Dayton Blaine, a woman in her midsixties. She was taller than six feet and built like an army tank. Dayton had short, dark blond hair with a hefty showing of gray roots, a wide mouth, and a blunt nose. She wore a no-nonsense beige suit with an aqua blouse and an aqua and gray silk scarf around her neck.

Dayton was a well-known figure in New Chapel. Her prominent family owned a manufacturing business that employed what seemed like a quarter of the population, and their donations to worthy causes were legendary. People didn't usually cross the Blaines and, in fact, went out of their way to court their favor.

The other three women were unfamiliar to me, but the signs in front of them indicated that one was the board secretary, one the treasurer, and one the vice president. Like everyone else in the room, the four women, too, were talking, and no one appeared ready to start the meeting.

I checked my watch. It was ten minutes after seven o'clock, so I leaned closer to Marco and whispered, "I hope this isn't an indication of how the organization runs, or we'll be here all evening."

Finally, Dayton Blaine went to the podium and tapped her finger on the mic to see if it was on. After fiddling with it for a minute, she leaned in to it and said in an annoyed voice, "We apologize for the delay, but Beverly Powers is not here to run the meeting. I can't imagine why she's late and we're unable to reach her, so please bear with us for a bit longer. If she isn't here soon, we'll let Emma Hardy, her second in command, start it. Emma?"

At that moment, a woman of about my age came hurrying up from the rear of the room. "I'm here," she said breathlessly, taking a seat in the front row. She was tall and curvaceous, with thick, curly brown hair that seemed disheveled, as if she'd just jogged a mile. She wore a fitted black linen blazer over a pink blouse, with gray pants and black flats.

"You're late, too?" Dayton remarked, still sounding annoyed. "Is there something in the air tonight?"

People in the audience laughed lightly, as though they

weren't sure if Dayton meant it in a humorous way or not. The woman I assumed was Emma seemed not to notice. Once she was seated, she took a mirror out of her purse and pushed her hair into place, then checked her makeup.

"I'm going to call Mom," I whispered to Marco, taking out my phone. "She should be here by now. She hates to be late for anything."

I tapped in her speed-dial number and listened. The phone rang four times, then went to voice mail. I waited for the message, then said, "Hey, Mom, where are you? We're at the meeting."

"Maybe your mom is driving and doesn't want to answer her phone," Marco said.

"That's possible." Except that my inner antennae were vibrating, and when that happened, I knew to expect the unexpected.

While we waited, Marco and I chatted about his PI cases for at least another ten minutes until Dayton Blaine went to the podium again and said sharply, "We're going to start the meeting. Emma Hardy is PAR's development director and she's agreed to take over."

The young brunette with the disheveled hair rose from her seat in the front row and walked around the table to the podium, seeming much more composed now and, in fact, almost happy to be speaking.

"Hello," she said with a smile. "Thank you for coming to the monthly meeting of PAR. We'll start with the minutes from the last meeting read by the board's secretary."

As the elderly lady seated at the table on the stage rose, my cell phone vibrated. I pulled it out of my pocket and checked the screen. "It's Mom," I said to Marco, and slipped out of the room.

"Abigail," she whispered, a note of desperation in her tone, "would you and Marco please come down to the police station and pick me up?"

"The police station? Why are you at the station?"

"It's Bev Powers," she whispered. "She's dead. And I was the one who found her body."

CHAPTER THREE

"You found Bev's body?" I whispered back to my mom, motioning for Marco to join me. "Where?"

"At the shelter. I was the only other person there," Mom explained in a hushed voice. "It was awful. Poor Bev. But I'll tell you all about it when you get here. The police want to question me again. Hurry, Abigail. I'm nervous."

"Mom, if you think the police are harassing you, don't answer their questions. Remind them that Dad was a cop on the force, and if that doesn't do the trick, tell them you want an attorney, okay?"

"If you think that's necessary."

"Trust me on this, Mom. Remember, I clerked for a public defender, and by the way, if you want me to call Dave, I'm sure he'd be willing to come down to the station right now."

"What's happening?" Marco asked.

I covered the phone. "Beverly Powers is dead. Mom found her body, and now she's at the police station answering questions."

Marco already had his car key in his hand. "Let's go."

"Okay, Mom, we're on our way. Should I call Dad and let him know what's going on?"

"Not yet, honey. Better let me tell him when I get home."

My father, retired sergeant Jeffrey Knight, had been a cop on New Chapel's force for twenty-four years when a drug dealer shot him during a pursuit. The subsequent surgery to remove the bullet had gone badly, leaving my dad paralyzed and for all practical purposes wheelchair-bound. I was devastated, as was my mom, but my dad was stoic about it. He made the best of his life, setting an example for my two brothers and me. But back to the situation at hand, Mom was right. Better to tell Dad after the fact.

I ended the call and hurried out to Marco's car, where we took off for the five-minute drive to the police station. At the station, I found my mom sitting on a bench, looking pale and upset.

She sprang up as soon as she saw us and came forward to give me a hug, holding on tight for a long time and then stepping back with a heavy sigh. Her worry line was deeper yet, and her eyes troubled. "The police officer said I could go home, but I have to make myself available to come back down for further questioning. They fingerprinted me. Can you believe it?"

"I'm sorry you have to go through this, Mom," I said. "It's traumatic to see a dead body, especially when it was someone you know."

"Let's talk in the car," Marco said, and put his arm around her to escort her to the Prius.

We tucked Mom in the passenger seat and I slid in the backseat, leaning forward to talk to her. "Start from the beginning."

"Oh, let me think. I'm so distraught, it's hard to focus."

"Explain to Marco what you do at the shelter," I said.

Starting with a routine description seemed to help. "Every day after closing time at five o'clock, two volunteers sort through and distribute boxes of donated supplies to the various pet wards and play with the kittens and puppies to socialize them. On Mondays, that's Susan O'Day and me. Then around six thirty, we check to be sure all the cages are shut and the security lights are turned on, and we leave."

"Volunteers are in charge of locking up?" Marco asked, clearly surprised.

"That's the system. Today Susan couldn't make it, so I just concentrated on distributing supplies and playing with the kittens. Bev Powers was there when I arrived, and she told me not to bother locking up because she had work to do and would handle it when she was done. She asked me to let her know when I was leaving. So after I finished with the kittens, I checked the cages in the cat ward, then went into the back hallway where the administrative office is. I called her name, but she didn't respond, so I looked around in the office. Her purse was there, but she wasn't.

"I finally went to the dog ward and looked inside. I noticed that two cages at the back were empty. That was strange because I knew that the dog ward was full beyond capacity. The whole shelter is overflowing with animals. So I walked farther into the ward, and that's when I realized that those particular cages housed our red-zone dogs—animals that are considered dangerous and, in a regular shelter, might have been put down. We're a no-kill shelter, so the staff attempts to rehabilitate red-zone dogs. Then I noticed that the small doors at the back of those two cages were open. Those doors let the animals out into the exercise pen.

"I knew all dogs were supposed to be inside at night, so that concerned me. I tried calling the dogs, but there was so much barking going on, they didn't hear me. So I got a dog treat for each one and placed it inside the cage, then knelt down and whistled. I could see the dogs outside pacing nervously and sniffing at what looked like a mound of clothing—and then I saw it had legs!

"I called the police and they came right over, as did the veterinarian who helps care for the animals. He used a tranquilizer gun to drop the dogs; then I let the police inside the exercise pen. You can imagine my shock when I finally got a look at the body." She let out a shaky breath. "Poor Bev!"

"Mom, you're getting paler by the moment. Marco, let's stop at Starbucks and get her some iced tea."

"No, dear," Mom said. "I just want to go home. I'll get something to drink there."

We took her home and explained the situation to my dad while Mom changed into a soft robe and made herself a cup of chamomile tea. By the time she sat down on the sofa with us, she looked a little better, although her hands were still shaking.

"There was no reason for Bev to be inside that exercise pen, Jeffrey," Mom said to Dad. "Nor was there a reason for those two dogs to be let out of their cages after hours. It seems obvious to me that someone did it deliberately. Bev has certainly made enough enemies."

"From what you've described," Marco said, "it has to be someone who had access to the shelter and knew Bev was there."

Mom set her cup down with a clatter. "That could be me! She and I were there alone."

"You merely found the body, Maureen," Dad said, taking her hand in his. "Put that out of your mind."

I knew he was trying to reassure her. It wasn't possible to think the police would believe my mom could harm anyone, yet I knew better. Anyone connected with Bev's death would be on the suspect list until they were ruled out. With no eyewitnesses, no one to prove Mom had been in the cat ward, she'd be a suspect for sure.

"Did you hear the cops call it a homicide?" Marco asked.

"No. They were talking in hushed voices. But Bev knows—knew—animals. There's no reason she would have released dangerous dogs into the pen, then gotten in there with them."

"So," I said, "let's think this through. Sometime after everyone except you and Bev had gone for the day, someone forced Bev into the pen with the red-zone dogs while you were busy in the cat ward. But how and why?"

"Was it Bev's habit to be at the shelter at closing time on any other days?" Marco asked.

"I couldn't tell you, Marco," Mom said. "I'm there one day a week. But here's what I know about the shelter. Bev's sister, Stacy Shaw, is the manager, a position she assumed nearly a year ago to turn the shelter around because it had been mismanaged. Unfortunately, the town council is still getting a lot of complaints, but now they're about Stacy."

"What kind of complaints?" I asked.

"That the animals continue to suffer from the poor conditions. Bev has been responding to those complaints by stopping by frequently to see that everything is running smoothly."

"Has it made a difference?" Marco asked.

"Maybe a little bit," Mom said. "But the two main problems are lack of space and lack of adequate staff, and that can be solved only by more donations to PAR."

"Or by changing the no-kill policy," Dad added.

"Unfortunately, you're right, Jeff," Mom said. "The latest rumor is that Dayton Blaine is the one pushing for a policy change. She supposedly has the board on her side, as well as Stacy Shaw, and it was only Bev who was resisting. With her gone, I don't know what will happen."

"How could she have prevented a change?" I asked. "The board sets policy."

"Since Bev's no-kill stance was reported in the newspapers, she's been wildly applauded by the voting public," Mom explained. "That's her political muscle. Dayton would have had to convince Bev to change her mind, which would mean she'd have to persuade the members of PAR that it was in everyone's best interests, including the animals', to adopt the new policy. I'd heard the matter was going to be up for a vote at tonight's meeting. I'll have to call one of the other PAR members to find out what happened. I'm praying that they tabled the matter until the next meeting."

"Explain again who locks up at night," Marco said.

"Here's the normal procedure," Mom said. "At five o'clock, two volunteers come in and the staff members leave, locking the door that the public uses. It's up to the volunteers then to make sure everything else is locked up tight before they go home, which can be anywhere from six to seven o'clock."

"That sounds like a risky way of running things," Marco said.

"Actually, it's worked well for years," Mom said. "Naturally, the volunteers are trustworthy or Stacy wouldn't accept their help. She insists that all applicants are screened, and anyone who is accepted has to take a two-hour class on how to work with the animals."

"So tonight it was just you?" I asked.

"Right."

"When did your partner call off?" I asked.

"This morning. Susan suffers from migraines, and today was a migraine day."

"Was Bev's sister at the shelter at closing time?" Marco asked.

"Stacy was just leaving when I got there," Mom said.

"So we have Stacy leaving at five," I said, "the staffers leaving at five, and you preparing to leave around six thirty. Sometime in that hour and a half, Bev was killed. Did the cops mention how she died?"

"Not that I heard."

"Did you see the rest of the staff leave at five o'clock?" Marco asked.

Mom shook her head. "Only Stacy, whom I saw heading out the door."

"Did you hear any unusual noises while you were working?" Marco asked. "Were the dogs barking more than usual?"

"The dogs bark all the time, and the cat ward is some distance away, so I don't really notice that noise unless I'm in that part of the shelter." Mom paused for a sip of tea. "The cats and kittens meow a lot for my attention, and they're what I was focusing on." She glanced at my dad and sighed. "I'm exhausted, Jeff. What a horrible night, and I can't get the image of Bev's body out of my mind."

"How about if I make you a hot toddy, Mo?" Dad asked. "That should put you right to sleep."

"Let's take off, Abby," Marco said, rising. "We should let your mom rest."

"What will happen next?" Mom asked, as she walked us to the front door.

"You'll probably be called back to the station for another interview," Marco said. "And don't be alarmed if the police label you a person of interest. Once they check you out, you'll be off their list. You might want to have an attorney present just for your own peace of mind."

Mom gave Marco a hug. "Thank you. My biggest concern now is what the board is going to do about the no-kill policy. You'll still look into that, won't you?"

"You bet," I told her. "I don't want to see the policy changed, either."

"Were you and Bev friends?" Marco asked.

"Not really," Mom said. "Bev didn't have any close friends, just some hangers-on. I don't like to speak ill of the dead, because she did work hard for PAR, but she was a loudmouthed bully who caused a lot of people to leave the organization. I put up with her because I love helping animals. The bottom line is that Bev was not a nice person."

"You didn't say that to the cops, did you?" I asked.

Mom picked at a thread on her sleeve. "I might have said something along those lines."

Great. Mom was the last one to have seen Bev alive, and she'd made disparaging remarks about her. My antennae were up and waving, but I said nothing until we were on our way to the car.

"Marco, I think we should investigate, and before you say anything, here's why. One, Mom was there alone with Bev and, as such, was the last one to see her alive. Two, it sounded like Mom made it clear to the police she wasn't a fan of Bev's. Three, if we don't, Mom will worry even more and she'll never get back her creative edge. Four, I'd rather have to sell her art projects than hear her complain about not being able to make them, and five, if it's true about the change in the no-kill policy—"

"You don't have to convince me this time, Abby. I agree that we need to step in quickly and find out what happened for both of your parents' sake. Plus, we have a wedding coming up, and I don't want this to cast a shadow on it."

"Our wedding was my number six," I said, and threw my arms around him for a hard squeeze. "You're the best, Salvare. It's no wonder I'm madly in love with you."

He opened the car door for me. "So let's figure out our plan of attack."

"Wait a minute. I just said I'm madly in love with you. That was your cue to chime in with something along those lines."

"I'm a man of action, Sunshine, not a man of words."

I knew that, I thought, as I got into the car, but it didn't stop me from pouting just a little.

"Hey." He propped his elbows on the open window. "If you can't wait for the action, how about a little preview?" He leaned in and pressed his lips just below my ear.

I shivered in delight. "That'll work."

Marco went around the car and slid in behind the

wheel. "What do you say we plan our strategy back at my place?"

"That'll work even better."

Marco's phone buzzed, so he answered it with a snappy "Salvare here."

He listened for a minute, then whispered to me, "It's Rafe. We've got a problem at the bar."

There went the plan.

"Okay, Rafe, keep me posted. I'll be just a phone call away." Marco hung up and slid his phone back into his pocket, worry lines between his eyes now. I was beginning to think an epidemic was afoot.

"What is it, Marco?"

"Nothing. Now, back to our plan of attack. Here's what I'm thinking . . . or wait. Let's see how good you are at the PI business. Tell me what you'd do."

"Okay," I said slowly, forcing my brain back into work mode. "First, I'd find out the cause of death. Then, if the death is labeled a homicide, I'd try to get the particulars on how Bev died."

"Because?"

"Because that could indicate whether the murder was premeditated and give a clue about the person who's responsible."

"Good. And then?"

"Hold on. I'm thinking. Okay, I'd interview the staff at the animal shelter to see what I could find out."

"As far as?"

"Means, motive, and opportunity for each of them."

"Who else?"

"Next we turn to the family, especially the sister, Stacy."

"And then?"

I had to think for a minute. "Chairman of the Board Dayton Blaine."

"Okay, and there's one more major avenue we should look into."

"I've got nothing."

"Sure you do. What was Bev Powers infamous for?"

"Suing people. So we should see if she's got any current suits in progress."

"With what stipulation?"

"It has to be someone with access to the animal shelter. I'll get a list of volunteers from my mom."

Marco lifted his hand to give me a high five. "You've come a long way, baby, from that very first case we worked on together. So what do we do tomorrow morning?"

"Talk to our buddy on the force, Sergeant Reilly, to find out the cause of death. You'll make that call, right? He thinks I'm too nosy for his own good."

"Which you are, and that nosiness makes you a better PI."

"It helps that I have my very own private tutor. But do me a favor and point that out to Reilly when you talk to him."

Marco turned into my apartment complex's parking lot and pulled into a visitor's space. Turning off the motor, he said, "Let's get upstairs. Class is about to begin, and I'm not talking about detective work."

CHAPTER FOUR

Tuesday

I woke in the morning to the aroma of freshly brewed coffee and toast. In the kitchen, I found my roommate, Nikki, sitting down at the counter to eat, while her white cat, Simon, was underneath the counter chowing down his breakfast of canned tuna.

"Hey, big boy," I said, crouching to scratch him behind the ears. Simon stopped swallowing long enough to give me a *Can't you see I'm busy?* glance, twitch his tail, then resume eating.

"You're fickle, Simon. If Nikki wasn't here, you'd be winding around my legs begging for food."

Simon ignored me. I knew it was temporary. Tomorrow morning he'd be back.

"'Morning, Nik," I said on my way to the fridge. "What are you doing up so early?"

"I have to take my car to the mechanic's. It's making weird noises." Nikki was wearing her favorite purple pj's and looked like a tall, lanky version of Lisa Simpson, with her short, spiky blond hair sticking out at all directions. I'd known Nikki since third grade, when she skated past my house, tripped and fell, and needed first aid. We'd been best friends ever since.

"I didn't even hear you get up," I said, taking out the orange juice.

"You were snoring. No wonder Marco left so early."

"Was not. I don't snore. Marco had work to do, is all."

"Maybe it was me then."

It wasn't often that Nikki and I saw each other at breakfast because I hit the sack early and she worked from three until midnight at the county hospital, where she was an X-ray technician. I'd lived with Nikki since I got booted out of law school, when I showed up at her door with only a suitcase full of clothing. I'd thought my dramatic exit from law school was the worst thing to happen to me until my then fiancé, Pryce Osborne II, dumped me *for* getting booted out of school.

It had been a rough year.

But then Nikki had opened her home to me, and we'd been great roomies ever since. Now that was coming to an end, because after the wedding next Saturday, I'd be moving in with Marco, and Nikki would have her spare room back. And as much as I couldn't wait to get married, there was a part of me that dreaded leaving the cozy two-bedroom where Nikki and I had shared good times and bad. I was leaving a part of me behind that I'd never get back.

I put a piece of bread in the toaster and pushed the lever down just as my cell phone rang. I picked it up, checked the screen, and said cheerfully, "'Morning, Marco."

Nikki gave me a wave, so I said, "Nikki says hi."

"Hi, back," he said. "Listen, I just talked to Reilly, so I thought I'd share the news with you now. The coroner's preliminary findings lists multiple bite marks on the victim's legs, but the cause of death seems to be a broken neck. That's all he could tell me so early into the investigation, but it's enough to get going."

"But does that mean Bev was murdered?"

"It doesn't indicate it by cause of death alone, just by circumstance. It appears that Bev may have crawled up the fence of the exercise pen to get away from the dogs, then fell from some height. I'm going to make an educated guess and say that they're going to call it manslaughter. So let's start interviewing at lunch today—if you can get away from the shop."

"Unless we get a sudden influx of orders, that shouldn't be a problem."

"Okay, I'll pick you up at noon."

The call ended and I stared at the phone for a second. Wow. Marco was all business. He hadn't even said goodbye. It was another of those moments that gave me pause.

"Who was murdered?" Nikki asked.

"The executive director of PAR, Beverly Powers."

"That poor woman," Nikki said, rinsing her plate at the sink.

"I know. She died in the prime of her life. And it happened while my mom was volunteering at the animal shelter. She found Bev's body."

"Oh, your poor mom! I'm glad nothing happened to her."

I hadn't even thought about something happening to my mom, but now that Nikki brought it up, it seemed more evident than ever that Bev had been the target, not that it had been a random attack.

"I've got to run," Nikki said, "so catch me up on this later."

When I walked into Bloomers, Grace was in the parlor behind the coffee counter preparing for the customers who would line up just before nine o'clock. The scone's flavor of the day depended upon her whim, and today I caught a whiff of almond.

Grace Bingham had been attorney Dave Hammond's secretary when I clerked for him during my one year of law school, but she had decided to retire about the time I bought Bloomers. Her retirement had lasted two weeks, when, bored to tears, she came to work for me. Running the parlor was a labor of love for Grace, which was fortunate since I couldn't afford to pay her much.

"Good morning, Grace," I called, following my nose straight to the pile of delicious-looking scones on the counter.

"Good morning, love," she said, looking up. "How are we today?" Grace had once been a nurse and still often talked in first person plural.

"We are gearing up for a murder investigation. You know the little matter my mom came to me about yesterday?"

"About the trouble with the PAR group?" Lottie asked, walking into the parlor. She had her arms full of daisies destined for the glass display case in the shop. "I heard on the radio that Bev Powers was found dead yesterday evening, and they're calling the death suspicious."

"That's not all. My mom found her body."

"Oh, the poor dear!" Grace cried, hands to her face. "How utterly dreadful for her. But how did she come to discover the body?"

"She volunteers at the animal shelter on Mondays," I said. "It was after hours, and she and Bev were supposed to be the only two there, but someone forced Bev into an exercise pen with two dangerous dogs. It appears that she died trying to escape them."

"The radio said the dogs mauled her," Lottie said. "What a terrible way to die."

For a moment none of us said anything, imagining the horror that Bev had experienced. After a sad sigh, Grace said, "I do hope they're not treating your mom as a suspect."

"Not so far. Marco and I are starting a full-fledged investigation today to keep that from happening. No one is going to accuse my mom of anything but being a helpful citizen and calling in a crime."

Grace cleared her throat and took hold of the sides of her jacket in what we called her lecture pose. "As that brilliant scholar William Jennings Bryan once said, 'The humblest citizen of all the land, when clad in the armor of a righteous cause, is stronger than all the hosts of Error.'"

We clapped and she nodded regally. Grace was an amazing repository of quotations and took pride in having an appropriate quip for every occasion. I didn't always understand them, but I still appreciated her contributions.

"Sweetie," Lottie said, "are you going to have time for a full-fledged investigation, what with your wedding coming up and all?"

"I've got everything under control on that front," I assured her, "and I promise to keep the time that I'll be gone from the shop to a minimum."

"Everything under control, huh," Lottie snickered.

"That's what you said about your bridal shower. Remember how that almost turned out?"

"But this time it's different. I really do have everything lined up for the wedding. I only have to go for a dress fitting and make my bouquet and Marco's and his groomsmen's boutonnieres, which will be a piece of cake. And I've got almost two weeks. My goal is to find out what happened to Bev by the end of this week."

"Good luck with that," Lottie said. "You know what happens when you make plans, right?"

"I know," I said with a sigh. "It makes God laugh."

"Speaking of your dress fitting," Grace said, "a sales clerk from Betty's Bridal Shop called to remind you of your appointment. The memo is on your desk."

"Perfect," I said. "Really, Lottie, everything will be fine. We planned the wedding to be small and efficient so our families couldn't ruin it."

"Speaking of trying to ruin your wedding," Lottie said, "your cousin Jillian is coming over today. Want to lay bets what for?"

"Never mind Jillian," Grace said. "Tell us more about Bev Powers's death."

Over cups of coffee, I filled the women in on the details of the crime as I knew them; then we went our separate ways to get ready for the store opening. Back in my workroom, I had a chance to get online and read the full newspaper account, which the paper was already labeling a homicide. Unfortunately, the article also included my mom's name, so as soon as I saw it, I called their house to alert them.

"Hello, Abracadabra," my dad said when he answered, using my childhood nickname. Apparently I had been good at disappearing when it was time for chores. "Yes, we saw the newspaper and yes, the phone has been ringing off the hook. Luckily for us, we have caller ID so I can screen the calls."

"Good, Dad. Don't talk to any reporters either."

"I was a cop, Ab. I know the drill. I just wish your mom felt better. She's still really upset, but she insisted on teaching school today. I hope she's not hounded by the media there."

"If the reporters find out where she is, she probably will be. I'll send her a text message and tell her to alert the school administration of her situation so they can screen her calls there, too."

"Thanks, honey. She'll appreciate it. Keep me posted of any updates, will you?"

I hung up just as the bell over the door jingled, signaling our first customer of the day. I waited for Lottie's cheerful greeting but heard nothing. Assuming she was on the phone taking an order, I listened for Grace's *halloo*, but again, all I heard was silence.

Unable to stand the suspense, I pulled back the curtain and saw Grace standing in the parlor doorway, hands to her face, and Lottie standing behind the cash counter, jaw dropped. And then I saw Jillian, my newly pregnant cousin, wearing a loose shirt with something the size and shape of a large cantaloupe tucked underneath.

"Ugh," Jillian said, tossing back her long copper locks, "I've got to get off my feet. Carrying around five pounds isn't easy."

"Jillian, what are you doing?" I asked, stepping into the shop.

"Rehearsing. Duh." She waddled past me and disappeared behind the curtain.

I glanced at Grace, then at Lottie. Both stared at me in surprise, proving that Jillian had not lost her ability to shock and awe.

"Rehearsing?" Lottie whispered. "For a pregnancy?"

"This is Jillian, after all," Grace said.

Jillian Knight Osborne was my only female cousin and as close as a sister. She was a year younger, a head taller, and twenty pounds lighter, plus she had a mere sprinkling of freckles instead of a waterfall like mine. But our differences didn't stop there. Unlike me, who'd had a distinctly middle-class childhood, Jillian had grown up in a humongous house, vacationed in exotic locales, and had a father who is a stockbroker and a mother who golfed daily.

About the only thing we had in common, other than our surnames, was that we were both business owners, Jillian's being a personal shopping service that she operated out of her apartment. It combined her two favorite activities, shopping and spending money.

I trailed after my cousin and found her perched on a wooden stool at the worktable. Always the fashionista, my cousin wore a roomy top in a pattern of big red poppies against a white background and black linen pants. She carried a red leather purse trimmed in black. The outfit looked terrific even with the huge bulge in front.

"Why do you have to rehearse? Can't you just let the pregnancy happen naturally?"

"Not according to the book I'm reading by Dr. Ben Baybee. He recommends a well-informed, well-rehearsed transition into motherhood. See? I've even started my wardrobe." She lifted her top and showed me the maternity slacks she had on. Beneath the stretch fabric that covered her abdomen, I could see what appeared to be a small beach ball.

"That can't weigh five pounds," I said, and pressed against the ball with my fingertip.

"It's not a beach ball. It's a rehearsal ball, and yes, it weighs five pounds. I had to order it from Dr. Baybee's Web site. Once I'm accustomed to this one, I graduate to the eight-pound, watermelon-shaped size."

"Which you also have to order from his Web site, I'm betting. Are you sure this doctor is on the up-and-up?"

"He wrote a book, Abs. Of *course* he's on the up-and-up." She cradled her hands beneath the bulge. "This ball makes my back ache. Maybe I should unstrap it for a while. Do you want to try it on? You're going to have children soon after you're married, right? I mean, at your age you can't afford to wait long."

"Thanks for the reminder, but I'll pass."

"Suit yourself, but it's an experience everyone contemplating children should have." She paused. "You're at least contemplating children, aren't you?"

"At this moment, Jillian, all I'm contemplating is the next order on my spindle." Unfortunately, there were only four, but I wasn't going to worry. I had enough with all the wedding details. Speaking of which, I still had to work on my vows. Marco had written his a week ago. And had I confirmed our reservation at Adagios for our postwedding dinner?

"Abs," Jillian said, standing up and putting her hands on my shoulders. She crouched down to look me in the eye. Since I was five feet two, everyone had to crouch to look me in the eye. "Do you even know if Marco is in favor of children?"

"Jillian, we are not having this discussion. I have orders to get out and I'm sure you have somewhere to go." To prove that I was indeed busy, I snatched the order from the spindle and read it out loud. "A fall anniversary arrangement for a thirtieth wedding celebration."

"Okay, fine," she said with a pout. "Then let's talk about this minuscule wedding you're having. You *are* inviting my in-laws, right?"

"No, Jillian. It's just our immediate families, plus Lottie, Grace, and Nikki. I've already explained why, so I'm not going to repeat myself."

"How about your wedding dress?"

"Ordered. As is the cake that we'll be eating at Adagios."

"So there's nothing left to do."

"Nothing." That I wanted her to know about.

"What about my bridesmaid dress? Now that I'm pregnant, what if it doesn't fit?"

"You're not even showing yet, and don't you dare say you want to wear that ball under it."

At that, Jillian burst into tears and sat down at the table, laying her head on her arms.

"What's wrong?" I asked in alarm. "What did I say?"

"I feel so useless." She sobbed. "You don't need me, Claymore doesn't need me, and the baby doesn't need me. I'm blue and sleepy and grumpy and I don't know what else."

I tucked a tissue in her hand. "Come on, Jillian, you know it's just hormones kicking in. Doesn't Dr. Baybee talk about hormones in his book?"

"I don't know. I only got through the first chapter."

"Then go home and read more. I'll bet the doctor will clear it all up for you. Besides, don't you have clients to outfit?"

"No," she wailed, and laid her head down again. "I'm between clients."

I heard the bell over the door jingle, and then Marco's mother called out, "Good morning, everyone. What a *bellissimo* day, eh?"

Just the visitor I needed, another person not happy with the size of our wedding.

CHAPTER FIVE

A moment later, the curtain parted and Francesca Salvare swept into the room, taking in my miserable cousin in one glance. "*Bella*, Abby," she said, and kissed both my cheeks. Turning to Jillian, she said, "What is it, *bella*? Don't say you are no longer a bridesmaid." Then to me she said, "You *are* keeping your bridesmaids in this tiny wedding ceremony, yes?"

"I'm keeping my bridesmaids. Jillian is having a hormone surge."

Francesca Salvare, Marco's mother, was an energetic fiftysomething woman who could have been Sophia Loren's child. She had luxurious waves of dark brown hair, big brown eyes, an olive complexion, a sensuous mouth, and an hourglass shape. Most often she wore outfits in black, but today she had on a pale blue silk blouse with black slacks and sleek black flats, with jewelry to complement them.

Francesca had lived in New Chapel years back, when Marco and his five siblings were growing up, then had moved to Ohio after her husband passed away. Now she was staying with her daughter, Gina, Marco's younger sister, who had two very young children. Francesca was supposedly there to help Gina raise them, but I suspected her real reason for staying in New Chapel was to oversee our wedding.

"What is it then, Jillian?" Francesca cooed, draping one arm around Jillian's bowed shoulders. "Why are you so sad?"

Jillian merely shrugged, so I said, "She feels useless. She's in that early pregnancy stage where nothing much is going on except morning sickness."

"But I *am* rehearsing," Jillian announced, and rose from her chair to show off her baby bulge.

"Rehearsing?" Francesca repeated, giving me an incredulous glance. "For a big stomach? You need to rehearse for this?"

While Jillian explained Dr. Baybee's theory, I took the opportunity to slip into one of the big coolers to pull stems for the anniversary arrangement. I wanted to get all the orders done since I'd be gone over the lunch hour and I never knew how many would be waiting when I returned.

For the arrangement, I decided on a low-profile, oval-shaped light brown basket filled with gently muted blossoms, so I chose soft green and soft peach roses, white gladioli, sprigs of rosemary, a sprinkling of waxflowers, jasmine vine, and lily grass. The subdued hues and feathery foliage would capture both the romantic and sentimental feeling of the anniversary celebration.

I came out with my arms loaded and spread everything on the counter. My cousin and Marco's mom were gone, thankfully, so I was able to create to my heart's content. When Grace came in later with a cup of green tea for me, she informed me that Francesca had taken Jillian into the parlor for a talk and from there they had left to go shopping.

Breathing a sigh of relief, I started on the next order, and by the time lunch came around, I had cleaned off the spindle, confirmed my reservation at Adagio, and taken the time to organize my desk. I hoped there would be more orders waiting when I got back.

At noon, Marco picked me up and we headed to the animal shelter on New Chapel's southern boundary. Marco was unusually silent during the ride, and during my pauses in the conversation, he said nothing.

"Marco, is something wrong? You haven't uttered more than a few words since I got into the car."

"I'm just thinking about business. Nothing to worry about, Sunshine. Let's plan our strategy for the shelter."

"We've got about forty minutes to work with. Should we divide up?"

"I'm guessing there aren't more than a handful of people working, and I'd be very surprised if Bev Powers's sister is there, considering the state the family must be in, so I think we'll be able to get them all. We'll keep it to a preliminary questioning of the staff, alibis mainly, and I want to get the layout of the crime scene."

"Okay. But just so you know, it's all right if we run over a bit. I finished all my orders this morning, and Lottie's not taking a lunch break today. She's on a new diet, so she's skips lunch every other day." I took my sunglasses off and polished them with the hem of my shirt. "I haven't been able to finish orders in one morning in quite a while. I hope it doesn't mean I'm having a downturn in business."

"Hmm," was all Marco said, his mind clearly on that mysterious business matter again. Should I pester him until he told me or drop the subject and pretend I hadn't noticed?

Since I'd used the word *pester*, I'd obviously answered my own question. I held my glasses up to the light to make sure I'd gotten off all the smudges. If what was on Marco's mind was important to the two of us, he'd tell me eventually . . . I hoped.

The PAR Animal Shelter was a long, low-slung, yellow brick building that had once been an elementary school. It had sat unused for years until PAR had raised enough money to lease it, and now they relied on an annual fund drive to keep it running.

As we pulled into the parking lot, I caught a glimpse of a chain-link fence through a tall hedge at the back of the building. "The exercise pen must be behind the shrubs," I said, pointing it out to Marco.

"Let's check it out," he said.

We walked around the building until we reached a row of boxwoods that shielded the nine-feet-tall cyclone fencing on two sides, making it nearly invisible from the street. The pen was attached to the rear of the building, where a series of small doors cut into the brick wall led to the dog cages, just like the big cat house at the zoo.

"See this?" Marco asked, pointing to a latch about four feet off the ground at one end of the pen. "This end should swing open like a giant gate, but someone put a padlock on it."

We walked around to the front and entered the building on the right side, finding ourselves in a small, shabby reception area. Behind a wooden counter with peeling green paint on it, two women in kelly green T-shirts sat talking. Neither one looked up at our entrance.

"Excuse me," I said to get their attention.

Both turned their heads. Neither seemed surprised to see us there. "Can I help you?" one of the women asked in a toneless voice. If she wanted to help us, she certainly didn't demonstrate it.

"I'm Marco Salvare," Marco said, showing them his PI badge, "and this is my assistant, Abby Knight. We're investigating Beverly Powers's death. Would you have a few minutes to talk to us?"

The women looked at each other; then one of them said, "We need to check with Stacy."

"She's in today?" I asked.

"She just got here," the woman said, picking up a phone from its base.

I raised my eyebrows at Marco. Stacy was certainly dedicated to her job.

"There are two detectives here who want to talk to us," the woman said into the phone. "What should we do?"

Marco didn't bother to correct her about the detective label.

She put the phone back and said in her flat voice, "Stacy will be right up. You can talk to her about your investigation."

While we waited, I took the opportunity to look around. The room had three chairs in it, old green vinyl models that were cracked and brittle, with a square table in the corner, on which sat a faded blue ceramic lamp and a stack of magazines that looked like they'd been there for years. Animal posters, yellowed and curling with age, filled the dingy walls and paint flaked from the low ceilings.

"Are you clenching your jaw?" Marco asked quietly.

"I have the strongest urge to bring in a Dumpster and empty this room out," I whispered.

"May I help you?" said a voice behind us.

I turned to see a woman with short bouffant blond hair, heavy black eye makeup, dark red lipstick, a white lab coat, tight jeans, and silver sandals coming toward us. A tiny golden brown puppy was tucked in the crook of her left arm.

"Stacy Shaw?" Marco asked.

"Yes," she said.

He showed her his ID. "Marco Salvare. I'm a private investigator, and this is my assistant and fiancée, Abby Knight. We'd like to ask you a few questions about your sister."

With a frown, she asked sharply, "Who are you working for?"

"My mother is the one who found your sister," I said. "We want to be sure she's not labeled a suspect, so I guess you can say we're working for her."

"Your mom is Maureen Knight?"

Stacy had a way of snapping out her words that was slightly unnerving.

"That's right," I said.

"This won't take long. I promise," Marco said. "Just some routine questions for you and your staff. I hope it's not an inconvenient time. I understand you just got here."

Stacy hesitated for only a second. When Marco spoke with a slight upturn of his sexy mouth and a downturn of his soulful eyes, hardly a woman in the world could say no. "I suppose so," she said, "as long as you understand that I'll be leaving soon."

"We'll keep it brief," he replied in his husky voice, causing Stacy to smile at him in spite of herself. Marco was not above using his charm to get what he wanted.

"How many employees are here right now?" I asked.

"Four. Two are in back with the animals," Stacy said.

"We'd like to start with you, if you don't mind," Marco said.

Stacy straightened her shoulders and gave him a confident smile. "I'll take you to my office. Peggy, would you take Seedling in the back for his vitamins?" She handed the puppy to one of the women, then walked smartly up a short hallway.

In contrast to the reception area, Stacy's office was a cozy retreat. While still not decorated with expensive furniture, it was obvious she'd taken pains to make it comfortable. She had a cherrywood desk and chair and two chairs with wooden backs and upholstered seats that looked like they'd come from a dining room set.

Against one wall stood two bookcases filled with books about animal care, several framed photos of Stacy with two large dogs that looked like shepherd-collie mixes, and a collection of cat and dog sculptures of all sizes. Next to her desk was a small empty cage with a bowl and a furry blanket inside. It appeared to have been recently used. I wondered if it was for the puppy she'd called Seedling.

"Have a seat," she said, slipping off the lab coat to reveal a tight coral blouse underneath.

"We appreciate your seeing us at this difficult time," Marco said, taking out his small notebook and a pen, which he handed to me. "Please accept our condolences."

Stacy attempted to look appropriately aggrieved, but she didn't do a very good job of it. "Thank you. I'm still in shock. I hope you understand that I don't want to discuss the details of"—she sniffled and gazed at us with sad eyes—"you know."

"We'll be as tactful as possible," Marco said. "Frankly, we didn't expect to find you in today. Your devotion to your job is impressive."

"Actually, I needed to get my mind off"—she sniffled again—"you know."

"I'll get right to the questions so we can stick to our promise," Marco said. "I understand that you left at five o'clock yesterday while your sister was still here."

"That's right. Bev arrived about ten minutes before I left. She said she had some administrative work to do. That was the last time I saw her alive." Stacy pulled a tissue from the box on her desk and dabbed the corners of her eyes, which looked dry to me.

"Who was here when you left?" Marco asked.

"*Her* mom," she said, pointing to me, as though I should feel guilty about it. "Also my two employees, Brian and Carol, and the two women at the reception counter, sisters Sharon and Peggy, who left right after I did. In fact, I was in my car when they came out. I spoke with Brian and Carol today, and they said they left about five minutes later. Maureen Knight was the only one here with my sister when she . . ." Stacy let the sentence fade, as though she couldn't bring herself to say *died*.

"Do you know if anyone can corroborate their stories?" I asked.

"All my employees have spouses. I'm assuming they can give you the corroboration you need," Stacy said.

"And what about you?" Marco asked.

"Unfortunately, I don't have a significant other," Stacy replied, gazing straight at Marco as though she wanted to be sure he got the *available* message. "I've been divorced for thirteen years now."

Time for me to jump in. I scratched my nose so she'd get a gander at my engagement ring. "Did you go straight home?"

"I drove out to the mall in Maraville," Stacy said. "I was hoping to find a jacket to wear to the meeting. I feel it's always important to be properly dressed for business. It lets people know who's in charge." She ended her little spiel by sweeping her gaze over my khaki-colored short-sleeved shirt, which I had always liked until that very moment. I glanced over at Marco, who had on a neat button-down white shirt. Naturally, he looked very professional. I sank lower in my chair.

"Did you buy anything? Have any receipts?" Marco asked.

"No, I looked but didn't buy," she said.

So far, she had no proof of her alibi. "Did you see anyone you know?" I asked.

Stacy thought for a moment, then shook her head. "No one. That's not to say someone I know didn't see me, if it comes down to needing to provide an alibi, but why should it? I have no reason to want to harm my sister. I loved her. We were best friends."

"I understand," Marco said. "What time did you get home from the mall?"

"I didn't go home before the meeting. I stopped to grab a burger and went straight to the town hall."

I finished writing it down, then glanced at my watch. Marco caught the movement. "Just a few more questions," he said. "Did your sister have any enemies?"

Stacy laughed. "She was a politician. What do you think?"

"Are the enemies you're referring to political opponents?" Marco asked, and at Stacy's nod, he said, "What about more specific enemies? Someone who might have threatened her. Someone who she might have mentioned was giving her a hard time. Anyone like that come to mind?"

"Yes," Stacy said instantly. "Dayton Blaine and Emma Hardy."

I noted their names, then asked, "Do you think either one could have been a serious threat to her well-being?"

"There's been a great deal of animosity between Dayton and my sister for a few months now, and just lately there's been the same between Emma and Bev."

"Animosity doesn't necessarily equate to a threat to a person's well-being," I said.

"Animosity may not be the right word," Stacy said. "According to what Bev told me, Dayton Blaine has been blindsiding her on everything she wanted to do at PAR. I actually thought they were going to come to blows at one meeting. As for Emma, for the past week all I've been hearing about was how my sister was ready to fire her because of what Bev termed 'Emma's outrageous audacity.'"

"Audacity about what?" I asked.

"I don't know. She didn't share it with me."

"Do you think there was strong enough animosity between your sister and those two women for us to consider them potential murder suspects?" Marco asked.

Stacy toyed with a pen on her desk, her gaze averted. "Yes," she said slowly.

"You don't seem certain," Marco said.

At that, her gaze sharpened angrily. "I'm certain each of them had it in for my sister."

"Then what you're suggesting," Marco said, "is that a young woman just a couple of years out of college or an older woman who's an icon in New Chapel may be a murderer. Am I stating that right?"

Stacy again averted her eyes. "Maybe murder is too strong a word."

"In what respect?" Marco asked.

"Pulling on a cord to open a doggy door isn't like pointing a gun and squeezing a trigger," she said. "Maybe the intent was to scare Bev instead of kill her."

Boy, was she backpedaling. I was about to mention that to her, but Marco, levelheaded as always, took over.

"Would you explain how the cords on the cages work?" he asked.

"There is a cord on the outside of each cage that operates a doggy door cut into the back wall," Stacy explained. "Pulling on the cord opens the door so the animal can get out into the exercise pen."

"Is that the only way the doors can be operated?" Marco asked, as I scribbled notes.

"There are handles on the outside of the doors, too," Stacy said. "In cases where an animal gets overexcited, the staff can access its cage from the exercise pen."

"In your sister's case," Marco said, "how do you know that the dogs were released by pulling the cords? Couldn't they have also been released from inside the exercise pen?"

"Well, yes," Stacy said, "but who would be reckless enough to do that?"

I could tell by the way Marco shifted forward in his

chair that he was getting ready to make an important point.

"Then whoever pulled that cord," he said, "had to get your sister inside the pen and somehow prevent her from escaping before releasing a pair of vicious dogs. No one would view that as an act that was meant to merely scare. I can't say for certain, but the police may even call it premeditated murder."

I knew Marco's intent was to rattle Stacy, and it did indeed seem to have that effect. Her eyes widened and her lips formed each syllable of the word *premeditated* as though the idea astonished her. Then, as though she were grasping at straws, she said in a more hopeful voice, "So you're saying Bev was killed by a professional?"

"No," Marco said. "This was definitely not an experienced killer. In fact, it was extremely amateurish. The plan wasn't well thought out at all. What if someone had heard your sister's cries? What if she hadn't fallen from the fence? She might have been safe until help arrived."

Stacy suddenly burst into tears and covered her face. "She wouldn't have been able to stay on the fence. Those dogs jump high. They"—she sobbed harder—"pulled her down."

Why wasn't I moved by her outburst? Fake, perhaps?

CHAPTER SIX

Stacy pulled several tissues from the box and said through her sniffles, "It's hard to believe Bev was despised that much."

"Considering what I've said about how your sister died," Marco said, "do you still think Dayton Blaine and Emma Hardy should be suspects?"

Stacy nodded almost too eagerly this time, using a tissue to wipe her nose.

"Why is the gate on the pen padlocked?" Marco asked.

Stacy turned to drop her tissues in a waste can behind her desk. "We had a problem with neighborhood kids opening the pen when the dogs were out. The padlock took care of it."

"Who holds keys to the shelter?" Marco asked.

"Besides the staff and me, it would be Bev, Dayton, Emma, and the volunteers who come in after hours, so"—she paused to add them up—"that would be eighteen people."

"That's a lot of keys," I said.

"We all work for the animals' welfare," Stacy said. "There was never a reason not to give a trusted employee a key, and the volunteers have been screened."

"Has Dayton been screened?" Marco asked.

Stacy laughed sarcastically. "Dayton Blaine, from *the Blaines*? Of course not."

"Why does the PAR chairman need a key?" Marco asked.

"Ask her," Stacy said.

"And Emma Hardy?"

"She's PAR's development director," Stacy said, looking at her watch. "She comes here in the evenings sometimes to work on our computers. She's our Web developer. She set up our Internet Web site and does marketing for both the shelter and for PAR."

"Is there any truth to the rumor that there's a move under way to change this shelter's no-kill policy?" I asked. I felt Marco's gaze on me, so I gave him a glance to let him know I would make it quick.

Stacy looked away. "It's being considered."

"How seriously?" I asked.

"The board of directors is scheduled to vote on it at the next meeting. If they approve, we're ready to implement it."

"In other words, you're prepared to start euthanizing," I said, the thought nauseating me.

Wordlessly, she looked at me. Thank God there was still time to organize a protest.

"Who's pushing for this change?" I asked.

Marco cleared his throat, impatient to move forward.

"The board of directors," Stacy said.

"Was your sister in favor of it?" I asked.

"No," Stacy said, glancing at her watch.

"I noticed your dog photos back there," I said. "You strike me as an animal lover. Surely you can't be in favor of euthanasia."

Stacy lifted her chin, a sure sign of defiance. "I'll do whatever is fiscally best for the shelter. Our goal is to keep it running so we can help as many animals as possible."

"*Help,* as in putting healthy animals down?" I asked, and felt Marco give me a nudge.

With a scowl, Stacy pushed her pen aside, clearly uncomfortable with my questions. "Yes, if that's what it takes. Now I really need to leave."

"Can you think of anything else we need to know to investigate your sister's death?" Marco asked.

"Yes," she said without hesitation. "Don't let Dayton Blaine's money and influence in this town deter you from asking tough questions. Same with Emma Hardy's innocent act. She's not, believe me." Stacy thought for a moment. "That's it."

"Here's my business card," Marco said. "Please call if you think of anything else."

Stacy put his card on her desk. "I will. Thanks."

"And thank you for your candid answers," Marco said. "We'd like to talk to the two workers in the back next, and if it's possible, get a look at the dog ward."

Stacy rose. "I'll take you there."

As we followed her up the hallway, Marco said to me quietly, "Do me a favor. Stick to the subject this time."

I didn't have time to reply, so I just gave him a scowl. Stacy stopped in front of a warped wooden door with a window in it, tapped on the glass, then waved someone over.

"Brian can show you around," she said, opening the door to barking dogs and the strong smell of animal fur, Lysol, dog food, and urine.

We stepped into a room crammed with cages—large cages standing alone, small cages stacked on top of one another. Every cage housed at least one dog, depending on its size, and they all wanted to sniff us. It appeared as though the area had once been two classrooms with walls removed between them. Judging by the number of dogs contained in the room, they could have used a space double or triple that size, and I immediately felt sorry for the cramped animals.

Stacy introduced Brian, a young man with thick, curly black hair, thin sideburns, black-rimmed glasses, and an honest face. He had on a green T-shirt with the PAR logo and worn blue jeans with sneakers. He didn't shake our hands because he said he'd been working with the dogs and didn't want to get us dirty.

"Answer any questions they have," Stacy directed, and saying a quick good-bye, shut the door behind her. I had the feeling she couldn't get away fast enough.

"Where are the pens that the two dangerous dogs were in?" Marco asked.

"You mean *are* in," Brian corrected. "We still have them. We're a no-kill shelter, at least for now."

"You still have the dogs?" I asked.

Brian pointed to the end of the row. "We're not supposed to let anyone near them. They're quarantined."

"Are they that dangerous?"

"They're just highly excitable," Brian explained. "It doesn't take much to rile them."

"Were they used as fighting dogs?" Marco asked.

"I'm guessing they were guard dogs," Brian answered.

"We found them tied to the front door handle one morning, poor guys. We were hoping to rehabilitate them and adopt them out, but that's all in question now. I guess a judge has to decide or something."

"Would you explain how a dog gets into the exercise pen?" Marco asked.

"See the cord here?" He pointed to the end of a white cord visible at the top of the cage. "As you pull it, the door in the back lifts. It's just like raising a shade. You pull the cord until it catches, then tie it around this wing nut."

"Looks kind of haphazard," I said.

"Yeah," Brian said, scratching his head. "Kind of how this whole shelter is. I mean, it was designed as a school. We've had to jury-rig a lot of it. There's always talk of finding a better space, but so far that's all it's been. Talk. I'm just hoping they keep it a no-kill shelter."

"Why do you say that?" Marco asked.

He put his hand to one side of his mouth to whisper, "Certain people want to change the policy."

"Who would that be?" I asked.

Brian shrugged one shoulder. "I can't say. It's my job, you know?"

"Is it your boss?" I asked.

At that, Brian's face stiffened. "I really don't want to say."

"Who has access to this room?" Marco asked.

"Anyone with keys to the shelter," Brian said.

"Who has access to the exercise pen?" Marco asked.

"Anyone in the building, if they know where to find the key," Brian said.

"Tell me where to look," Marco said.

"Down at the end of the main hallway, there's a door that takes you outside and straight into the pen," Brian explained. "Beside the door are two keys hanging from a nail. One works the lock on the door, and the other works the padlock on the outside gate into the pen."

"Does the door automatically close behind anyone entering the pen?" Marco asked.

"No. It has to be locked from the inside," Brian replied.

"Does everyone with access to the shelter know about those keys?" Marco asked.

"Yep," Brian said. "A tour of the facility is part of the two-hour training class."

"Are those the only keys to the pen and gate?" Marco asked.

"There's another set in Stacy's office," Brian said.

"Did you go home after you left work yesterday?" Marco asked.

"Straight home. My wife can verify that."

"Who usually cares for the dogs?" I asked, craning my neck to get a look at the red-zone dogs. I saw two mostly black German shepherds, both beautiful animals.

"That's my job," Brian said, pointing to his chest. "When I'm sick, Carol can do it, but she's really better with the cats."

"So it's just you two caring for all these animals?" Marco asked.

"For the time being at least. That's all PAR can afford."

"Why don't they use more volunteers?" I asked.

"We used to, but then Stacy decided there were too many people who came only to play with the kittens and puppies and didn't want to do any work." He shrugged. "It is what it is, I guess. Carol and I do the best we can. All I can say is thank God this is a small shelter."

"Okay. Thanks, Brian," Marco said. "You've been a big help. Would you take us to Carol?"

We were led to a room that was identical to the first, except that it was on the front side of the building and there were more cages, though they were smaller. At the back were two large pens that housed the kittens, and it was all I could do not to open one and climb in, but I knew I'd probably end up going home with an armful, and Nikki's cat, Simon, would definitely not welcome the company.

Carol was a small woman in her midthirties with brown hair pulled back in a ponytail, no makeup, the same green T-shirt that the other staffers wore, with black jeans and sneakers. She answered the same basic questions we'd asked Brian with the same responses, prompting me to write "Ditto Brian" in Marco's notepad.

Our next stop was the reception desk, where we asked the Friendly Sisters if anyone could verify their whereabouts after they'd gone home for the evening. Both gave their husbands' names and acted highly indignant about being questioned. Marco didn't bother asking them anything else.

"So what did we learn?" he asked on our ride back to Bloomers.

"That I need to call my mom so she can organize a protest march and that I'm going to need to eat something when I get back. Other than that, let me get out the notes."

"A protest march because of the euthanizing?"

"You bet. We've got to stop that from happening."

"Sunshine, let your mom worry about that. We've got a wedding coming up, remember?"

"You're right. I'm sure Mom can handle it without me."

"What did you think of Stacy?"

"Too early to make a judgment call, but off the top of my head, it seemed odd that she was so dry-eyed after just losing her beloved sister-slash-best-friend. Also odd was that she didn't know what Dayton had done to make Bev so angry and why Bev wanted to fire Emma. I mean, if Bev ranted about Emma in front of her, you'd think she'd tell her why. And wasn't Stacy quick to name Emma and Dayton Blaine as suspects? Exceedingly quick?"

"But you're not ready to make a judgment call?" Marco teased.

"Ha. You caught me. Okay, I'd call her a viable suspect. Stacy has no proof of her alibi, just her word that she went to the mall."

"What's your gut feeling about her?"

"I don't trust her. I don't think she's being up-front with us."

"About what specifically?"

"First, about her sister being her best friend. If they were close, Stacy would be red-eyed and crying at the mere mention of her sister's tragic death. Instead, she grimaced twice. It wasn't until she described the gruesome detail that did her sister in that she showed any emotion, and I'm still not sure that was real.

"Second, she basically called Dayton Blaine and Emma Hardy killers, then backpedaled, like she was trying to find a way to soften her accusation. And would she really come into work the day after her sister died? Shouldn't she be calling family or making funeral arrangements or something?

"Then there was her defensiveness when I asked about the change in shelter policy. That woman loves animals.

Did you see how she was cuddling that puppy when she first came up to the front counter? I'll bet she keeps the dog in the cage beside her desk while she's in the office. And she had several photos of her with two big dogs. That's not a woman who would push for a kill shelter. So why did she lie about it?"

"Good," Marco said. "Then we're on the same page."

I loved being on Marco's page. "Who's our next interviewee?"

"Dayton Blaine, if I can pin her down."

"Doesn't she work for the Blaine family business? Can't we find her there?"

"She's a member of the board there. I don't think either she or her siblings work, per se. The problem is that she serves on many boards, so she's always on the go."

"If you can get her on the phone, you can pin her down, Marco. You know how to use your charm."

"We'll see. Dayton may be used to people trying to work their charms on her. It goes along with the territory of being megarich."

My cell phone rang and I checked the screen: Jillian. I took a deep breath to psych myself up for the call. "Hello, Jillian. What's going on?"

"Abs," she said in a chiding tone, "know what I learned today? That Dr. Baybee has a word for people like you."

"People like me? What did I do?"

"It's not what you *did*; it's what you're *not* doing."

"Okay, I'll bite. What am I not doing?"

"You're not supporting my intention to rehearse my pregnancy. You're what is known in the industry as a non-supportress. A *non-supportress,* Abs."

"I'm a non-supportress," I said to Marco.

"Sounds like a bad mattress," he said.

"Do you know what having a non-supportress around a pregnant woman can result in?" Jillian asked.

"No, but I'm sure you'll tell me."

"Gastric distress and depression. *Depression,* Abs! Does that ring a bell?"

More like the scrape of nails down a blackboard.

"What Dr. Baybee is saying is that it's not hormones causing my problems, Abby Knight. It's you."

"So what can I do to help you, Jillian?"

"Embrace the ball. That's what Dr. Baybee says."

"What does that even mean?"

"Pretend that the ball is a real baby growing in my womb. That's all. See how simple that is?"

I had no choice but to say yes or those nails would just keep on scraping that blackboard. "Fine, Jillian. I'll embrace the ball. Does that make me a supportress?"

"Wait."

I could hear pages turning; then she said, "Now you're an embracer."

"I'm relieved."

"Okay, that's all I wanted," Jillian said happily, and hung up.

"What was that about?" Marco asked, as he pulled up in front of Bloomers.

"Jillian thinks that I'm the cause of her depression because I wasn't supporting her pregnancy rehearsal, and do you really want to hear this story? If you do, I'll fill you in at dinner. We are having dinner together, aren't we?"

"Um," he said, "let me get back to you on that."

I hadn't imagined *that* pause.

Gripping the door handle, I stopped to glance over at him. He'd get *back* to me? I felt like one of his beer reps.

But Marco was checking his cell phone for messages and didn't even notice, so I got out of the car and shut the door. "See you," I said through the open window, leaving off the word *later*.

"Okay, babe," he replied without looking up.

I waited on the sidewalk outside the flower shop until he pulled away, hoping for a wave. He never even looked over.

CHAPTER SEVEN

Back inside Bloomers, the coffee-and-tea parlor was filled with customers, which was great to see, since the front shop was empty. Lottie was using the time to dust the shelves while Grace handled the parlor with her usual aplomb.

"Hey, sweetie. How'd it go at the shelter? Did you have time to get everyone interviewed? And why is there a wrinkle between your eyebrows?"

"Because I inherited this stupid wrinkle from my mom, and I'm not happy about it."

"Seriously, Abby," Lottie said, coming toward me. "Did something happen? You look concerned."

"Nothing happened, per se, but I think Marco might be"—I shrugged a shoulder to show that it wasn't a big deal, which was a bald-faced lie—"keeping things from me."

"What kind of things?"

"Business problems maybe? Or personal? I don't know, but whatever problems he's having, he's not sharing, Lottie, and that hurts. Doesn't he trust me?"

Lottie guffawed, just the kind of reaction I was hoping for. "Sweetie, that man is crazy about you. What's he doing that makes you think he's keeping things from you?"

"Lately he seems distracted and not interested in what I have to say. And just now, when I asked him about us having dinner together, which we almost always do, he said he'd get back to me."

"Who said he'd get back to you?" Grace asked, stepping out of the parlor.

"Marco," Lottie said. "He's distracted, and Abby thinks he's keeping his problems from her."

"She shouldn't worry about it," Grace said, "because he's made it clear he's madly in love with her."

"That's just about what I told her," Lottie said.

And exactly what I wanted to hear.

"Did you tell her that men are easily distractible?" Grace asked.

Suddenly I felt like I'd stepped out of the room. "Hello. I'm still here. You can talk directly to me."

"Abby, dear," Grace said, putting her arm around my shoulders, "you mustn't take every little thing as a sign that something's amiss."

"I don't take every little thing as a sign, but there've been a *few* of these little signs and they're starting to add up. It isn't like Marco to ignore me, which is what it feels like he's doing. I mean, I thought I knew him, but lately—"

"Ah, there's the problem," Grace said to Lottie. "Do you see it?"

"You betcha," Lottie said.

Having no sweater edges to hold, Grace folded her hands together and put her shoulders back, assuming her alternate lecture pose. "As that wise man Friedrich

Nietzsche once said, 'One should never know too precisely whom one has married.' And what that means is, you'll never know Marco completely, nor should you want to. Let him be a little mysterious. You're always going to discover new things about him, and perhaps one of those things is that he doesn't always pay attention. I've practically got to stand on my head to get my Richard's attention during a sports game."

"And I've told Herman my birth date a hundred times," Lottie said, "but he always gets it wrong. Thing is, he doesn't do it on purpose. He just has a lousy memory."

"So you're saying I should ignore it when Marco doesn't listen?"

"Unless it becomes habitual," Grace said. "Then it would need to be addressed. Always keep those lines of communication open, love."

I let out a sigh of relief. "Thank you both so much. I feel much better now."

"Then our work here is done and I must get back to my customers," Grace said. "I could use a hand in there, Abby, if you wouldn't mind."

I was about to ask Lottie if I had orders waiting, but before I even opened my mouth, she gave a little shake of her head, so I followed Grace into the parlor and grabbed a pot of coffee.

Bummer.

At three thirty, the bell over the door jingled, and I heard my mom's voice up front, so I left my cleaning project in the workroom and stepped through the curtain. In Mom's hand was a large plastic bag, which she held up with a smile.

"Guess what I've been doing, Abigail."

"I hope you're going to say working on an art project." Wait. Had I actually said that?

"Yes!" she exclaimed excitedly. "I felt so much better knowing you and Marco were on the case that I stayed up late working. This is just a prototype, but I wanted you to see it before I made any more."

As always when Mom showed me a new project, my stomach knotted, knowing she would ask me to sell it in the shop and that I probably wouldn't want to. Once she'd made a footstool that looked like a giant bare foot, toe hair and all. Another time she'd made a hat stand that looked like a giant bowling pin with a Homer Simpson face, with pegs sticking out of his neck, à la Frankenstein. And then there was the beaded jacket, made out of giant wooden beads, and the brightly hued feathered picture frames. So I braced myself as she pulled something out of the bag.

"Ta-da!" she said, holding out a rooster-shaped water pitcher.

It looked remarkably like the one on a display shelf behind her, which was handcrafted in Italy. My version had a rose-colored cock's comb, a soft yellow beak, and a leafy vine in a pale green that twined around it. The top was open, as was the rooster's mouth, which functioned as a spout. I had it displayed as a vase.

Mom's rooster, on the other hand, had a bright red cock's comb, a shocking yellow beak, and neon green leaves on the twining vine.

"What do you think?" she asked, hope shimmering in her eyes.

Bunching my shoulders into an *I'm so sorry; please don't hate me* shrug, I pointed to the pitcher behind her.

She turned around, saw the Italian version, and her

shoulders slumped. We Knights were definitely shoulder people. I wondered if the medieval armor makers had problems suiting up my relatives.

"Well, that's that," she said dejectedly, letting her rooster dangle from her fingers. "I still don't have my creativity back."

"You'll get it," I said, putting my arm around her. "Give it time. And meanwhile, I have a request. Would you make a list of all the volunteers who work at the shelter? With phone numbers?"

"Of course, honey. Anything to help."

"While we're on the subject," I said, "did you hear that the vote to start euthanizing was postponed until the next board meeting?"

"Yes, I heard it from Susan O'Day, and we've already organized a protest for the meeting."

I gave her a hug. "I knew you'd be on top of this."

"I'm worried, though, Abigail. When Dayton Blaine pushes for a change, she's usually powerful enough to make it happen."

The phone rang and Lottie answered at the cash counter. "Bloomers Flower Shop. How may I help you?" She listened a few moments, then said, "Until five o'clock. You're welcome." She hung up and glanced at me with a smile. "Wedding customer coming in later."

If my mom hadn't looked so down in the dumps, I would have done a pirouette.

At five minutes before five o'clock, Marco called to see what time I would be down for supper, as though there had never been a question about me coming at all.

"I can be there in five minutes," I said. "Business has been slow today."

Not only slow, but disappointing. The wedding customer was interested only in shopping for prices, so she'd been in and out in thirty minutes.

"Good," he said, which I thought was pretty insensitive. Or was it just another example of him not paying attention? "I've got an appointment set up with Emma Hardy here at six, and that will give us time to plan beforehand."

"She agreed to meet at the bar?"

"She seemed pretty eager to clear her name. She said she and her friend were looking for a place to eat anyway, and she'd never been to Down the Hatch."

"Okay. I'll see you in a few."

The bar wasn't busy yet when I got there, so Marco and I were able to grab the last booth in the row, or "our booth" as we called it, and have a quiet meal. It would have been quieter except I kept up a steady stream of chatter to fill the blank spaces, because again, Marco seemed distracted until we began to discuss the murder investigation.

"From what I could find out about Emma Hardy," Marco said, reading from his notes, "she's had the position of developmental director for a little more than a year. Before that, she worked at a marketing firm in Maraville for just over a year, and before that she was in college. She's single, an only child, and has an apartment here in town.

"Also, I spoke with Reilly about the police investigation. So far they've done basic interviews but are waiting for more autopsy and tox results before they go any further."

"Tox results? Do they think Bev might have been drugged?"

"Toxicology reports are standard police practice. The main thing is that we're ahead of them, which is exactly what we want. How's your mom doing?"

"Still nervous but relieved that we're investigating. On a different topic, we never finished our discussion on how all my clothes are going to fit in your apartment."

"They'll fit. I'm cleaning out drawers and my closet is half empty."

As though that would be enough room. Marco had so much to learn.

He checked his watch. "If you want to freshen up before Emma gets here, you'd better go now. I'll go get the notepad and pen."

When I returned from the washroom, Emma had already arrived. She looked curvy and cute in an aqua off-the-shoulder knit top. Taking in her glistening, wavy golden brown hair falling onto her bare shoulders and her peaches-and-cream complexion, I suddenly felt every freckle on my face and, but for my hair, totally colorless in my drab shirt and khaki pants. It made me wish I'd brought a change of clothing to work. And maybe a mask.

I slid in next to Marco and reached out my hand to Emma as he introduced me.

"Emma Hardy, this is Abby Knight," he said, putting his arm around me. "She's my assistant and my fiancée and owns Bloomers Flower Shop."

He said that with so much pride, I didn't feel quite so colorless. Still freckled, though, especially when I shook Emma's creamy-skinned hand.

We exchanged the normal pleasantries; then Gert came to take our drink orders, which Marco said were on the house. "A peach margarita for me," Emma said in a way that made the drink sound exhilarating.

"I'll just finish my beer," I said. Boring, colorless Abby.

"I *love* your mother, Abby," Emma gushed. "I got to know her at one of our rallies. She is *so* sweet. You're *so* lucky to have her. My mom is bor-*ing*."

That was one thing I couldn't say about my mom. Anyone who could create a Dancing Naked Monkeys Table was definitely not boring.

Emma gazed at me with twinkling blue eyes, waiting for my bright, bubbly response. I had a feeling she'd been a cheerleader in high school.

"Thanks." That was all I had. Super-exuberant women like Emma stunned my system.

"Let's get started," Marco said, sensing that I was not on my game. "We appreciate your meeting with us, Emma. As I told you on the phone, we want to make sure Abby's mom isn't considered a suspect, so we're taking precautions by running our own investigation."

"All my mother did was find a body and call it in," I felt compelled to add.

"Oh, for sure," Emma said. Her hands were folded on the table in front of her. I was sitting on mine. "I *totally* get it. I'm just relieved you're not looking at me as if I had something to do with Bev's death. I mean, me? Really?" She held out her arms. Apparently that was so we could see she wasn't carrying any weapons in her armpits.

"Bev was my boss," she continued, "and we had a solid working relationship. I did everything she asked and more. Isn't that the kind of employee everyone wants?"

She focused her smiling face and twinkling eyes first

on Marco, until she got his nod of agreement, then on me. I quickly obliged, though a red flag went up. Why was she trying to convince us that she was a wonderful employee? Could it have anything to do with what Stacy had told us about Bev wanting to fire her? Was Emma laying groundwork in case we'd heard anything?

Rafe appeared with a tray bearing our drinks. He didn't normally deliver drinks when Gert was around, but by the way he was smiling at Emma, I knew why he'd made an exception.

"I've got a beer for Marco, nothing for Abby, and a peach margarita"—he set it in front of Emma with a flourish—"for the beautiful lady here."

"Oh, thank you," she said with gusto, twinkling up at him. She turned her head to look at Marco, then back at Rafe. "You *have* to be brothers."

"I'm the handsome younger model," Rafe said, balancing the tray on one finger. "Rafe Salvare," he said, holding out the other hand. The tray clattered to the floor. He ignored it and Marco's scowl, but beamed at Emma's giggle, as if that had been his intention all along.

"Emma Hardy," she said. "Nice to meet you."

Marco finally caught Rafe's eye and gave him a slight frown.

"Nice to meet you, too, Emma," Rafe said. "If you need anything, just give a wave. I run the bar." He gave me a wink, Marco a nod, and then sauntered off.

Emma looked at me and mouthed, "He's so cute!" Then she took a sip of her margarita and glanced over at Rafe, who was already chatting with a customer and pouring a beer. "Is he single?"

"He sure is," I said.

"What we're interested in knowing," Marco said, getting us back to the topic, "is what kind of relationship Bev had with the board of directors."

"By the board," Emma said, still with her cheery demeanor, "I'm assuming you mean Dayton Blaine."

"Why?" Marco asked.

"Because Dayton controls the board. Whatever Dayton says, the board does. They sit quietly, nodding their heads at her, during most of the meetings—when they're not dozing off, that is."

"How do you know this?" Marco asked.

"I attend board meetings. I see it all the time. All. The. Time." Emma smiled. I wondered if she could keep her eyes from twinkling.

"Then I'll work under the presumption that the board is represented by Dayton Blaine," Marco said, while I wrote it down. "Did Bev and Dayton usually agree on PAR business?"

"When I first started working for PAR, they did. But that changed about three months ago. Dayton was getting flack from the newspapers about the conditions at the animal shelter and didn't like her name connected with the *abominable shelter business,* as she put it. And she placed the blame squarely at Bev's feet."

"What was Bev's reaction?"

"She didn't like it at all. She was used to everything going her way." Emma leaned forward to say quietly, "Bev was a control freak, if you want to know the truth. But she knew the shelter was in bad shape, so she started going there after she finished at the PAR office for the day. Personally, I think it was all for show."

"Let's go back to the board meetings," Marco said. "How did the other members of the board react when Dayton criticized Bev?"

"I think they were very glad Dayton was dealing with the situation, because no one liked going up against Bev. Very few of them spoke at the meetings anyway, and if one of them did, it was just to back up Dayton.

"Last month, with no explanation given, Bev ran the meeting, not Dayton. Honestly, Dayton sat through the meeting acting uninterested in what was going on. In fact, she seemed withdrawn. I don't know. Maybe she was ill. In any event, she said only one thing that evening, and that was at the social hour afterward. She thought the no-kill policy needed to change."

"Did she give a reason?" I asked.

"Finances," Emma said with a shrug. "And that was only after someone questioned her. But here's what I don't understand. Dayton loves cats. She supposedly has several of them, which is why I don't see her sanctifying a shelter that euthanizes. And besides, Blaine Manufacturing gives a lot of money to PAR specifically designated to keep the shelter running. You'd think they'd just give more rather than change the policy."

"Let's talk a little more about Bev's sister, Stacy," Marco said. "What kind of relationship did she have with Bev, if you know?"

"Oh, they didn't get along at all," Emma said with a frown, which did not cause her eyes to dim. I looked up at the ceiling. Was it the lighting?

"Would you elaborate as to how you know this?" Marco asked.

"Bev had me working at the shelter during my off hours to set up a Web site that people could actually understand and use. You should have seen the one they had before. It was a mess. No tabs, links missing . . . So anyway, I was there when Bev and Stacy were there on at least"—she stopped to count on her fingers—"ten occasions."

"Did they argue?"

"Not in front of me. Always in Stacy's office, but those walls are really thin."

"What did they argue about?" I asked.

"Mostly how to run the shelter."

"What's your opinion of the shelter?" I asked.

"I don't know anything about anything, other than what I saw on their computer, and that was pretty sloppy." Emma wrinkled her perfect nose. "But it could have been that way when Stacy took over management. Those conditions didn't happen overnight."

"So you heard them argue on ten occasions?" Marco asked.

"Oh, yeah. Bev was tough on Stacy. Bev wanted to be able to go back to the board and show improvements, and it just wasn't happening. About two months ago, Bev wanted to hold a big fund-raiser for the shelter so she could make more changes to the physical environment, but Dayton told her no one was going to donate money unless they could see that things were changing. Otherwise, as Dayton said in a meeting, it would be throwing good money after bad." Emma folded her hands on the table again and smiled. "Isn't that just the best saying? Throwing good money after bad?"

I realized I was humming "Twinkle, Twinkle, Little Star" in my head. I had to stop looking into Emma's eyes.

"How did Stacy react to the arguments with Bev?" Marco asked.

"Stacy would just stop talking after a while, and pretty soon Bev would come out and go into another room to work."

"What did she work on?" I asked.

Emma shrugged. "I wasn't a part of that."

"How did the shelter staff react to Bev?" Marco asked.

"The women at the counter are dull. I've never seen them react to anything. And the two in the back never had much contact with Bev that I could see."

I wrote: *Shelter staff a nonissue.*

"Did you ever feel that Bev and her sister were close?" Marco asked.

That got a laugh. "You never met Bev, did you?"

"No," Marco said.

"Believe me," Emma said in a dramatically low voice, "it would be hard to be close to her."

"Even for her own sister?" I asked.

"Especially for her sister."

"Why do you say that?" I asked.

Emma toyed with the straw in her drink, as though deciding what to tell us. "I don't know how they were outside of work, but from what I overheard at the shelter, the sisters didn't like each other."

Just as Marco was about to ask his next question, Rafe appeared with a fresh margarita.

"Look what I have here," he said, setting the drink in front of Emma and whisking the old one out from under her hand.

"Aren't you sweet?" Emma said, tilting her head coyly and gazing up at him.

Rafe beamed. "I hear that all the time, but never from someone as gorgeous as you."

Emma giggled and put the straw between her lips. She took a sip, then said, "Yum. You make wonderful margaritas."

"I make the best daiquiris in town, too."

"There might be a customer waiting for one right now, in fact," Marco said, giving Rafe a scowl.

"See you later," Rafe said, and strutted off as though he was sure Emma was watching him, which she was. I thought it was pretty amusing, but Marco didn't. I could tell by the way he stared at the table that he'd lost his train of thought. That was unusual for him.

I was about to remind him when he said, "Let's talk about the PAR staff. Who besides you works for Bev?"

"Just two others—the fiscal director and the administrative assistant."

"Would you give me their names, please?" I asked.

"John Bradford is our fiscal director," Emma said, "and Holly Jankowsky is the admin assistant." She followed that with a spelling of Holly's full name.

"Would you explain your duties and the duties of John and Holly?" Marco asked.

"I'm in charge of fund-raising, social media, publicity, and networking," Emma said. "And can I tell you how much I *love* my job?"

She watched as I wrote it down, then pointed at the words and said, "Underline *love*."

Now she was editing my notes.

"The fiscal director," she explained, "is PAR's chief financial officer, which is self-explanatory, and the administrative assistant handles all the little tasks the three of us give her, or at least I *try* to give her. Bev keeps her—make that *kept* her—pretty busy."

"How did the other two get along with Bev?" I asked.

"John's work is nonconfrontational, so he got along with Bev just fine. Holly is a sweet girl who just graduated from college and is super efficient. Bev loves her. I'm sorry. I mean she loved her."

"Did you get along well with Bev?" I asked, remembering that red flag from before.

After a split-second hesitation, Emma nodded. "I didn't have any problems with Bev."

Another red flag. She changed the meaning of my question. I wrote: *PAR staff—check with admin asst. and CFO re: Emma's relationship with Bev.*

"Did Bev ever have a problem with you?" Marco asked.

Emma shook her head and followed that with a firm "No."

"Was your job confrontational?" I asked, and then, at her puzzled look, I reminded her what she'd said about the fiscal director.

"My job involves a lot of marketing tasks, and they can be open to interpretation, so sometimes how I interpreted something differed from how Bev interpreted it."

"Did she ever threaten to fire you?" Marco asked.

Emma finally lost her smile. "She never threatened me."

That time she hadn't answered the exact question.

"Did she ever get angry over something you did?" Marco asked, changing his angle.

"That happened all the time to everyone," Emma said, waving her hand. "Bev was always angry at *someone*."

That time Emma had deflected the question. She was a lot cannier than I'd first thought. "Even Holly?" I asked.

Emma turned to look at me as though she suspected a trap. "She might have been on occasion. I don't know. I wasn't around Holly all the time." With a frown, Emma stirred her margarita, looking uncomfortable enough to call it quits. I knew Marco would switch tactics now to prevent her from ending the interview.

"Emma, can you think of anyone who might have been a danger to Bev?" Marco asked, his hands folded on the table, his expression earnest. "Anyone we should be investigating for her death?"

She gazed into his eyes for a long moment, as though considering his question. Then she nodded. "Stacy. For sure."

"For what reason?" Marco asked.

"Stacy hated Bev," Emma said, "and not just because of problems at the shelter." She sat back and waited for one of us to ask the obvious question, so I obliged.

"What was the other reason—or reasons?"

"From what I gathered, a long time ago Bev had an affair with Stacy's husband." Emma lowered her voice and leaned forward again. "In fact, Bev is the one who broke up the Shaws' marriage, and I *know* Stacy has never forgiven her for it because I heard her say those very words."

I glanced at Marco's face and knew Stacy had just moved up to the number-one-suspect position.

CHAPTER EIGHT

Marco leaned forward, his gaze intent on Emma's face. "Did Stacy tell you that she had never forgiven her sister?"

"No, not to my face," Emma said, wrinkling her nose. "Remember those thin walls I told you about? Well, while I was working on the computer, on several evenings after the staff was gone, I heard Stacy and Bev get into it."

"Would you relate the conversation as you heard it?" Marco asked.

"You know how certain words are said louder than others in an argument?" Emma asked. "Well, I heard enough of those louds words to piece together what they were talking about."

"Which is," I said, writing, "that Stacy blamed Bev for breaking up her marriage?"

"Oh boy, did she blame Bev—and still hasn't forgiven her. From what I heard, Stacy was crazy about Justin—

that's her ex-husband—and accused Bev of ruining her life fourteen years ago and wanting to ruin it again now."

"By doing what?" Marco asked.

"I don't know. Every time Stacy got to that point, she lowered her voice." Emma smiled and shrugged. She was relaxed again.

"Was anyone else around to hear? Any volunteers?" Marco asked.

"No. The volunteers are always in the animal wards."

"Do you know anything about Stacy's ex-husband?" I asked.

Rafe suddenly appeared with a basket of tortilla chips and a dish of salsa. "I thought this would go with your margarita," he said, gazing adoringly into Emma's blue eyes. "Need another refill?"

"Are you trying to get me drunk?" Emma teased with a flirtatious shake of her wavy hair. "I should warn you, it doesn't take much."

"I like a woman who can't hold her liquor," Rafe said, crouching down so he could feast upon her beauty.

Emma laughed, light and tinkling. "I like men who like women who can't hold their liquor."

"I like men who do their jobs," Marco said, prompting Rafe to stand and salute his older brother, then wink at Emma.

"Don't leave without stopping at the bar to say good night," Rafe said.

"I won't." Turning back to Marco, Emma said, "I'm sorry. Please go on."

"What do you know about Stacy's ex-husband?" Marco asked.

"Nothing. I don't even know if Justin lives in town."

I wrote: *Interview Justin Shaw*

"You said Bev was hard to get close to," Marco said, picking up an old line of questioning. "Did you try to get close to her?"

"Believe me, I tried for months after I started working there," Emma said, then sipped her fresh margarita from the straw. "I finally gave up and just did the best job I could. There was no pleasing her."

"How does her assistant do it?" I asked.

"By letting Bev walk all over her. By being her slave girl." Emma shook her head. "Poor Holly. I felt sorry for the way Bev treated her, but she didn't seem to mind. She fell into the game of pleasing Bev."

"But you found that impossible?" I asked.

"Totally. She'd give me a project to work on one day, then get angry that I was spending time on it the next day. Or she wouldn't like the way it was done and do it herself. No matter what I tried, I couldn't seem to please her."

Emma was stirring her drink fast, clearly agitated. I saw Marco's focus sharpen and knew he was about to put pressure on her.

"Why didn't you quit?" he asked.

"The job pays well, and I have lots of student loans, lots of expenses. Do you know how hard it is to find a well-paying job in today's market? It's nearly impossible. I don't even want to think about trying."

"Is that why you took on projects for private clients outside of work?" Marco asked.

Emma's eyes widened, clearly shocked that he knew. "I was helping a friend with publicity for her new shop, that's all. I got paid minimally."

"Did Bev find out?"

Emma looked down at her drink, as though ashamed. "Yes. I tried to explain that I never worked on it during work hours, only on my free time, but Bev said it was a conflict of interest."

"How would that be a conflict?" I asked.

"I don't know," Emma said, looking as puzzled as I felt. "She wouldn't explain it."

"Did she say she was going to fire you over it?" he asked.

At first it appeared that Emma was going to say no, but then she let out a heavy sigh, as though deciding it wasn't worth lying about. "Bev said if I didn't stop, she would have no choice but to fire me. I tried to explain that I desperately needed more income to keep my head above water, but she didn't want to hear it. She said my financial problems weren't *pertinent* to the work at PAR."

Emma's last remark was said with a lot of bitterness.

"So she did threaten you," Marco said, causing Emma's peachy complexion to glow a hot red.

"I saw it as more of a warning," she said.

"When did this happen?" Marco asked.

Emma shrugged. "Sometime last week, I think. I'm not sure what day it was."

If I were warned that I could be fired, I was fairly certain I'd remember that day for a long time to come.

"Did you do as she requested and stop?" Marco asked.

"What choice did I have?"

Easy answer. She could stop moonlighting, or she could *put* a stop to Bev. I studied Emma as she pressed her lips together, clearly angry at the memory of the argument she'd had with her boss. But could Emma have been angry enough to pull two cords to raise the doggy doors?

Emma checked the time on her watch, then glanced around the bar. "Are we done yet? I'm meeting a friend."

"Just one more thing," Marco said. "Where were you Monday evening between five and seven o'clock?"

"You're asking for my alibi?" Emma cried, causing a few heads to turn our way.

"It's a routine question," Marco said in a soothing voice. "We have to ask everyone we talk to."

"So basically you're treating me as a suspect."

"No," Marco said patiently. "As I said, it's a routine question. Would you answer it please?"

Emma shoved her drink away, clearly angry. "I went home to change and eat dinner."

"Is there anyone who can verify that?" Marco asked.

"Okay, that's it," she said abruptly. "You *are* trying to make me a suspect, and don't pretend otherwise. So write this down." She pointed to my notes. "I had nothing to do with Bev's death. *Nothing.*" She slid toward the end of the bench. "Tell your brother good-bye for me. My friend and I will go somewhere else for dinner."

She got up in a hurry and headed for the door, threading among people, as the bar had filled up since she'd arrived. Poor Rafe caught sight of her just as she left and came over to find out what had happened.

"I think we made her nervous," Marco said.

"Thanks a lot," Rafe said in disgust. "I was hoping to ask her out."

I motioned for Rafe to come closer; then I said quietly, "She's a suspect in a murder investigation. You might want to hold off dating her until she's been cleared."

Marco motioned for him to come even closer. "When

you see us interviewing someone, would you not interrupt, please?"

Rafe straightened, coloring. "Fine," he said, and stalked off.

Marco sighed. "Sorry, Sunshine, if he annoyed you, because he sure did me."

"I agree with you, although it was kind of funny. So what did you think of Emma?"

"I'd like to hear your opinion first."

I looked over my notes. "She's good at deflecting questions she doesn't want to answer."

"Check."

"She withheld the big news about Bev and Stacy's relationship until she felt more comfortable around us, like she didn't trust us at first."

"Yep. Caught that."

"She's harboring a lot of anger toward Bev for threatening to fire her."

"Enough anger to kill Bev?"

"I hate to agree with a suspect, but I'm having a hard time thinking about what happened to Bev as a pure killing, Marco. So I asked myself whether Emma could have pulled two cords to let the dogs loose."

"Why does that make a difference?"

"After listening to Stacy's rationale on the subject, I tried to put myself in the mind-set of a person who would probably not be prone to violence but might have gotten so angry she just wanted to get even. In pulling on the cord, the killer wouldn't have had to stick around and see the results, making the deed less gruesome somehow. As weird as it sounds, I could see it being a female-style killing."

"Still, that female is taking a big risk that it might not do the job intended."

"I know. It obviously wasn't well thought out, so it must have been a spur-of-the-moment decision."

"What's your answer on Emma?" Marco asked.

"I can't answer it yet. The interview was too short. What about you?"

"Same here. I'm going to withhold judgment until I get more information. I'd like to talk to the other two members of the PAR staff tomorrow, hopefully in the morning while you're working."

"*If* I'm working."

Marco glanced at me sidelong. "What does that mean?"

"It means I hope I have orders to work on."

"Is business that slow?"

"It was today. I hope it's not a trend."

"Can you have a sale or something? Print coupons? Hire Lottie's boys to distribute flyers around town?" Marco was intent on solving my problem. "Didn't you run a contest a long while back? Can you do that again?"

"I'll figure something out."

He took my hand. "I don't want you to worry about your business, Abby. It's a good, solid business. It'll bounce back."

"Thanks. I appreciate your support." And that's all I really wanted, his support. But typical of most guys, he needed to solve the problem, not just listen to me vent. Now I had to hope he was still listening because I wanted him to open up.

Giving his hand a squeeze, I said, "Isn't it great when we can share our concerns like this?"

"Sure is." He pulled the notebook closer so he could read it.

"That's what a team is all about, right?"

He turned the page. "Team Salvare."

"So what's our next step in the investigation after you talk to the staff at PAR?"

Marco closed the notebook. "Interview Stacy's ex-husband, Justin Shaw. I'm going to do a search on him tomorrow morning, so maybe by noon I'll have something lined up. I need to set up a meeting with Dayton Blaine, too, but she's proving difficult. I called Blaine Manufacturing today and got transferred around until finally a secretary somewhere said I'd just missed her, but I could try her office at PAR headquarters. So I did, and she hadn't arrived yet.

"I left a message for her to call me, and of course she didn't. I called back later and was told she'd already left. She was supposedly on her way to a Blaine subsidiary, but I couldn't reach her there, either. I'll probably have to go camp out at the Blaine headquarters and wait for her to show up."

"She may not agree to see you."

"Who are you talking about here?" Marco asked, putting his hands to his chest and acting offended. "Are you talking about the man you claim can charm any woman?"

"Oops. I forgot. You're right. One look at you and she'll grant you an interview. But that means I should stay away so I don't ruin the Salvare magic."

"Are you kidding? If she shows up, I'll have you come right down with a bouquet of flowers. What woman can resist flowers delivered by the cutest redhead in town?"

"Naturally, she's cute," came a woman's voice from behind us. "Why would my son marry her if she weren't?"

Francesca Salvare appeared at the end of the table and leaned down to wrap her strong arms around me for a lung-squeezing hug. "Abby, *bella*," she said, smiling down at me. "You're adorable. Who is questioning it? Give me their names and I will straighten this out at once."

"No one is questioning it, *Mama*," Marco said, as his mother slid onto the bench opposite us. "I was talking theoretically."

"Never mind your theories," she said. "Let's talk specifics."

"About what?" Marco asked.

"About your wedding."

Oh no. Here it comes. Another harangue about the guest list.

"Where are you holding the ceremony?" she asked.

"In the gazebo at Fairfield Park," I replied.

"Oh," she said, looking crestfallen.

"What's wrong?" I asked, glancing at Marco in bewilderment.

"Well," Francesca said, folding her hands on the table, "there's nothing much around it except for farm fields and rural county roads."

"That's why we chose it," I said. "Not many people visit Fairfield Park because it's a county park outside the city limits. The gazebo is set in a beautiful, secluded location. It'll give us plenty of privacy."

Francesca looked baffled. "On a beautiful September afternoon, why would you want to hide your wedding? Aren't you proud to be getting married to my son?"

"Ma," Marco said, putting his arm around me, "of course Abby's proud, and we're not hiding. We just like the privacy. We don't want gawkers."

"You're going to be married in God's cathedral," Francesca said, gesturing broadly, "so why not hold your ceremony where He can see you? Like on the dunes at Lake Michigan? You know those quaint outdoor shelters they have at Indiana Dunes State Park?"

Quaint as in old. All I could think of was getting sand in my new shoes and having to live with it for the rest of the day.

"Or at Community Park in the heart of the downtown area," she said, "in full view of all the wonderful people in New Chapel."

Trying to be tactful, I said, "Both sound lovely, but I'm sure it's too late to change locations now."

"So here is what we can do—" Francesca said.

"*Mama,*" Marco said, "why don't you let us handle it?"

"Because both of you are simply too busy to see what's important," she said, then noticed my expression. "Oh, I'm not criticizing, *bella*. I'm just stating facts. I have a lot of time on my hands, so let me do this for you. Yes?"

"No," Marco said, which only made Francesca more desperate to convince us. He was using the wrong tactic. The right one would be to let her try to book a different location and see that it was just too late. Then she'd have to concede.

"Ah," Francesca said happily, "I can see by the light in Abby's eyes that she's in favor of this, yes?"

"With a caveat," I said. "This is a simple wedding, as you know, for family and friends only, so I don't want anything fancy, like a country-club setting." Beneath the table, I took Marco's hand in mine and gave it a conspiratorial squeeze. "Right, Marco?"

"Right." He gazed into my eyes and I knew he understood what I was doing. "Keep it simple."

"Don't worry," Francesca said. "You will be happy with the results."

That was what I was counting on.

CHAPTER NINE

Wednesday

When I woke up in the morning, the knot in my stomach had moved up to the lymph glands in my neck, or so it seemed when I saw my reflection in the mirror. I pressed on the swollen flesh and drew in a sharp breath. *Ouch!* It hurt *and* I looked like a frog.

My glands always got lumpy when I was coming down with something, so as a precaution, I took extra vitamin D and C before heading out the door. That would foil any germs hanging around.

Driving with the top down on my beloved old 'Vette, I turned up the radio and sang along with the music as I made the ten-minute trip to work. It was a beautiful September morning, and I wasn't going to waste it worrying about a potential cold. I wasn't going to fret about the wedding's location, either. We'd made it clear to Francesca that she could line up a setting for the ceremony and that was it. I was praying that she got the picture.

I pulled into the city parking lot, put up my ragtop, just in case the weatherman was right about the chance of rain, and headed up the street to my shop, still feeling froglike, yet positive. Jingles the window washer was busy scrubbing the plate-glass window on Marco's bar, so I called hello and continued on by. He barely glanced my way.

Jingles was an older man who'd been washing windows on the square since I was a child, and well before, I was sure. He'd gotten the name Jingles because when he talked to people, he jingled the coins in his pocket. I didn't think anyone knew his real name.

When I got to Bloomers I saw why Jingles had been so intent on his job. My window had been egged, as had the window of the insurance company beyond Bloomers. I was betting the same thing had happened to Marco's bar.

"Jingles, can you do my shop next?" I called, returning to Down the Hatch.

"Yes, miss. Four shops got hit last night. Yours'll be next in line for a cleaning."

Refusing to let a few eggs or swollen glands ruin my good mood, I entered my flower shop, cheered as always by the bell over the door. "'Morning, ladies," I called.

No one answered. The shop and the parlor were both deserted.

I continued on through to the workroom. There I found both women on their hands and knees, sopping up water with big towels.

"What happened?" I asked.

"Bad news," Grace said, rising. "There's a leak in one of the coolers—and, dear me, what happened to your neck?"

Lottie stood up, too, and clucked her tongue. "Looks like you swallowed a couple of giant marshmallows."

Grace palpated my painful glands, eliciting winces from me, then put her palm on the back of my neck. "No fever at present. Did you have chills in the night?"

"Now that I think about it, I did wake up once shivering, but I feel fine now, except for my glands. Which cooler is leaking?"

"This one," Lottie said, tapping on the right door. "I called the plumber and he'll be out as soon as he can squeeze us in."

Inventory: swollen glands, egged window, leaking cooler. If trouble came in threes, I'd just had mine.

"We're going to have to move our stock to the other cooler," Lottie said.

"We don't have much room," I said, circling the wet floor to get to the cooler on the left.

"We'll have to make room or we'll lose our flowers," Lottie said.

I pulled open the insulated door and stepped inside. It would be tight. If we needed something in the back, I wasn't sure how we'd reach it, but what choice did we have?

My positive attitude was starting to erode.

We spent the next hour transferring containers of flowers and greens, finishing up just in time to open for the day. My assistants took their places and I opened the door to a large crowd that couldn't wait to get their morning coffee and scones.

As soon as the rush was over and Grace could handle the parlor alone, I returned to the workroom and glanced at the spindle. Two orders hung by their lonesome, but at least I had something to work on.

I pulled the first order slip and read through it. Naturally, the blossoms I needed were at the back of the first cooler and I had to remove a number of tall containers so I could climb past the others to reach them. And then I had to put them all back again.

I had just finished moving the last container back inside when I turned around and found my mom standing at the worktable, beaming. Then she saw my neck and gasped, "Abigail, what happened?"

"Just swollen glands," I said, and touched them to find that they were even larger than before. And more painful.

"My poor little girl," Mom said, clasping my shoulders for a better look. "Does it hurt to swallow?"

"No, it just hurts to touch the glands."

She stopped probing my neck and went into the whole fever-chills interrogation until she pronounced me ill with a virus. "You should be home in bed."

"I don't feel that bad, Mom. I just look bad."

"You look cranky, too."

And I was starting to feel cranky. "So why aren't you teaching today?"

"We had half a day of in-service training and the other half off." She picked up a plastic bag from the floor. "I made something last night that I think you'll like."

Before I could blink, she pulled a pair of flowerpots from her bag. They were made to look like two giant sunflowers, with the yellow flower petals bending backward from the centers to form the interiors of the pots. They were connected at the bottom by green metal stems, and, um, they weren't pretty.

"What do you think?" she asked, handing me her creation.

I set her pots on the worktable and stepped back to study it, stalling while I thought of something positive to say. Before I could answer, Lottie walked through the curtain, took a look at Mom's artwork, and assumed I had pulled it out for the order I was working on. "Oh, good. You finally found a use for those old sunflower pots. I thought we'd never get rid of them."

Mom looked from Lottie to me. "What?"

Realizing she'd said something wrong, Lottie glanced up at a high shelf on the back wall and her eyes widened to about the size of Frisbees. Mom followed the direction of her gaze and her jaw dropped as she saw another pair of sunflower pots similar to hers.

"Oh no. I did it again!"

"I'm so sorry, Maureen," Lottie said. "Now that I see them both, yours are much prettier."

Mom's shoulders sagged. "Thanks, Lottie. I appreciate you trying to make me feel better. I just can't figure out how I could have spotted your pots all the way up there to copy them."

"They used to sit on the table in the middle of the shop," Lottie said. "Speaking of the shop, I'd better get my roses and head out front."

While Lottie climbed over containers in the cooler, Mom pulled out a stool at the worktable and sank onto it. "What's the matter with me, Abigail? That's the second time I've copied something unknowingly."

"You're still stressed out, Mom," I said, putting my arm around her shoulders. "You need to relax."

"It's true. I *am* still feeling stressed," she said. "I keep waiting for the police to call me in for questioning."

The phone rang at that moment, startling both of us. I

picked it up at my desk and assumed a cheerful voice. "Bloomers Flower Shop. How may I help you?"

"I can think of several ways," Marco said in a seductive growl.

I turned my back on my mom to answer in a low voice, "So can I, Salvare. And my mom is here."

"Okay, then. How's it going today, Sunshine?"

"To tell you the truth, things could be better."

"What happened?"

"Do you want the entire list?"

There was a pause on Marco's end. For a moment I thought we'd lost the connection. Then he said, "Can it wait until lunchtime?"

It stung just a little that he didn't have time to hear my tale of woe now, but then I didn't want to burden my mom with it either. "Of course. What are we doing at lunch?"

"I tracked down Justin Shaw. He owns a towing service just outside the city limits. I thought lunchtime would be a good time to catch him in the shop."

"Okay, but I have to prepare you for my appearance. The glands in my neck are a little swollen. Mom thinks it's a virus."

"I'm sure it's a virus," Mom corrected. I gave her a thumbs-up.

"Are you contagious?" Marco asked.

"I'm not sneezing or coughing, and I feel fine."

"Then I'll tough it out," he said.

"Sandwiches on the way there?" I asked.

"I'll bring them along. See you here at noon."

"Abigail," Mom said, clearly chagrined, "surely you're not going out looking like that." She pointed to my neck.

Just the confidence boost I needed. "Mom, the interview process is the best part of the investigation. That's where we really get to see what people are like. I'd hate to miss this one."

"But your glands!"

I held up a stainless-steel flowerpot to check my reflection. "They don't look that bad, do they?"

"Your jawline is disappearing."

"I'll take some aspirin. That should help the swelling. Go home and sit down at your pottery wheel and see what you come up with. I'll bet it'll be something brand-new."

Mom sighed wearily. "I'll give it a try. And before I forget"—she dug through her purse—"here's the list of volunteers you asked for."

"Thanks, Mom." I took the list and put it in my purse. "How's the protest coming?"

"We have twenty people signed up for it," she said.

"Abby," Lottie said, sticking her head through the curtain, "remember the bride-to-be from yesterday? She's back. I think she's ready to choose Bloomers for her flowers."

I wanted to clap and do a happy dance. Instead, I escorted Mom out of the workroom and went to meet with my new—I hoped—client.

Feeling jubilant at having a wedding to do, I left the shop—its front window now egg free—at noon and found Marco already waiting in his car out front. I climbed in and turned to look in the backseat, spotting a small red cooler there. "Yum. I'm starving."

"Wow. Those glands really are swollen. Do they hurt?"

"A little bit. The aspirin is helping. What kind of sandwiches did you bring?"

"Nothing wrong with your appetite. Turkey and Swiss."

He pulled away from the curb, shooting me what he thought were discreet glances, until I flipped down the visor and opened the mirror for a look. *Yeesh.* Mom was right. My jawline was almost nonexistent, and now my skin was beginning to itch, too.

I snapped the visor back in place. "Any news to report?"

"Here's the update," Marco said, as I unwrapped a sandwich for him. "I spoke with Emma's coworkers on the phone this morning, but neither was free to talk because Emma was in the room. I have personal cell phone numbers so I can call them after five today."

"That's good. And Mom gave me a list of the shelter volunteers along with their phone numbers."

"I'll start researching them this afternoon, see if anyone is involved in a lawsuit with Bev."

I unwrapped my sandwich and took a bite. I was surprised he hadn't asked about my list of troubles. Had he forgotten? "Any more news from Reilly?"

"I haven't heard a word." Marco turned onto Lincoln Avenue and headed west.

Still nothing about my list, so I decided to jump right in with it.

"Jingles said your window got egged this morning. Mine did, too. And one of my coolers sprang a leak. So on top of having these swollen glands and finding my window egged, there was water all over the workroom floor when I got there. I'm hoping it's fixable. I'd have to go into debt to buy a new cooler. Those suckers are expensive."

"Mmm," was all he said. He hadn't glanced my way. Was he even paying attention?

He finished his sandwich, took a swig from a water bottle sitting in the holder, then said, "How's business been today?"

"I had two orders waiting for me when I got in this morning, and a woman wants me to do her wedding."

"That's great news about the wedding, Abby. Congratulations."

"Thanks. I just wish I had more orders. I think I'm going to have to have those flyers you mentioned printed and have Lottie's boys plaster them all over town. I can offer a ten percent discount on them. At this point, I can't afford anything more."

We drove in silence for the next five minutes, Marco with a look of concern on his face. But when we pulled into the gravel parking lot of Shaw's Towing, he shut off the motor and looked over at me as though nothing were wrong. "Ready, Kermit?"

"Thanks a lot," I said, pretending to be offended but secretly relieved that he seemed back to his usual kidding self.

Shaw's Towing was in a building that had once been a car-repair shop. It was a low brown brick structure with two garage bays on one end and plenty of windows. On the other end was a fenced-in lot where the tow trucks were kept. As we got out of the car, two large Dobermans ran up to the fence and began barking at us, baring their teeth as though they would've loved to rip us apart.

"Why do people have dogs like that?" I asked Marco, giving them a wide berth.

"They must be there to protect their trucks after hours."

"Right. Like someone's going to hot-wire a tow truck and joyride through town."

"Good point. Let's ask."

We stepped inside a small reception area and saw a long-haired man in stained blue overalls and a red plaid shirt standing behind a glass counter watching a tiny television propped in front of him. He seemed to be working on either a big wad of chewing tobacco or a large chunk of gum. I saw a coffee can sitting next to the counter and decided on the chewing tobacco.

"Those your dogs?" Marco asked.

"Naw. They belong to the business," he replied, bending over to spit into the can. "Justin got them 'cause sometimes we hold cars here till the owners come for 'em."

"I'd hate to see what those dogs would do if anyone broke in," I said.

"Wouldn't be pretty," Tobacco Man said. "Those are actually our second set of dogs. First ones got so that even Justin couldn't handle 'em. We had to put 'em down."

"You did it yourselves?" Marco asked in surprise.

"Naw." *Spit.* "Justin took them someplace."

"Is Justin here?" Marco asked.

The guy hitched a thumb over his shoulder. "In his office. Want me to get him?"

"Please," Marco said. "Tell him it's a business call."

Tobacco Man disappeared through a door behind the counter and returned a few moments later. "He'll be right up." The guy noticed me for the first time and did a double take at my neck. I swiveled to stare out the window.

We waited five minutes until a pleasant-looking man in a casual yellow-and-white-checked shirt and tan pants came out. He had thinning brown hair cut short, thin sideburns, and a well-trimmed goatee. He glanced at Marco, then at me, then at me again. Now I was really feeling self-conscious. "Justin Shaw," he said, reaching out a hand toward Marco.

"Marco Salvare. This is my fiancé and assistant, Abby Knight."

He gave me a nod but kept his distance, as though afraid to shake my hand. "What can I do for you?"

"Give us about ten minutes of your time," Marco said, displaying his PI license.

"What's this about?" Justin asked, sounding wary.

"Beverly Powers. We're investigating the circumstances of her death."

Justin held up his hands, palms out. "Hey, I don't know anything about what happened to Bev."

"I believe you," Marco said. "We're here because Abby's mother found the body and may be considered a suspect, so we're collecting as much information about Bev's life as we can. As I said, it'll take about ten minutes; then we'll get out of your hair."

"I don't know what you think I can tell you," Justin said, glancing at me again.

"My mom is sick with worry," I told him. "We're really hoping some tiny detail about Bev or Stacy will make a difference."

"Stacy?" Justin asked, looking at me with suspicion. "If Stacy is involved, I'm definitely staying out of it."

My error. I should have let Marco explain. By the tone of Justin's voice, he was mistrustful now.

"I talked to Stacy just yesterday," Justin continued.

"She told me she left before Bev was killed. Are you telling me that's not true?"

Marco glanced over at the man in overalls, who was listening intently. "Can we talk in your office?"

Justin studied Marco for a moment, gave me a wary glance, and finally said, "Ten minutes."

We were led up a short hallway to an office consisting of dingy white walls, gray metal filing cabinets, and a tan metal desk. On the walls were photos of Justin with various people. One showed him with two handsome German shepherds on leashes. I wondered if those were the dogs that had had to be put down.

Justin walked around behind his desk and sat down in an old chair that needed a good dose of WD-40. He indicated the two brown folding chairs in front of his desk.

"Now, what's this about Stacy?" Justin asked, crossing his arms over his chest as we got situated.

"All we know is what Stacy told us," Marco said, "and that is that she left at five o'clock."

Justin gave a nod, apparently satisfied that our facts matched his.

"Had you had any contact with Bev recently?" Marco asked, as I took notes.

"Nope."

"Do you know of anyone who might have been a threat to Bev?" Marco asked.

"Nope."

"Do you know if she made any enemies?" Marco asked.

"Nope, but I'm sure Bev did have enemies," Justin said. "She was that kind of person."

"By *that kind,* what do you mean?" Marco asked.

"I'll spare the lady here from the language I'd normally use to describe her," Justin said. "I'm sure anyone who knew her well would say the same thing."

"Did you know her well?" Marco asked.

Justin reddened, realizing his mistake, and said quickly, "Once upon a time I knew her—or I should say *sort* of knew her—as well as anyone knows his sister-in-law."

The woman he'd had an affair with? Yeah, right. I couldn't wait to see how Marco would pull out the truth. I always enjoyed watching his artful tactics.

"That was when I was married to Stacy, of course," Justin added, smiling as though relieved to have cleared that up. Obviously he didn't want to be associated with Bev. Did he have reason to worry that he'd be a suspect?

"What kind of relationship did Bev and Stacy have?" Marco asked.

"Rocky," Justin said, toying with a paper clip on his desk.

"According to an employee who worked with both Bev and Stacy, the sisters hated each other," Marco said. "Would you say that's a fair assessment?"

"Yeah, that's about right," Justin answered.

"Was their relationship that bad while you were married to Stacy?" Marco asked.

"They'd never had what you'd call a close relationship, but it got to the point of hatred by the end of our marriage."

"Do you know the reason for the hatred?" Marco asked.

Justin shrugged, but wouldn't meet Marco's eye. "Sisters. What can I say? I never had any, so I can't tell you any more than that."

More like he didn't want to, no doubt because the sisters' hatred had everything to do with their affair.

"If I told you that Stacy now claims she loved her sister," Marco said, "and that they were best friends, what would you say?"

"That she must have been drunk when you talked to her," Justin said. "But hey, I haven't been around them for years, so maybe I'm way off base and some kind of miracle happened."

My cell phone beeped, so I pulled the phone from my purse and read the message from Marco's mom: *Be law, e-coli donut gets halters at the dunes.*

What?

The phone beeped again, and instantly another text message popped up: *Stupid autocorrect.*

It was followed by a third message. *Bella, I couldn't get any shelters at the dunes.*

Which was just as I'd predicted. I texted back, *Darn it*, suppressing the urge to add *LOL*.

That left the most popular wedding site in town—the gazebo at Community Park—which I knew was booked at least a year in advance.

Marco glanced at me, his eyebrows drawing together at the wide smile on my face. Turning back to Justin, he asked, "What can you tell us about your relationship with Bev?"

"She used to be my sister-in-law. End of story."

"Is that the whole story?" Marco asked.

Justin checked the time on his watch, keeping his gaze averted. "Pretty much."

I slipped my phone back into my purse. This was getting good. Now Marco would tiptoe closer to the truth, pushing Justin inch by inch until he cracked wide open.

"When were you going to tell us," Marco said, his gaze focused intently on Justin's face, "that you had an affair with Bev that broke up your marriage?"

Wow. No tiptoeing today.

CHAPTER TEN

"Whoa, whoa, whoa!" Justin said, trying but not succeeding in smiling. "Where did you hear that?"

"From one of Bev's employees," Marco said.

"And this employee knew it how?" Justin asked, tilting back on the hind legs of his chair.

"She heard Bev and Stacy arguing about your affair," Marco said. "This happened on several occasions."

Justin appeared stunned, shaking his head as though he couldn't believe it.

"We'd like you to validate that the affair did indeed happen," Marco said.

Justin came down on all four chair legs. "Yeah, it happened, something I've regretted every day of my life since. I won't even call it an affair because it was just the one time and then I told Bev to back off. I knew immediately afterward that I'd made a big mistake because Bev isn't— *wasn't*—one you could say no to and get away with it."

"How long ago was this?" I asked.

Justin rubbed his eyes with his thumbs. "Happened

about a year before we moved to New Chapel, so let's see . . . I guess it's coming up on fifteen years now."

"How did Stacy find out about the affair?" I asked.

For a second, Justin's expression hardened, his lips flattening into thin, colorless lines. "Bev told her, the bi—" He caught himself and quickly cleared his expression of anger. "But hey, that's water under the bridge now."

"When did Bev tell Stacy?" I asked.

"About a week after I told Bev to back off." Justin shook his head, as though he still couldn't believe it. "Stacy and I tried to make a go of it, even moving here to start over, but Bev followed us. Stacy was so convinced that we were still having an affair that she filed for divorce."

"Did you have any idea that Bev was going to tell Stacy?" Marco asked.

"She warned me she was going to do it," he said. "Said she had to clear the air, which I've never believed. She wanted to ruin my marriage to get even with me. I tried to talk her out of it, but when Bev makes up her mind to do something, nothing stops her."

He blew out a breath noisily, as though trying to shake off his tension. "I guess I should be putting everything into the past tense now, shouldn't I? Damn, it's so hard to believe Bev's really gone."

He had completely switched tones, from angry to light. I had the unfortunate feeling that Bev's death had been welcome news to a number of people.

"Did you have any contact with Bev after the affair?" Marco asked.

"None," he said emphatically. "I kept my distance. Bev could make things miserable if she was of a mind to, and she usually was. I wanted to protect myself and my son from her as much as possible."

"You have a son?" I asked.

Justin grew red-faced again. "I thought you knew that. Didn't Stacy tell you?"

"She didn't mention any children," I said.

"We have only the one child."

"How old is he?" I asked.

"He turns fourteen next week. He was born shortly before we relocated here."

"Why did you want to protect your son from Bev?" Marco asked.

"For the reason I told you earlier. I didn't want him to be around someone like her."

"Did it work?" I asked.

"I had no control over the situation while Kyle was with his mother, only when I had him every other weekend—and your ten minutes is up," Justin said, displaying his watch face.

"Just two more quick questions," Marco said. "Are you positive you haven't had any contact with Bev in the fourteen years since your son was born?"

"She might have been at the house a time or two when I dropped Kyle off, but believe me, I've tried my best to keep away from her—and keep my son away from her, too. She was poison."

"Have you ever been to the PAR Animal Shelter?" Marco asked.

"No reason to."

"I thought maybe you got your dogs there."

"Nope. Got them through a breeder."

Marco rose. "That should do it, then. Thanks for giving us your time." We walked to the door; then Marco turned back. "Sorry. One more detail. Where were you Monday evening between five and seven o'clock?"

"Monday?" Justin rubbed his chin as I whipped out the notepad and pen. "I don't remember . . . Oh, wait. Monday! I got a service call on my cell phone as I was leaving for the day. My guys had all gone home, so I took one of the trucks out myself to respond."

"Can you verify that?" Marco asked.

"I can give you the customer's name," Justin said. "He'll verify that I responded."

"Would you do that now, please?" Marco asked. He waited while Justin searched through receipts stuck on a spindle, then, as Justin wrote down a name, asked, "Do you recall what time you got to him?"

"Not exactly, but I'd say somewhere around six o'clock. His car broke down outside of town."

"That'll do it, then," Marco said, handing me the piece of paper. "Thanks again."

"Marco, your mom couldn't book a shelter at Dunes State Park! Isn't that great?"

He opened the car door for me. "Was that what the text message was about?"

"Yep. See how much better it is to let her find out for herself that you can't change locations at the last minute? Just think of it, Marco. Soon we'll be married in that cute little white gazebo with flowers all around it and shady trees overhead." I sighed dreamily. "How perfect it'll be."

He patted my knee. "Good, babe. I'm glad you're happy."

"Aren't you happy?"

"Sunshine, as far as I'm concerned, we could be married in the back of a pickup truck." Seeing my horrified expression, he quickly recanted. "Of course I'm happy. It'll be beautiful, I'm sure."

"Way to backpedal, Salvare."

Marco's mouth curved up at one corner as he glanced my way. It was another of those endearing traits I loved so much.

As we headed back to town, I turned the topic back to our wedding plans. "Have you confirmed the dates of our honeymoon with the bed-and-breakfast in Key West?"

"Yep. Air travel is lined up and I've rented us a car for the week. We went over this a few days ago, remember?"

"Sorry. I've got so many details crammed into my brain that I forget."

"Not a problem. What's your opinion about Justin Shaw?"

Obviously, Marco wasn't as focused on the wedding plans as I was. "I thought Justin was being honest for the most part, but I'm glad we talked to Emma first or we wouldn't have known about the affair with Bev. Justin sure wasn't going to bring it up."

"I can't fault him for that," Marco said. "He probably doesn't care to revisit it."

"But when we pinned him down, he seemed to be straight with us," I said. "I didn't get any negative vibrations from him. Stacy is the one who wasn't being honest. I didn't believe her when she said she and her sister were best friends, and this interview reaffirmed that."

"She's protecting herself. Stacy clearly fears she will be a suspect, and rightly so. Her alibi won't stand up in court. With that said, I wouldn't cross Justin off the list just yet either. I'm going to call the customer on that piece of paper this afternoon to check out his story, and

I want to be certain that the shelter staff has never seen Justin there."

"Did you think he was lying about it?"

"I never take a suspect's word on anything. Check every statement, Sunshine. Remember that. I also want to find out if there was any way Justin could've gotten access to a shelter key through his son."

"How do we do that?"

"We need to talk to Stacy again."

"Think we can catch her at the shelter at five o'clock? Unless the funeral is today."

"The coroner hasn't released Bev's body yet, Abby. Nothing happens until that final autopsy report is done. Reilly will let me know when it's in. So I say it's worth a try. There's a photo of Justin on his Web site that I'll enlarge and copy. If you can leave work twenty minutes early, we can question the staff about him and then we'll be in the reception area when Stacy is ready to leave for the day."

"Weren't you going to talk to Emma's coworkers at PAR at five o'clock?"

"I can do that later this evening. When we finish at the shelter, do you want to go back to the bar for dinner?"

"Will you be embarrassed by my fat neck?"

Marco smiled. "You will always be the most beautiful woman in the room to me, Abby. So the answer is no, I won't be embarrassed. Will you be upset if I tell you I need to work at the bar this evening?"

"Of course not, but isn't that what you're training Rafe to do?"

Marco scratched his nose, as though the question made him uncomfortable. "It's taking a little longer than I expected."

"Don't worry about it, Marco. I understand."

He pulled up in front of Bloomers and reached for my hand, bringing it to his lips. "You're my sweetheart, you know that?"

"Yes, but it's always good to hear you say it. I'll see you before five."

"Get out those flyers," he called, as I exited the car.

"Yes, boss."

Inside Bloomers, two women were browsing the gift items on the display shelves, so I said hello and continued on into the workroom, where I immediately checked the spindle. This time three pieces of paper fluttered there.

"Hello, dear," Grace said, sailing through the curtain. "How did it go?"

"I'll give you a rundown when Lottie's free," I said. "How's business been?"

"We had a nice afternoon in the coffee parlor, but for the shop, only a few customers here and there."

I sagged onto a stool. "A few customers and a whopping three orders on the spindle. I'm starting to get nervous, Grace."

"I don't think you should be worried just yet, love. You know the economy is still struggling."

"So is my bank account. We had such a good month in July, I was hoping the trend would continue."

"What needs to continue, love, is your determination to succeed. Let me tell you what famed businessman and entrepreneur Richard M. DeVos said." Grace cleared her throat and lifted her chin. "'If I had to select one quality, one personal characteristic that I regard as being most highly correlated with success, whatever the field, I would pick the trait of persistence. Determination.'"

Lottie walked in, clapping with me.

"That was fantastic, Grace," I said. "I don't know how you remember all those quotes."

"It *is* a gift, isn't it?" Grace said.

Lottie put her arm around me. "You've got pluck, kid. You'll make it. And those two ladies you saw out front just dropped a cool hundred and twenty dollars on a pair of crystal candlesticks and a bouquet of roses. How about that?"

"That's great. How can I feel down when I have you two around?" I asked, giving them each a hug.

"Um, Abby," Lottie said, pulling back to look at me, "take a look at your neck in the bathroom mirror. Looks like you have a rash now, too."

Oh, boy, did I have a rash. It went from my neck down my torso all the way to my ankles, and it itched. I had become a freckled frog with a skin condition.

"Perhaps you should see your family doctor," Grace said, peering over my shoulder as I examined my swollen, bump-covered glands in the mirror. "It's probably nothing serious, but why take chances?"

Normally, I'd tough it out and wait for whatever it was to go away, but with my wedding right around the corner, I took her advice and made the call. Luckily, thanks to a kindhearted nurse, I snagged an appointment for first thing in the morning. Now all I had to do was keep myself from scratching so I didn't make my condition worse. To distract myself, I pulled an order from the spindle and set to work.

The arrangement was for a woman's forty-third birthday, a gift from her family. They gave me a budget from which to work but left the design entirely up to me, so I decided on a pastel palette with an oval cream-colored ceramic bowl.

Climbing around containers in the first cooler, I pulled out white carnations, Apple Blossom pink stock flower, Bellamosum light blue delphiniums, blue Veronicas, waxflowers, leather fern, and lily grass, then laid them all out on the worktable.

Grace came in with a cup of green tea for me, which she said would be good for my rash, and admired the blossoms. "Those should be lovely together."

"Thanks. Any word on when our cooler will be fixed?" I asked.

"The plumber indicated the part he needed would be in at the earliest tomorrow afternoon," she said. "By the way, you have your dress fitting this evening."

Wouldn't that be fun in my condition?

At ten minutes before five o'clock, Marco and I walked into the animal shelter's reception area and were greeted by the Friendly Sisters in the same lackadaisical manner as before. Marco showed them the enlarged photo of Justin, but neither of them had ever seen him.

"You know who's his spittin' image?" one of them asked the other. "Stacy's son."

"Who are you looking at?" asked a voice behind us.

I turned just as Stacy came up to the reception counter for a look, cradling the same golden brown puppy in her arms. She took one peek at the photo and her features stiffened. "What are you doing with that picture?"

"We wanted to know if your staff had ever seen him here," Marco said.

She snatched the photo and threw it onto the counter

in front of the women. "Have you?" she snapped. Both women shook their heads, looking alarmed. Stacy gave them a satisfied nod and turned back to Marco. "That's because he wouldn't dare show his face around here."

"Could we step into your office to finish this conversation?" Marco asked, retrieving the photo.

"This conversation *is* finished," she said. "I've told you everything I know."

"Not everything," Marco said, "but your ex-husband filled us in on what you left out. I think you know what I'm talking about. We can talk about that here, if you prefer."

Stacy's eyes narrowed as she did some fast thinking; then she handed the puppy to one of the women, did an about-face, and marched up the hallway.

I glanced at Marco. "Are we supposed to follow her?"

"After you," he said.

CHAPTER ELEVEN

"**W**hat did Justin tell you?" Stacy demanded, settling behind her desk. She was trying to look relaxed, but I could feel the tension radiating from her body as she clutched the armrests on her chair.

"He told us you have a son," Marco said.

"How is that important?" she snapped.

"I understand his name is Kyle," Marco said. At her nod, he asked, "Is there any way your ex-husband could have gotten a copy of your key from Kyle?"

"Kyle would have told me if his dad had asked for the key."

"Are you sure?" Marco asked.

"Are you implying that Justin may have murdered my sister?" she replied.

She sure was quick to jump to that conclusion. Judging by her expression, it almost seemed as though she was hoping we'd say yes.

"We're checking every possibility," Marco said evenly.

"Is there any other way Justin might have accessed the shelter?"

"I wouldn't know that." Stacy tapped her fingers on her desk. "Is that all?"

"Justin also told us he tried to shield your son from your sister," Marco said.

"What a liar," Stacy said venomously. "*I* tried to shield Kyle from my sister, not Justin. *I'm* the one who raised him, who protected him. Don't be fooled by Justin's pretense of being a good father. There isn't a paternal bone in Justin Shaw's body."

"Why did you feel the need to protect Kyle from your sister?" Marco asked.

Stacy started to answer, then closed her mouth. She clearly hadn't been expecting that question.

"Yesterday you told us you loved your sister," Marco said, "that you were best friends. Now we find out that both you and Justin felt a need to protect your son from her. Do you see my confusion? So why the disparity?"

"I don't have to answer your questions," she retorted. "You're not the police."

"No, but we work closely with them," Marco said, pulling out his cell phone. "If you'd like verification, I'll give you the name and number of Sergeant Sean Reilly and let you talk to him. Abby, would you write down his number and give it to her, please?"

I jotted it down and handed it across the desk. Stacy looked at it for a moment, then placed it in front of her. "What are you saying? That you're going to report this back to them?"

"We're trying to find a murderer," Marco said. "*They're* trying to find a murderer. Naturally, we collaborate. We have the same goal. So if you want to clear this up, I'm sure the detectives investigating the case will be grateful. If you don't feel the need to clear it up, we'll report that back to them."

It was a gamble, but Marco knew how to play it cool. He waited a few seconds, then touched my arm. "Let's go."

"Wait," Stacy said, rubbing her forehead. "Can you give me a minute to think?"

"There's no reason you have to think about your answer if you're telling us the truth," Marco said.

"Okay, look," she said. "It's true that Bev and I didn't always get along, especially in the years following the affair. But in the past year or so, with Kyle being older, more on his own, there was less need to—" She looked around, grasping for a word, and used a shrug instead. "When Bev put me in charge here, we grew close again."

I wasn't buying it, not because of what she'd said, but because of what she'd omitted—having less need *to protect her son*. How could she go from not trusting her sister around Kyle to being close to her simply because the boy was a teenager? Where had her mistrust gone? Had it suddenly dissolved in a bubble of goodwill? That didn't match up with what we'd heard from others.

"Let's go back to when Kyle was young," Marco said. "What were you protecting him from? Was Bev abusive?"

"She could be verbally abusive at times, yes," Stacy said. "I didn't want Kyle subjected to that."

"Was she verbally abusive to you or to Kyle or to both of you?" Marco asked.

Stacy said slowly, "Me . . . at times."

Reading off my notes, I said, "So she had an affair

with your husband *and* she was verbally abusive to you, and yet at the end you were close?"

Stacy said nothing, obviously realizing how inane that sounded, so I continued. "I'm surprised she had the nerve to visit you after you found out about her affair."

"That was Bev," Stacy said with a tinge of bitterness. "Our parents died years ago and we had no other siblings. Bev didn't want to lose the connection."

"How did you feel about it?" I asked.

"After she and Justin betrayed me, I never wanted to see either of them again. Unfortunately, divorce doesn't work that way, and neither did Bev."

"She forced herself back into your life?" I asked.

"Bev didn't take no from anyone," Stacy said. I wondered if she realized how weak that made her sound.

"How does Kyle feel about his aunt?" I asked.

"He doesn't . . . didn't really know her. Oh, he knew her to say hello, but I always made sure he had something else to do when she was coming over. Now he has the chess club at school and friends to hang out with. I hardly see him myself."

"Didn't he have questions about this aunt whom he wasn't allowed to be around?" Marco asked.

"I told him we'd gotten into a huge argument and weren't on good terms. He accepted that."

"Would it be all right if we talked to Kyle?" Marco asked.

Stacy's expression hardened. "No. I'm keeping him out of this."

"The detectives will want to interview him," Marco said.

"I won't allow it. I'll hire a lawyer if I have to."

"Lawyer or not," Marco said, "you can't stop the detectives from interviewing your son if they believe he's a material witness. And just so you know, they'll want to take him down to the station and put him in an interrogation room, where they may keep him for several hours. Are you willing to put him through that, or do you want to let us save him that agony by talking to him at home — or here in your office, if you prefer?"

"If the detectives were going to talk to him," she countered, "they would have done so already. I've been questioned and no one — got that? — *no one* has asked to interview Kyle."

"That doesn't mean they won't," I said.

"I'll take my chances," Stacy said, folding her arms. "There's absolutely no reason why he has to be interviewed. He's a thirteen-year-old kid, for God's sake. He doesn't know anything about the operations here at the shelter because he suffers from severe allergies and isn't allowed near animals. Anyway, he didn't know his aunt's habits, so there's nothing he could tell you. So my answer is an absolute no."

"Okay, then let me ask this again," Marco said. "Is there any possibility that Kyle took your key to the shelter to make a copy for his dad?"

"Same answer as before," she said. "Besides, my keys are always with me."

"Even at night?" I asked.

"I don't sleep with them, if that's what you mean," Stacy snapped.

"Are they in your purse?" I asked.

"That's right."

"And you keep your purse where?"

"In a closet," she said.

"In your bedroom?" Marco asked.

"No." Realizing that Kyle had access to her keys, she looked away uneasily.

"Would you do me a favor?" Marco asked her. "Would you ask Kyle if Justin approached him about getting the key?"

"As I said before," Stacy said, "Kyle would have told me if his father had asked for the key."

"So Kyle doesn't keep secrets from you?" Marco asked. "He shares everything?"

Stacy hesitated long enough for me to sense that her honest answer was no, yet she stubbornly answered, "He tells me everything." Stacy rose. "I'm through here. You'll have to go now."

Marco touched my arm, so I closed up the pen and prepared to leave. "If you change your mind, give me a call," he said. "You have my number."

"Won't happen," she muttered as we left her office.

"Well, Sunshine, what do you think of Stacy now?" Marco asked as we rode back to Down the Hatch.

"She's overly protective of Kyle, and that makes me wonder why."

"Wouldn't your mom be that way under similar circumstances?"

"I think she'd let me answer questions but maybe with a lawyer present. Why not?"

"That's what I keep asking myself," Marco said. "Why won't Stacy let Kyle be interviewed? What is she afraid of? And the answer I come up with is that Kyle has some knowledge about the events of Monday evening that Stacy doesn't want to get out."

"So why doesn't she just instruct him not to say anything to us about it?"

Marco pulled up to a railroad crossing, where a train was moving at a snail's pace. "Stacy can instruct him as much as she likes, but if we were to ask him a question she hadn't thought of, she has no way of predicting how he'd answer."

"I wonder if she realizes that protecting him makes her look guilty."

"Sunshine, this mom is worried enough to take her chances. She would rather have us think she had something to do with her sister's death than have her son open his mouth and prove it. And she believes she's safe because the detectives haven't asked to speak to Kyle."

"So all we have to do is put a bug in Reilly's ear so he can pass that along to the detectives and let them contact Kyle. That'll scare Stacy into letting Kyle talk to us."

"I'd rather not. We'd run the risk of Corbison actually interviewing the boy."

I couldn't help but shudder. Al Corbison was the detective who'd gone after me for the murder of a law professor, and I was still sore about how poorly he'd handled my interview. "So what do we do? Put more pressure on Stacy?"

"I'm thinking about working from the other end. Justin still sees his son every other weekend. Maybe we can impress upon him how important it is we talk to Kyle."

"If he did get a key from Kyle, he won't want us talking to the boy either."

The crossing gates went up, so Marco put the Prius in gear and started across the tracks. "What did you think about the rest of Stacy's interview?"

"I can't decide if she was purposely trying to confuse us or not. She told us she had to protect her son from her sister because Bev *could* be verbally abusive, not that she *was*. So was she or wasn't she abusive to Kyle? Then Kyle hit the teenage years and suddenly Stacy didn't need to protect him any longer, like he'd grown armor.

"And at that point, she claimed she and her sister grew close again. Yet from what Emma claims to have overheard, the sisters fought over the affair up until Bev's death. So how could Stacy feel close to her sister with all that pain still being dredged up?"

"Stacy is a puzzle," Marco agreed. "We'll have to get back to her eventually, but in the meantime, let's see if Justin is willing to arrange a meeting with Kyle."

"Is it legal to go behind the mother's back?"

"We're working for ourselves this time, Abby, so we can fly under the radar. I say we go see Justin tomorrow and find out when he'll have contact with Kyle next. After dinner tonight, I'm going to call Emma's coworkers and see what they can tell me."

"Does that mean we get to eat now?"

"Are you sure you feel like eating with that swollen throat and itchy rash? You're scratching all the time."

"I need to soak in an oatmeal bath, but I need food even more. I've got my wedding gown fitting after dinner."

"With a rash?"

"I'll manage somehow. I can't afford to delay."

After a miserably itchy dinner with Marco, I took advantage of the warm, breezy evening to walk four blocks to the beautifully restored Victorian home that was Betty's

Bridal Shop. I sat on a red tufted settee in the front parlor scratching my arms and legs until Betty came out front to get me.

Betty Dale was a slender woman in her late forties whose soft-spoken voice and small frame belied a hard-driven saleswoman. I'd met Betty before, when I was one of Jillian's bridesmaids, and I'd admired her strong business sense then. Now she came forward with her hand extended, then took a good look at me and pulled her hand back, her eyes widening in surprise. "What's wrong with your neck? And your arms?"

"It looks worse than it feels," I told her. "It's just swollen lymph glands and a rash."

Betty took a discreet step backward. "Are you contagious?"

"I don't think so, but I'm going to see my doctor in the morning just to be sure."

"Why don't you call me after you see the doctor and we'll go from there?"

She couldn't get out of the room fast enough.

"Hey, babe, how'd the fitting go?" Marco asked when he called later that night.

I stuffed the last bite of Ghirardelli Midnight Reverie chocolate bar in my mouth and chewed fast. "It didn't," I mumbled. "I have to go back tomorrow. Betty was afraid to touch me."

"Are you eating chocolate?"

"How did you know?"

"Besides hearing you chew, it's nine o'clock. You always eat chocolate at nine."

Was I that predictable? "Yes, Sherlock Holmes. I'm eating my usual dark chocolate squares." But only two because I really wanted to fit into my gown. "Did you have a chance to call Emma's coworkers?"

"I did. The fiscal director, John, was a little hesitant to talk about Bev, but he did admit she was a hard person to work for. Holly, Bev's assistant, was a little more open, but didn't have much to criticize. Holly did admit that Bev and Emma butted heads on several occasions and that Bev had called Emma on the carpet at least twice in the weeks prior to Bev's death, threatening to fire her, the last time on Monday. Apparently, it was Bev's habit to leave her office door open so the others could hear."

"Interesting." I wanted to lick the dark chocolate off my fingers but instead wiped them on a napkin. "What about the so-called outrageous audacity that Stacy mentioned?"

"John didn't know anything about it, but Holly believes it had something to do with Emma moonlighting. She said Bev was furious about it."

"I don't see why," I said. "So what if Emma took on some outside work in her free time?"

"According to Holly, Bev accused Emma of slacking off of PAR business so she could work on her outside projects during business hours."

"Do you think that is Emma's outrageous audacity?"

"It could be. Holly couldn't come up with anything else. Now I need to find out how far in debt Emma is to see how desperate she is to keep her job. By the way, I phoned Justin's customer, who verified that he did call Shaw's to tow his car and that it was indeed towed between five and seven p.m."

"That lets Justin off the hook."

"Not quite. The customer only spoke to Justin on the phone. He's never seen him in person, so he couldn't verify that the man driving the truck was actually Justin. The driver never introduced himself."

"Did you show him Justin's photo?"

"It's in your purse."

"Well, duh. So we'll need to do that."

"Right. That's on tomorrow's list."

Ah, tomorrow's list. I still had to get online to change the address on my driver's license and credit cards, call my insurance company, write my vows, reconfirm the reservation at Adagio, and get back over to Betty's Bridal Shop. In a weird way, a business slowdown was a blessing. I prayed it was a temporary one.

"Also on the list is another visit to Justin's business to see if we can set up a meeting with his son," Marco said. "Think you'll feel up to going along?"

"As long as I don't croak in the night." I waited for a chuckle. It wasn't forthcoming. "My frog neck? Croak? Get it?"

"Got it. Threw it out. Good night, Buttercup. Feel better."

Thursday

Feel better, Marco said. If only.

Instead, I felt itchier, and my rash was definitely worse. On the positive side, the swelling in my glands had gone down, so my jawline was visible again. Thankfully, the rash had avoided my face, so as long as I wore my khaki pants and a long-sleeved shirt, I looked presentable.

Being the first patient at the doctor's office was an advantage. I was in and out within fifteen minutes and on my way to the lab in the basement to have blood drawn.

Dr. Chen thought I had a virus but didn't want to take any chances with my wedding so near, so he'd ordered routine tests designed to rule out any bacterial infections.

Half an hour later, with a bandage above the crook of my arm, I headed to Bloomers. The rain that had been promised for the day before had materialized, so I had to keep my ragtop up, then use the umbrella I kept in the car to make the block-long dash to Bloomers. I got there shortly after eight o'clock and was greeted by Grace, who handed me a cup of coffee and informed me that Lottie was in the workroom with the plumber.

"Be prepared, dear," Grace said. "You may want to shield your eyes."

"Why? Is the plumber using bright lights?"

"No, not that. Are you aware of all those indelicate jokes about"—Grace sighed—"how shall I put it? The plumber's posterior view?"

"Grace, are you referring to the butt jokes?"

"Forgive me, love, but I just couldn't say it. Yes, that's what I'm referring to. Sadly, our plumber has become a cliché."

"Thank you, Grace. I'm prepared now."

"Your neck looks better, dear. What did the doctor say?"

I unbuttoned my shirtsleeve to remove the bandage while I gave her a rundown on my doctor's appointment. As I finished, Lottie came through the curtain making a face. "You've heard of a sight for sore eyes? Well, I just came from a sight that *causes* sore eyes. Why on God's green earth would a fella with his waist size wear jeans tight *and* low? When you got a belly, you need larger pants. There's no two ways about it."

"Is the plumber done?" I asked.

"He's just finishing up. I think the bill's gonna be high, though, sweetie, because he said something about the part being expensive."

Wonderful way to start the day—a blood draining *and* a wallet draining.

I walked into the workroom and found the plumber writing out a ticket at the table. "Okay, here you go," he said. "All done."

I picked up the ticket and my stomach knotted. "That part cost five hundred eighty-six dollars?"

"Yeah, you got an old cooler here. The parts aren't easy to come by. You might want to think about replacing it."

Three hundred for labor, plus the cost of the part? I wanted to cry.

After the plumber had gone, Grace and Lottie came into the workroom, where I was sitting in my chair staring at the bare spindle, the bill still clutched in my hand. "We've got to drum up more business."

Grace pried the ticket from my curled fingers and showed it to Lottie, who let out a low whistle.

"What about those flyers you mentioned?" she asked. "My boys will distribute them around town."

"And I can offer a two-for-one special on scones," Grace said. "Indeed, we can have a bake sale. That will draw in more customers."

"*That* many more?" I asked, pointing to the plumber's ticket.

Lottie took the bill and slapped it upside down on the desk. "Sweetie, don't you fret about this. I've seen bad times at Bloomers before and we came out of it."

Grace cleared her throat and assumed her lecture position. "It was the American poet Anne Bradstreet who said, 'If we had no winter, the spring would not be so pleasant: if we did not sometimes taste of adversity, prosperity would not be so welcome.'"

Lottie gave her a round of applause while I clapped halfheartedly. "I guess I'll start working on the flyer," I said.

"And I shall bake all evening," Grace said. "Lottie, tomorrow let's put out a signboard and see how many customers we can draw."

The bell over the door jingled. It was followed by the sound of something clattering to the floor and someone muttering.

"Oh, dear," Grace said quietly, peering through the curtains. "It's your cousin Jillian. Winter, it appears, is still with us."

CHAPTER TWELVE

"Hello? Where is everyone?" Jillian called.

"On the other side of the curtain," Grace said, and stepped into the shop. This was followed moments later with, "What in heaven's name do you have there, Jillian?"

"My baby," Jillian said happily. "Want to see her?"

At that point I had to go out to see what she had, because I knew very well it couldn't be her baby. I followed Lottie through the curtain and saw Jillian picking up baby rattles that had fallen out of a stroller and rolled across the floor.

"What are you doing?" I asked her.

"Shh! She's napping," Jillian whispered, tucking the toys into a side pouch.

"What is that smell?" Lottie asked, sniffing the air.

Grace bent over the stroller, which held a bundle wrapped in a pink print baby blanket. "Does someone have a dirty nappy?" she cooed, tugging the blanket away from the infant's head.

At Grace's gasp, I peered in for a look, then began to laugh. "You wrapped a sack of potatoes in a baby blanket?"

"Excuse me, please," Grace said, doing her best to hold back laughter as she rose and headed for the parlor. "I must see to my coffee machines."

Lottie gulped in air, fanned her face, and fled to the workroom.

Jillian placed her hands on her hips, arms akimbo, and glared at me. "Abby, are you going to be a non-supportress or an embracer?"

"Is this chapter two in Dr. Baybee's book?" I asked, pinching my cheeks together to keep from laughing harder.

"No, this is not chapter two," Jillian said snidely, clearly disgusted with me. "This is from a book by Dr. Charlton Harris-Easton Applewaithe-Paine." She pulled a hardback from a compartment in the stroller and showed me the cover. "It's called *Don't Muddle Motherhood: Be a Better Begetter*."

I pinched my cheeks harder. "A better *begetter*? And this doctor said to carry around a sack of potatoes to do that?"

"A ten-pound sack of potatoes is supposed to mimic the weight of a three-month-old baby, which Dr. Applewaithe-Paine says is how old an infant should be before he—or in this case she—is taken out of the house."

Jillian paused to carefully pick up the sack. "Would you like to hold your niece? Don't be afraid. She won't break."

"But will she grow roots?" I asked.

Simultaneous bursts of laughter came from the kitchen and the shop. Clearly we had eavesdroppers.

"Ha-ha," Jillian said drily. "Very unhumorous."

"Jillian, call me a non-supportress all you want, but I'm not going to hold that sack of potatoes and pretend it's a baby. Is Claymore going along with this charade?"

"Claymore," she said with a lift of her chin, "is proud to be an embracer, as are my parents. Once again it's you, Abby Knight, who is failing to do her kindred duty."

"Jillian, I do many things for my family, but I draw the line at cuddling a sack of potatoes. Now, I really need to get back to my desk because I have work to do."

As if she'd forgotten she was supposed to be holding an infant, Jillian tossed the sack back into the stroller and hurried to get in front of me before I could step through the curtain. "How am I supposed to be a good mother if I don't have my family's full support?"

I had a wry retort all ready, but then I gazed into her accusing eyes and saw a woman who was clearly afraid of impending motherhood.

Jillian, afraid of anything? I was shocked.

Then I was instantly transported back to our childhood years, when I had been the older cousin always looking out for the frail little girl with scoliosis. Jillian had gone through a lot in her short lifetime, and even though now she was a tall, thin, gorgeous but ultimately spoiled diva, underneath she was still that young child with the crooked back, counting on her tougher cousin to get her through scary times.

With a heavy sigh, I walked back to the stroller and wheeled it toward the workroom. "If I'm going to play aunt, I'll do it in private."

Jillian's face brightened into a wide smile. Clapping her hands together in a touchingly childlike gesture, she followed.

"So I'm thinking of some new baby names," she said, perching on a stool, while I sat on the other stool cradling the silly potatoes. "My current favorite is Cloud."

"Cloud Osborne?"

"Cloud Elizabeth Osborne," Jillian amended. "That way, her initials would spell out CEO, which I hope she will be someday."

"I don't know, Jill. Cloud sounds like a hippie name from the sixties."

"So what? I like it. I also like Air, Rain, Moonbeam, Sunshine—"

"Not Sunshine. You can't have that one."

"Oh, right."

I handed back the bundle, which Jillian promptly tucked into the stroller. "I really do have to get to work, Jill. I've got to come up with a flyer to advertise my business."

"Has it been slow?"

"It dried up practically overnight."

"I can help," she said eagerly. "Tell me what to do and I'll do it. Want me to distribute your flyers around the square?"

"Lottie's boys are going to do that."

"Oh." She looked crestfallen. Clearly she had too much time on her hands.

"If I think of anything, though . . ."

"Just let me know." She slid off the stool, put the sack back into the stroller, and gave me a shrug. "My business is slow, too."

"I'm sorry."

"That makes two of us."

The bell over the door jingled, and moments later my

thirteen-year-old niece, Tara, pulled back one side of the curtain. "Hi, Aunt Abby, Aunt Jillian."

The daughter of my brother Jordan and his wife, Kathy, Tara was nearly a carbon copy of me, with vivid red hair, freckles, green eyes, and a short stature. She even wore her hair in a long bob.

Her gaze instantly fell on the stroller. Crouching before it, she asked, "Who do you have in here?" Before Jillian could answer, Tara pulled back the pink blanket and fell on her haunches laughing. "Man, you really had me going for a minute, Aunt Jillian."

"It's not a joke, Tara," Jillian said with a sniff. "For your edification, I'm rehearsing. And if I didn't have to take Cloud home for a feeding—no, make that Air; I mean Rain—I'd tell you more about it. Suffice it to say I will be calling upon your babysitting services soon."

Tara stared at Jillian in amazement until the conclusion of her little speech, when she turned a puzzled gaze on me, as if to say, *Is she for real?*

"Bye, Tara. Let me know what I can do to help, Abs," Jillian called over her shoulder, then wheeled the stroller from the room.

I signaled for Tara to wait; then, after the bell over the door jingled, I said, "We have to be patient with Jillian. She's nervous about having a baby, so she's reading books on how to be a good mom. Just humor her. She'll get through it."

"That's fine, but I'm not babysitting that gross sack."

"I don't blame you. So what brings you here?"

Tara hopped up onto a stool, pulled out her cell phone, glanced at it briefly, and stuck it back in her pocket before answering animatedly, "Guess what I want to do. Never mind. You'd never guess it. I want to be a volunteer at the animal shelter. Isn't that awesome? Grandma asked if I wanted to go with her on Mondays and I said yes, yes, yes! She knows how much I love animals."

"Good for you, Tara. Will your mom and dad approve?"

"That's the only problem. I know they won't want me to work there because they'll be afraid I'll want to bring some of the pets home with me."

"That's why I was afraid to volunteer there," I admitted.

"The thing is, Aunt Ab, my parents would be right. There's already a mother dog and her puppy that I want."

"You've picked them out already?"

"Yes! I've been to see them twice. A friend asked if I would go visit them when he couldn't make it, so I did and fell in love."

"What kind of dogs are they?"

"They're mixed breeds. The mother dog is the ugliest thing I've ever seen—but so sweet and loving, Aunt Abby! She has lower teeth that protrude and a grizzled muzzle and pointy ears that have tufts of hair sticking straight up and raggedy fur that's brown and gray and black—oh, and she has only three legs, so she kind of hobbles."

"Tara, your parents will never let you bring home a raggedy three-legged mutt."

"Not right away maybe, but see, that's why I want to help out at the shelter. I'll get to see Seedy and her puppy while I work on Mom and Dad."

"Seedy?"

"That's her name. The shelter workers call her that because of how she looks. Her puppy is beautiful, though. His name is Seedling. Isn't that cute? So my plan is to convince my parents to let me bring Seedling home, and once they see how much she misses her mom, they'll let me adopt Seedy, too. They wouldn't want to split up a mother and child."

"Are you sure you can convince them?"

"See, that's where you come in. When it comes to an animal in the house, they'd never listen to me. It has to be you, Aunt Abby, and the first step is to talk my dad into letting me volunteer with Grandma."

"Whoa. Time out. What do you mean, it has to be me? Why can't Grandma talk your dad into it?"

"Grandma said her nerves are too shaky to put up a good argument. She said to ask you to do it because you badger people better than anyone else in the family."

"That was so sweet of her," I said drily.

Tara folded her fingers together imploringly and gazed at me with her big green eyes. "Please, Aunt Abby? My friend says no one is ever going to adopt Seedy because of her looks, but her puppy will be gone in a week. We can't let them be split apart. Not only that, but there's a rumor going around that the shelter may start putting unwanted animals to sleep." She took my hands in hers. "Seedy would be killed, Aunt Abby."

"You don't know that, Tara."

"You don't understand how pitiful Seedy looks, Aunt Abby, and she's been there for a month. Please help me save her."

As if I didn't have enough to do. "Tara, you're putting too much faith in your volunteer work. That will hardly guarantee that you'll be able to adopt Seedy or her puppy."

"Can you think of a better way?"

I sighed in exasperation. I didn't really need this extra burden.

But then I pictured the puppy being taken away from his mother, and at once the image in my head switched to one I didn't want to contemplate. What was Tara asking me, really, but to help her save a life? In my lifetime I'd convinced Jordan to do many things and I knew exactly which buttons to push.

I put my arm around my niece's shoulders and gave her a squeeze. I couldn't help but feel extremely proud of her for caring so deeply about a little dog's life. Somehow I had to help her succeed. "I'll give your dad a call and see what I can do."

"Oh, thank you, Aunt Abby," she said, throwing her arms around me. "You're awesome!"

At least to some people I wasn't dull, boring Abby.

"And just so you know," Tara said, "I hardly noticed that nasty rash on your neck."

I was just finishing up the flyer on the computer when Marco phoned.

"Hey, Kermit, how are you today?"

"Not froglike anymore, so you can drop the nickname."

"Buttercup, then. What's going on?"

"I just finished the flyer. All I have to do is take it to the printer and have a stack printed up; then Lottie's boys are going to distribute them around town."

"Is your printer broken?"

"It's just old and slow, and I have a credit at the print shop."

"How's business today?"

"We had a whopping five orders. I'm in a dry spell, Marco, and it worries me."

"The flyers will improve things," he said, as though it were no big deal. "Are you still open to going with me to see Justin at noon?"

"Nothing here to hold me back. I'll stop at the printer and then head your way. Have you had any luck tracking down Dayton Blaine?"

"None. She must have some kind of radar to know when I'm coming. I did find out that she and her husband hold season tickets for the Cubs baseball games, so we may have to go see a game one evening and see if we can find their box."

"That would be fun."

"It's a long shot, though, and we're operating on limited time."

Lottie stuck her head through the curtain. "Your brother Jordan is on the other line."

"Marco, I have to go. My brother is on the phone. I'll see you at noon."

I punched the button and said, "Hi, Jordan. Thanks for getting back to me."

"Yeah, what's up, Abs? I've got only a few minutes between surgeries."

Jordan was an orthopedic surgeon who worked for a private clinic in town. He was the middle child in our family and the one I was closest to growing up. Jonathan, my older brother, was a heart surgeon and had always been something of an enigma to me. I would never bet on being able to convince Jonathan of anything, but Jordan was a different matter.

"Jord, remember that scroungy mutt we found when we were kids, the one with mange?"

Jordan chuckled. "We fed him bologna and table scraps that we hid in napkins so Mom wouldn't find out."

"Do you remember what happened to that poor dog?"

"No, not really. Why?"

"Didn't it ever bother you that such a sweet-tempered dog had to go around begging scraps to stay alive? Don't you wish we could have adopted it?"

"Where are you going with this, Abby?"

Tactic one: Beat around the bush to work up to the point. "We've always had a soft spot for animals, haven't we? How many kittens did we rescue? Remember the whole litter we found abandoned in a box in the alley? How we fed them with doll bottles and found them all homes?"

"Two minutes, Abs."

Tactic two: Direct attack. "Why don't you have any pets?"

"You called to talk me into getting a pet?"

"So why don't you?"

"Because we're busy people. Hurry it up, Abby."

Tactic three: Talk fast. "You know Tara has been longing to help animals for a while now, and—"

"No, I didn't know that. Did she tell you that?"

"Would you just listen? Now there's a way for her to help without any obligation to you. And it would teach her social responsibility to give back to the community. I'm talking about being a volunteer with Mom at the animal shelter."

"You want my daughter to work at a murder site?"

"Oh, come on, Jord. Mom's not afraid to work there, and you know how spooked she can get. She'd love Tara's company, and Tara would get to play with the animals and help care for them."

"And ask to bring one home."

"Jordan, everyone who works as a volunteer doesn't bring animals home."

"Why don't you volunteer then, Abs?"

I should have seen that one coming.

Tactic four: Tell a white lie, then revert to tactic three. "Because I work late hours here at Bloomers and there's no time to volunteer. But your daughter would be so happy if you let her do it. Will you promise to think about it and talk to Kathy tonight? Or I can call her if you'd like. Hey, that's what I'll do, so don't even bother yourself—"

"Don't you have a wedding coming up?"

"This is so important to Tara that I'll make time for it."

"Why didn't Tara come to me about volunteering?"

"I think you know the answer."

"Because she knows I'd say no."

"And if you say no, Kathy would say no, and that would be the end of it. You'd have one brokenhearted girl."

"But if I say no to you, you'll just keep picking away at me until I cave in. So what are my options here really, Abs?"

Tactic five: Pluck the patriotic chord. "Let Tara do her civic duty, Jord. That's all. Your daughter will love you forever if you say yes. Talk Kathy into it; then call Tara in and let her know how proud you are of her wanting to volunteer. You'll be teaching her so much."

He sighed wearily and after a pause said, "Okay, Abs.

You win. I've got to get back into surgery now, but I promise I'll talk to Kathy about it tonight."

"Great! I'll call tomorrow to see how it went."

"Tell you what. I'll have Tara call *you* tomorrow, okay?"

"You're the best brother in the world, Jord."

"Yeah, right," he said with a laugh, then added, "Better than Jonathan?"

"Way better."

I said good-bye, hung up the receiver, and checked to see how long I'd been on that call: one minute forty-nine seconds. I took a bow to the empty room. I really was the best badgerer in the family.

At fifteen minutes before noon, I carried my flyer prototype up Franklin Street and across to Lincoln Avenue to Big Red Quick Print, a shop that had been in business for more than forty years. I stopped to chat with Bonnie, one of the owners, who commiserated about business being slow; then I retraced my steps to get to Down the Hatch.

"Hi, Gert," I called to the waitress as I started toward Marco's office.

"Oh, hey, hon. You might want to wait out here," she said. "The boss is in a meeting with his brother." She leaned closer to whisper, "It's a little warm in there, if you get my meaning."

I was tempted to ask Gert if Marco was having problems with Rafe, but then I decided that Marco would not want me discussing his business with the staff.

In a few minutes Rafe came out of the hallway and went around behind the bar, a none-too-happy look on his face. He saw me and called, "Hey, hot stuff. How's it going?"

"Look!" I said, stepping up to the bar. "No more froggy neck."

He gave me a puzzled glance.

"Didn't you notice how swollen it was the other night? Oh, right. You were too busy ogling Emma Hardy."

"A lot of good that did me," he said grimly.

Marco came striding out at that moment and said to me, "Ready to go?"

"See you, Rafe," I called. Once we were outside, I asked casually, "What was your meeting about?"

Marco scratched his nose, a sure indication that he didn't like the question. "I was going over a few things with Rafe."

"Everything okay between you two?"

"Of course. Why wouldn't it be?"

"You said before that it was taking longer than you thought to train him, so I was just wondering if that was putting a strain on your relationship."

There was the slightest hesitation before he said, "No. Business as usual." Marco opened the car door for me, and I slid inside. And those were the only words he said on the subject.

At Justin's towing shop, the same pair of Dobermans bared their teeth at us and the same long-haired man in the same stained blue overalls and red plaid shirt worked on a wad of chewing tobacco—a fresh one, I hoped—as he watched a tiny television propped on the counter in front of him.

He glanced up and nodded in recognition. "Hey, how's it going? You want to see the boss?"

"Please," I said.

He ambled through the door behind him and was back in a minute. "Boss says to go on in."

Marco escorted me around the counter, through the doorway, and up the hallway to Justin's office, where we found him seated behind his metal desk. He rose to shake Marco's hand and give me a friendly nod. "What can I do for you today?"

"We'd like to ask you a favor," Marco said. "We want to talk to your son. Can you set up a meeting for us?"

Holding his good-natured smile, he asked, "Why do you want to talk to Kyle?"

"Same reason we came to see you," Marco said. "To gather information about Bev Powers."

"Tell you what," Justin said, leaning forward in his chair as though sharing a confidence. "You'd be better off going to Stacy for that meeting. She's got primary custody of Kyle. I see him only every other weekend."

"To be frank," Marco said, "we asked Stacy, but she said no."

He sat back and smiled in such a way that I could almost hear his sigh of relief. "Well, then," Justin said, lifting his hands in a shrug, "there's your answer."

"She didn't say your son couldn't have a meeting with you present," I said.

"Still," Justin said, "I wouldn't go against Stacy's wishes."

"The thing is," Marco said, "Kyle may have useful information that will help us with this case."

Justin tapped his fingers on his desk, as though thinking it over. "Did Stacy mention why she didn't want you to talk to him?"

"She felt he was too young and innocent to be of any help," Marco said.

"Hey, she's his mother," Justin said cheerfully. "Mothers know best."

"He's a teenager," I said. "That's hardly young or innocent."

"Frankly, I'm puzzled by Stacy's and your reaction," Marco said, casually crossing one leg over his knee. "Neither of you seems to want to help find out who's responsible for Bev's death."

"I've been cooperative," Justin countered.

"Then what's the explanation?" Marco asked. "Are you afraid of what Kyle might reveal?"

"Me? No! I just don't want to cross Stacy." As if he were afraid of being overheard, Justin put his hand to the side of his mouth and said in a low voice, "She can be a real ballbuster, if you know what I mean."

"I'm not buying it," Marco said. "I think you and Stacy are protecting yourselves."

Justin's smile dissolved. He sat forward, serious now. "Look, man, all I'm doing is respecting Kyle's mother's wishes. If it were up to me, I'd let you talk to him. But if I set up a meeting and it got back to Stacy, which I'm sure it would, there'd be hell to pay. Been there, done that, got the scars."

"I can appreciate that you don't want to go against your ex-wife's wishes," Marco said, "so let's toss out the idea of a formal meeting. But what if we dropped by while you and Kyle were together and had an informal conversation with him with you present?"

"I don't want another court battle on my hands," Justin said, "so I'm going to have to go along with Stacy on this."

"Do you understand that by denying us access to Kyle," Marco said, "it makes it look like you have something to hide?"

"Hey, man, don't pin this on me," Justin said, placing

his open hands on his chest. "This is Stacy's decision. Have you considered that *she* might have something to hide?"

"Are you saying Stacy might have had something to do with her sister's death?" Marco asked.

"Interpret that any way you want," Justin said, rising. "Nice talking to you."

CHAPTER THIRTEEN

"We could always ambush the boy after school," I said to Marco as we drove back to town.

"Not ethical," Marco said. "We need an intermediary."

"Such as whom?"

"I'll have to work on it. What do you think of Justin now?"

"He really threw Stacy under the bus, didn't he, eager to put all the blame on her?"

"You said it, Sunshine. He could have set up a meeting between us and Kyle, and Stacy couldn't have done a thing about it."

"I don't know that she couldn't have done a thing about it, Marco. Exes have ways of making lives miserable. I saw plenty of that when I clerked at Dave Hammond's law office."

"You're right. So the question is, was Justin protecting himself from our further investigation or from his ex-wife's retaliation?"

"I can almost buy Stacy's protective reaction to our

request to interview Kyle," I said, "but not Justin's. He seemed relieved to have an excuse to deny us that meeting."

"My thoughts exactly. We'll have to turn up the heat and see what happens. As long as it's still early and we're on this side of town, let's stop at Blaine Manufacturing to see if we can catch Dayton Blaine in her office."

"It's twelve forty, Marco. She's probably out to lunch."

"Then where would she have lunch?"

"Adagios. It's the nicest place in town."

"Adagios it is."

But Adagios it wasn't, and we were unable to get any information from Dayton's secretary, so we returned to Down the Hatch for a quick soup and salad lunch; then I trotted up the block to Bloomers.

"How'd it go?" Lottie asked. "Make any progress?"

"We hit a wall," I said with a frustrated sigh. "We really need to interview a potential witness, but the teen's parents are being protective and won't let us. And then there's Dayton Blaine, who's never in and won't return Marco's calls."

"Why don't you and Marco take flowers to her?" Grace asked, coming out of the parlor. "We've delivered orders to Blaine Manufacturing before. If you stress that it's a time-sensitive arrangement, someone will make sure you get it to her right off. Then, once Marco gets a foot in her door, he can work his charm on her."

Grace was my Yoda. "Perfect. And if Dayton's not there, someone should be able to tell me where we *can* deliver the flowers. But won't it look odd for me to need a guy at my side to hand over a flower arrangement? I'm afraid we won't get any farther than the front desk."

"Then go alone," Lottie said. "You've interviewed suspects before, right?"

"But this is *Dayton Blaine* we're talking about," I said. "Do you know what people call her? The Donald Trump of New Chapel. She's merciless, and that frightens me a little—okay, a lot—and you know I don't frighten easily."

"Hey," Lottie said, "Dayton puts on her pants one leg at a time just like everyone else. Don't you be frightened by her."

"The thing is," I said, "I'm still not the most skillful interviewer in the world, and I can't afford to screw this up. It could be our only shot at talking to her."

Grace straightened my shoulders. "Stand tall, love, and remember these words by Eleanor Roosevelt. 'We gain strength, and courage, and confidence by each experience in which we really stop to look fear in the face . . . we must do that which we think we cannot.'"

"Remember who you're doing this for, sweetie," Lottie said. "Your mom is counting on you."

"And you know how you love a challenge," Grace said.

Grace and Lottie had just said the magic words. "You're right. I've never backed away from a challenge, and I'd do anything to help my mom." I took a deep breath and blew it out. "So what if Dayton is one of the most powerful people in town? That doesn't mean I can't talk to her woman to woman. Or I should say daughter to daughter. Everyone has a mother, right?"

"That's the spirit," Grace said.

"I'll make up a beautiful arrangement right now and take it over there," I said. "Maybe by suppertime, I'll have some news to report to Marco."

The bell over the door jingled and three customers

walked in, so while Lottie went forward to help them
and Grace returned to the parlor, I slipped into the
workroom to begin Dayton's floral arrangement.

Half an hour later, I turned the pale purple ceramic
container around to get a 360-degree view. I'd filled the
bowl with a striking arrangement of Iris Rendezvous, a
deep purple blossom, white pompom mums, and vibrant
pink hydrangeas edged with *Pelargonium graveolens*
"Lady Plymouth" greenery that I liked for its sweetly
scented, pale green leaves with frilly white edges. The
effect was just what I'd hoped—feminine yet powerful.

"Wow, sweetie, that's a knockout," Lottie said, coming
into the room. "If that doesn't get you in to see Dayton
Blaine, I'll eat my hat."

"Let's hope it doesn't come to that," Grace said, walking up behind us. "Remember, dear, persistence and determination will carry the day. If at first you don't
succeed . . . and all that."

"Got it. If Marco calls here, just tell him I'm out on a
delivery."

Blaine Manufacturing was a huge one-story brown brick
building that took up an entire city block, forming a big
U with a parking lot in the middle. Five reserved parking
spaces sat close to the main door, each marked with a
sign for the various Blaine family members. The one
marked *Dayton Blaine* was occupied by a big black Cadillac sedan with fancy chrome wheels. I hoped that
meant she was in.

I drove to the visitor parking area and pulled into a
space where I could see Dayton's car. With my nerves
strung tight, I carried the clear-wrapped floral arrangement into the beautiful lobby at Blaine Manufacturing,

crossed the shiny white-tiled floor, and approached the neatly dressed woman behind the reception desk. There was an older gray-haired man seated to her right who was watching a bank of television monitors.

"Delivery for Dayton Blaine from Bloomers Flower Shop," I called cheerfully, holding up the arrangement.

"You can leave it here," the woman said with a smile. "We'll see that she gets it."

Yikes. Not going according to plan. I put the arrangement on the counter so the receptionist could see it. "I'm Abby Knight, the owner of Bloomers, and this is time sensitive. I can guarantee the flowers for only so long. I'd prefer to deliver it myself so I know that it gets to Ms. Blaine right away."

"Don't worry," she said. "I'll send it right up."

Plan B: Try to look sweet and innocent and play on her sympathy. It was one of those rare times I was glad for my freckles because they made me appear younger. "Would it be okay if I took it? I'd really love to meet Ms. Blaine."

"Only those on the approved list can go up," the man said without glancing over at me. "Company policy."

"How do I get on that list?" I asked.

"Let me call Ms. Blaine's secretary," the receptionist said, pushing buttons on her phone. She listened a moment, then said, "Hi, Joan. Would it be all right for a florist to come upstairs to deliver an arrangement to Dayton right now?" She listened again, then said, "Okay. Thanks."

"Can I go up?" I asked.

"No. Ms. Blaine is in a meeting and has to leave for another meeting shortly, but I promise to get these up to her within the next few minutes."

Rats. I'd have to fall back on Plan C: Parking lot ambush.

"Okay. Thank you for your help." I handed her a flyer. "Remember Bloomers for all your floral needs. We have a great coffee-and-tea parlor, too."

Then I returned to my car to wait for Blaine to come out the door.

Promptly five minutes later, Dayton exited the building. She was wearing a navy pantsuit, a white shirt, and brown shoes, and with her short blond hair, bulldog face, and tall, thickset body, I nearly mistook her for a man.

I hopped out of my car and dashed over to hers, calling, "Ms. Blaine, hi! I'm Abby Knight, the owner of Bloomers Flower Shop. Did you like your complimentary floral arrangement?"

She gave me a cursory glance as she unlocked her car door with the remote. "Nothing in life is free. What's your angle?"

"I don't have an angle. I just wanted to talk to you for a minute."

She glanced at her watch, a heavy gold timepiece with a mother-of-pearl face. "I'm on my way to a meeting. Make it quick."

Oh geez. Here it went. I took a deep breath and dove right in.

"My mother found Bev Powers's body at the shelter and may be the police's top suspect unless I can clear her, so I was hoping you might be able to shed some light on the events of Monday evening." I took a breath. "Will you?"

She blinked at me several times, as though absorbing my words, then said, "No," and opened her car door.

"No, you won't help me?"

"That's right."

I was stunned for all of two seconds; then my indignation kicked in. "You won't help an innocent woman who may be wrongly accused of a crime? You can't spare even five minutes for a good cause?"

"Right." She got into the car, but I stepped forward so she couldn't close the door.

"I'm shocked, Ms. Blaine. *You*—the woman who is known for her philanthropy—*you* don't care about another woman's life? A *mother's* life?"

"I have a meeting across town. I don't *have* five minutes."

What bull. She had the power to hold up a meeting for as long as she wanted. "Could we set up a time afterward, then?"

"I'm too busy. Now, step away from my car, please."

"But what if your mother were in jeopardy? Wouldn't you want someone to help her?"

"My mother wouldn't be so foolish. Step back or I'll call security."

"Fine. You call security, and I'll call my friend Connor McKay, who writes for the *New Chapel News*. He's always looking for juicy celebrity news, and you *are* a local celebrity, Ms. Blaine. He'd love to hear how you wouldn't extend a helping hand to a gentle kindergarten teacher who may be wrongfully accused of murder, especially when she's been a loyal member of PAR and a long-standing volunteer at the animal shelter that you are supposed to be working for."

Dayton pulled her cell phone out of her jacket pocket and opened it. "You're pushing your luck, Miss Knight."

"That's what I do for people I love, Ms. Blaine, and if you'd only admit it, I'll bet you'd do the same thing if you were in my position. I don't really want to call the reporter, so won't you please talk to me after your meeting?"

She let out a frustrated sigh. "What is it you're looking for?"

"Not what, *who*. The killer."

"There's your problem. I don't know who killed Bev or anything about her movements on that day. A meeting would be a waste of time and money."

I had to pull out all the stops now. "Are you afraid to talk to me?"

Dayton let out a low, throaty laugh. "Young lady, I'm not afraid of you or anyone else."

"Then why won't you give me a few minutes of your time?"

"Because *time*," she said, enunciating the word as though I were slow, "is money. Got it? It's always about the money, Miss Knight."

"Please, Ms. Blaine, won't you at least talk to my boyfriend, Marco Salvare, a private investigator who's been trying to track you down for an interview?"

"Salvare is your boyfriend?"

"My fiancé, actually. Why?"

"He's making a nuisance of himself. Now—"

"Did you get along with Bev?"

"No. Now *back up*."

"What changed?"

She huffed in irritation. "What are you talking about?"

"I spoke with Emma Hardy, who said you and Bev got along until a few months ago."

"Don't tell me you actually consider Emma Hardy a reliable witness. Did Emma happen to mention that Bev caught her moving money out of the PAR account and into her own?"

I didn't want it to appear that we hadn't uncovered that important fact, so I just said, "See there? You do know things that would help us investigate Bev's death. All I need are ten minutes."

"So now it's *ten* minutes. You're a headstrong young woman, aren't you?"

"Please meet with us, Ms. Blaine. I'll bring you fresh flowers every day for a week if you'll just give us ten minutes of your time."

"Every day for a week, is it?" She looked me over. "You remind me of myself when I was your age— unstoppable and plenty of spunk. Okay, here's the deal. I'll meet with you tomorrow morning at nine o'clock right here in the parking lot. But for only ten minutes and only you alone. No professional PI tagging along. Got it?"

"Why by myself?"

"Because you're scared of me, and I want to see how you handle yourself. And don't bother with the flowers. I hate flowers." She motioned for me to step back; then she shut her door and started the engine. She backed out and pulled away without another glance in my direction.

"Marco, we need to come up with a list of questions," I said as I sat in my car talking on my cell phone. "I can't go to the meeting with Dayton unprepared."

"We'll do that over dinner tonight. Can I tell you how proud I am of you?"

"As many times as you want. I can't take credit for all

of it, though. Grace was the one who came up with the idea."

"But you executed it, Sunshine, and it worked. I'm going to open a special bottle of wine tonight to celebrate."

"Let's hold off on that celebration until the interview is over," I said. "I don't want to be premature. I could still fall flat on my face."

"You'll be fine. We'll rehearse until you feel comfortable"—he paused, then added in a sexy rumble—"even if it takes all night."

"What would I do without you, Salvare? Never mind. I don't even want to think about that. I'd better get back to Bloomers. I'm hoping some orders came in while I was out."

"Before you go, I spent the morning checking into the lawsuits that Bev had filed and none appear to have been against anyone connected to the animal shelter, so I think we're safe focusing our attention on Stacy and Justin Shaw, Dayton Blaine, and Emma Hardy. Unless another suspect pops up, of course."

"Oh, that reminds me. The one tiny bit of info I got out of Dayton today was that Bev apparently caught Emma Hardy moving money from a PAR account into her own. You might want to check with the fiscal director to see if he can verify that."

"What brought that up?"

"She was questioning why we would take Emma's word on anything."

"Got it. I'll contact John Bradford and see what he has to say. See you around five, babe."

I tucked away my phone and started the engine. The

rain had ended and the sun was out, so I put the top down, tuned the radio to a rock station, and sang along. I was still smiling from Dayton's compliments. She thought I had spunk. She thought I was unstoppable. Yep, that was me. Spunky, unstoppable Abby.

Maybe that was why the cop car was following me with its lights flashing.

CHAPTER FOURTEEN

Through my side-view mirror, I watched as the cop got out of his patrol car and removed his sunglasses. Sauntering up to my side of the 'Vette he said, "And just where do you think you're going? To a fire?"

"Reilly, it's you! Sheesh. You scared me to death."

Sergeant Sean Reilly and I went way back. When he first came onto the New Chapel police force, he trained under my dad and years later worked with Marco during his short stint on the force. Reilly had brown hair, intelligent brown eyes, a pleasant face, and was tall and sturdily built, all of which gave him an imposing presence. His only failing, as far as I could tell, was that he considered me to be a nuisance, always getting mixed up in murder investigations. But he'd been invaluable to Marco and me on a number of occasions, giving us just enough helpful hints to help crack open cases. With a scowl, he said, "I ought to give you a speeding ticket, you know that?"

"Ought to but won't, right? Because you wouldn't do that to a friend." I smiled up at him.

"Don't press your luck, Abby. You were going ten miles over the limit, and on busy city streets, that's a danger to you as well as to everyone around you."

"I'm really sorry, Sarge. My mind was"—I made a little twirling motion with my finger—"elsewhere. But you know I'm a good driver. I've never gotten a single ticket. That tells you something, right?"

"And that's why you're getting off with a warning. Pay attention, okay? Don't let your mind go"—he made the same twirly motion—"*elsewhere* when you're behind the wheel."

"I won't. I promise. Lesson learned."

"So," he said, dropping the angry cop role, "you and Marco still investigating the Powers case?"

"Yes, why? Got any new info?"

He leaned down, glancing around to see if anyone was watching. "Let Marco know the tox screen came back negative for drugs and alcohol and the final autopsy report will be in later today."

"Thanks, Reilly. I will."

"And no more speeding; got that?"

"Got it."

"Get out of here."

Not only did I watch my speed, I was also very careful to obey all the traffic signs on the way back, coming to a complete stop at each corner. I simply couldn't afford a ticket, not with that plumbing bill to pay.

When I got back to Bloomers, only one order had come in, but the good news was that Lottie had picked up the box of flyers and had called her sons to come down to the shop to distribute them.

"After work," she said, "I, personally, will get these

placed in as many shops on the square as I can, and I'll have the boys stick them under the windshield wipers of all the cars in the parking lots. By this time tomorrow, I'll bet you any money we'll have more business."

"I've already got my scone recipes selected," Grace said, "and I've even enlisted a dear friend's help in baking them this evening. Tomorrow we'll put out a signboard first thing."

"Thank you, ladies. You're the best assistants in the world. Now give me something to do."

"You can start by helping your mom," Lottie said. Dropping her voice to a whisper, she added, "She's in the workroom right now waiting to show you her latest art."

"Since you're whispering," I said, also in a whisper, "I'm assuming it isn't good."

"Be brave, love," Grace said quietly. "She's made worse."

I pulled back the curtain and walked into my oasis of paradise. Mom was sitting at my desk, staring at the computer, and when I drew nearer, I saw that she was on the Web site of a business that sold pottery and ceramic pieces.

"What are you looking for?" I asked.

"Oh, hi, honey. I was just making sure I haven't copied something I saw here. I often browse their site. Want to see what I made?" She jumped up, hoisted a shopping bag to the worktable, and reached inside. "Here it is!"

Out came a round, matte gray clay pot approximately ten inches tall with about an eight-inch circumference. The straight sides of the container looked like they were made of tiny blocks of concrete broken up by four small square openings spaced evenly around the upper perimeter. The openings were filled with tiny vertical bars painted black. The only thing Mom's creation lacked were miniature prisoners.

"What do you think?" Mom asked, gazing at her work of art with pride.

"It's unique," I said, then added gently, "If you're into prison art."

Her eyebrows drew together in a puzzled frown. She was clearly clueless. "Prison art? It's a flowerpot, Abigail."

"Mom, look at the block walls. Look at the bars in the windows. Rapunzel could have lived here."

She picked it up and turned it around, squinting her eyes as though trying to imagine what I was talking about. Then she set it down with a thump. "I made a jail cell, a round jail cell. What is the matter with me?"

"It's obvious what's on your mind, Mom. Look, why don't you take it home and paint it in a cheerful pink and make the bars yellow and then paint on some vines or something. You used to do tole painting. You can come up with something pretty that doesn't look so—prisonish."

With a dejected sigh, she put the pot back into the shopping bag. "It'll still be a jail cell to me. I'm sorry to have bothered you, Abigail. I know you're busy."

I wished.

Hoping to cheer her, as I walked her to the door, I said, "We're making progress on the case, Mom. I can't give out any details, but we do have several suspects."

"Thank you," Mom said, and gave me a hug, then leaned back and gazed into my eyes with gratitude. "It helps ease my anxiety on that front. But the PAR board just announced that they'll be holding a special meeting next Monday to decide on the shelter's no-kill policy.

They wouldn't do that unless there was going to be a change."

"You're going to organize a protest, aren't you?"

"Yes, but if they implement the new policy in spite of our protests, the shelter is prepared to start euthanizing unadoptable animals to make room for the younger, healthy ones that people want. The little mutt that Tara is so concerned about has been there a month, Abigail. I can't sleep at night for worrying. All I can say is, pray."

I could do more than that. I could corner Dayton Blaine about it — if I had the courage.

Shortly after five o'clock, I locked the flower shop and hurried up the street to Down the Hatch, which had no shortage of customers. Marco was standing with Rafe behind the bar, giving him what appeared to be a lecture. The look on Rafe's face said he wasn't happy about it.

"I *get* it, Marco," Rafe said irritably, as I slid onto a newly vacated stool. "You don't have to keep going over it."

"If you got it," Marco said in a low voice, "you wouldn't have made the mistake."

"Hi, guys," I said.

"Hey, hot stuff," Rafe said unenthusiastically.

Marco looked up and smiled. "Hey, babe. I'll be with you in a minute. You want to see if you can find us an empty booth?"

I swiveled to scan the wall behind me, but all the booths were filled. "Looks like we'll be eating in your office," I told him.

"That's fine. I'll meet you there in a few minutes."

Obviously Rafe's lecture wasn't over. I hopped off the stool and headed for Marco's office, taking a seat in one of the leather chairs in front of his desk. My cell phone beeped, so I dug it out of my purse and read the text message. It was from Tara: *Mtg w/Dad & Mom in 10 min. Xcited!!! :-D*

I texted back, *Good luck!*

The door opened and closed behind me, and a moment later Marco leaned down to kiss me on the cheek. "How's my favorite redhead?"

"Hungry and nervous, in that order."

"Nervous about the interview with Dayton?"

"That, and my mom said there's going to be a special board meeting to decide on the no-kill policy. I wish I had time to help her with the protest. The best I can do is try to convince Dayton to leave the policy as it is."

"You can't do everything, Abby. You're going to have to trust your mom with this one so you can focus on the case. I think your mom would prefer that, too."

The case, my wedding, my floundering flower shop . . . I massaged my neck. It ached just thinking about all there was to do. When was I going to squeeze in time to write my wedding vows?

"Tell me what you'd like to eat," Marco said, "and I'll go inform the kitchen."

"Whatever kind of sandwich you're having is fine with me."

"Want to try a new brand of microbrewed beer? We just got it in today."

"Sounds good."

While Marco was gone, I took the yellow legal pad from his desk and wrote *Questions for Dayton* at the top. Then I wrote:

> *How did you find out that Emma took money from PAR?*

My overworked brain refused to go any further on its own.

Marco returned with two bottles of beer, handed me one, then settled into the chair next to mine. "Food will be here shortly. What do you have already?"

I read the first and only question to him.

"Good start," he said. "Now, if Dayton sticks to her ten-minute rule, what is it we really have to know?"

"What her alibi is and why she and Bev were at odds for the last few months."

"Great. Put it on the list."

Collaborating with Marco made the process enjoyable. By the time our food arrived, we had come up with ten pertinent questions and ranked them in order of importance. We broke to eat; then I rehearsed while we finished our beers.

"Feeling better?" he asked, after we'd gone over the questions three times.

"Better, yes, but still nervous."

"That's okay. Nervousness will keep you on your toes."

My cell phone beeped to signal an incoming text message, so I checked the screen and saw Tara's name. "Excuse me just a sec," I said to Marco.

Tara's message was brief: *M&D ok'd it! I'm in! Thx, AA!!*

I texted back, *Congrats! Xoxo AA.*

"Sorry for the interruption," I said. "I helped Tara get the okay from her parents to help Mom do volunteer work at the shelter. She let me know Jordan and Kathy okayed it. Anyway, you were saying?"

"I just thought of something. Not to make you more nervous, but given your limited time with Dayton, you probably won't want to stop to write down her answers, so you'll have to remember them."

Like that would work. With so many things going on, I could barely remember my name. "I wish you were going with me, Marco."

"Come here."

He pulled me onto his lap and nuzzled my neck. "Just be your spunky, unstoppable self and you'll do fine. With luck, she may even forgo her ten-minute rule."

Friday

When I arrived at Bloomers at eight in the morning, I wasn't feeling spunky or unstoppable, but after two cups of coffee, an inspirational quotation from Grace, and a pep talk from Lottie, I did feel my old self again . . . until I saw pans full of scones sitting on a table in the parlor.

"The bake sale! I've been so nervous about my interview with Dayton, I totally forgot."

"Perfectly understandable, dear," Grace said, as Lottie carried the signboard out to the sidewalk.

"But I won't be here when we open," I said, "and it's bound to be busy."

"Why don't we see if Francesca can come in for the first hour?" Lottie asked as she stepped back inside. "I know you like to limit her involvement since she does like to run things, but she's been a great help in the past. I'm sure she'll be glad to lend a hand."

What could I say but yes? I couldn't very well leave them in the lurch.

"Great," Lottie said. "I'll give her a call right now. And FYI, we got one whole stack of flyers passed out last night. Let's watch those orders roll in today."

*   *   *

At eight forty-five, wearing neatly ironed coffee-colored pants with a crisp white shirt, I drove across town to Blaine Manufacturing and pulled into a visitor's space with five minutes to spare. Dayton's Cadillac was in her parking space, so I knew she was there. To steady my nerves, I sat in my car and reviewed the list of questions that I'd printed on a note card.

At a minute before nine, Dayton came striding out of the building wearing a black suit, a blue shirt, and black flats, carrying two paper cups with lids on top. I got out of my car and held up my hand in greeting.

"Follow me," she called, and strode up a brick sidewalk that led around to the side of the building, where there were shade trees and picnic tables. She sat down at a table and placed one of the cups in front of her and the other one across from her.

"Good morning," she said in a brisk but not unpleasant manner. "I brought you coffee, and for that, you should be greatly impressed. Dayton Blaine doesn't bring people coffee. People bring Dayton Blaine coffee."

"Then consider me impressed. Thank you, Ms. Blaine. That was very thoughtful."

"It's Miss Blaine, not *Miz* Blaine. I want to swat flies when I hear *Miz*. Don't just stand there looking sheepish. Have a seat and tell me how you like the coffee."

I sat down opposite her and reached for the cup, but before I could get it to my lips, she said, "I hope you like it black. Better for you than fattening cream."

Black coffee. *Yuck.* I lifted the cup to my mouth and braced myself so I wouldn't wince at the sharp bite of the brew. Then I took a sip—and found it smooth and sweet.

"To your liking?" she asked. "You struck me as a cream and sugar kind of girl."

"Thanks. It's perfect, but I thought you said it was black."

She wagged her finger at me. "You weren't paying attention. My statement was, I hope you like your coffee black. I did not say it *was* black. Important difference. Now, let's see how you do with this so-called interview." She tapped the face of her watch. "Ten minutes starting now."

I quickly set the coffee aside and placed the note card on the table in front of me. "Okay, first question."

"I'm fine. Thanks for asking."

I blinked at her for a moment. Had I erred? "I'm sorry. I guess I should have—"

"Never mind. Apparently, my well-being isn't important. Go on."

Wonderful. Dayton had rattled me right out of the gate. I drew in a steadying breath. "Okay, number one. Did you see or talk to Bev on Monday?"

"No. Next question."

I tried to steady my nerves by focusing on the note card. "Did Bev have any enemies that you knew of?"

"*That you knew of* is implied. You wasted time by adding it to your question. Did Bev have enemies, you should have asked. Lots. No one liked her. Next."

I wanted to yell, *Slow down!* But instead I took a quick breath and moved on. "Do any of her enemies stand out as likely to have harmed her?"

"Awkward sentence. Reword it, please."

I thought fast and blurted, "Should we be looking at any of her enemies as potential murderers?"

"Better, not great, but I'll answer it. Physically, I

wouldn't think so. Politically, I would have hoped so. She was a terrible councilwoman. Next."

Dayton's answers were so rapid, my brain was racing to keep up. "What was your relationship with her like?"

"She was a bitch. I dealt with her as little as possible. Don't waste any more time on that one. Next."

My stomach was starting to knot. How I wished I had a tape recorder. "How did you know about Emma taking money from PAR?"

"I made it my business to know everything that went on at the PAR office."

"But who told you?"

"Bev. Next."

"When?"

That made her pause a moment. "On, let's see. The Friday before she died? It wasn't Monday, of that I'm one hundred percent certain. Yes. It was Friday. Next."

"What did Bev tell you about Emma?"

"She called to tell me she was going to fire Emma and wanted the board's blessing. I told her she had to talk to the girl first, document it, and give her a chance to respond before she could fire her. SOP."

"Standard operating procedure?"

Dayton tapped her watch. "You're wasting time on the obvious."

"What was Bev's relationship with her sister, Stacy, like?"

"At the PAR meetings they were cordial, but it was as clear as the noses on their faces that they didn't like each other. Do I know why? No. Didn't care. Move on."

She was running through my questions so quickly, I was certain we'd finish before the ten minutes were up. "How often do you visit the shelter?"

"About twice a month, more if I hear of a problem. Bev was handling it, though, so I had no reason to interfere."

"Why do you have a key to the shelter?"

She had just lifted her cup to her mouth, but then paused to ask curiously, "*Do* I have a key?"

"I was told you do."

"Huh."

"Have you ever used it?"

Dayton took a swallow of coffee. "If I didn't know I had one, the answer is self-evident."

She was quickly eroding my confidence. I wished I had time to edit my questions so she wouldn't pick them apart. "When was the last time you were at the shelter?"

"Check with my secretary. I don't keep unnecessary details in my head." She glanced at her watch. "Clock's running."

Yikes. Maybe I wasn't going to finish after all. Instead of reading the next question on the note card, I inserted one of my own. "Are you in favor of changing the shelter's no-kill policy?"

Dayton opened her mouth to answer, then clamped it shut.

Finally, I'd slowed her down.

CHAPTER FIFTEEN

Dayton took a slow, noisy sip of coffee, gazing at me over the top of her cup with a lifted eyebrow, as though she suspected a trap. "What does my opinion on the no-kill policy have to do with Bev Powers's death?"

The thread was tenuous, but I forged ahead. "My understanding is that you and the board of directors, and Stacy Shaw, want to change the policy so animals can be euthanized, but Bev was the lone holdout against it."

"Is this your convoluted way of insinuating that everyone who wanted the policy changed is a suspect?"

"A kill shelter isn't humane, Miss Blaine. We shouldn't be playing God with animals' lives. PAR needs to raise more money to take care of the animals and work harder to adopt out those that might be labeled unadoptable."

"Platitudes, Miss Knight. You're spewing platitudes and have ventured off topic. But since you brought it up, let me ask you this. If an animal is brought in who is in terrible pain from being run over by a car, with no hope for recovery, what should be done? Should that animal be made to suffer even longer until it dies?"

"Well, no. But I'm talking about a shelter that euthanizes animals simply because they're unwanted."

"You have no idea what the operating costs of an animal shelter are, do you? Of course not. Don't think me heartless. I have four cats, all adopted from the shelter. One is near the end of her life, and if she should become in excruciating pain, you'd better believe I'd want to see her put down rather than suffer needlessly."

"Why not give her pain medication and let her end her life naturally?"

"Dope her up, do you mean? Sure, I could do that, if you want to call that natural, but is that humane? Who knows? Maybe that's the route I'll take. I won't know until I have to make that call. But that's beside the point. The shelter is operating under severely limited funds and a critical lack of space. Do we turn away young, healthy animals in desperate need of homes so we can nurse the old, the unadoptable, and the suffering indefinitely?"

"Some shelters do it. How do they manage?"

"They have more money than we do."

"More money than Blaine Manufacturing?"

"Blaine Manufacturing isn't in the business of running an animal shelter."

"Then why doesn't PAR have more fund-raisers? I can't even remember the last time there was one."

Good. I'd slowed her down again.

Dayton picked up her coffee and took a swallow, then another. Then she set her cup on the table and folded her arms. "Enough of this back-and-forth dickering. We could keep at it all day. I'm going to level with you now, so pay attention. I did *not* want to change the shelter's policy. Got that? I was *not* in favor of it. I had to go along with Bev because she convinced me it wasn't feasible to continue the way we were."

"*Bev* convinced you? I was told that Bev was the only one who *didn't* want to change it."

"Yes, yes," Dayton said brusquely, "you've already stated that. I'm telling you now that Bev was working behind the scenes to get it changed but didn't want anyone to find out. Bev was the consummate politician. She knew the voting populace wouldn't like it, so she convinced her sister and me to come out in favor of it and let us do her dirty work for her."

Then Stacy had lied to us. Another mark against Bev's sister.

"How did Bev convince you?" I asked.

"That's not important."

"It *is* important. It goes to your credibility."

"My *credibility*?" Her nostrils flared in indignation as she glared at me. "Young lady, do you understand to whom you're talking?"

Uh-oh. Now I'd done it. I had to get this right or the interview would be over. "A very influential and powerful businesswoman."

"You're damn right I am. I've helped make New Chapel the thriving town it is. I've turned struggling businesses like yours into successes *based* on my credibility. But if you think I'm not a credible source, *you* shouldn't be here talking to me, and I most certainly should not be talking to *you*."

I was on the verge of apologizing when Stacy Shaw's warning jumped into my head: *Don't let Dayton Blaine's money and influence in this town deter you from asking tough questions.*

With my heart in my throat, I said, "You're avoiding the question."

"And your ten minutes are up." She rose from the table and picked up her cup. Striding away, she called over her shoulder, "Not so spunky today, are you?"

Dayton Blaine wasn't going to get away from me that easily. I jumped up and hurried after her. "What about your whole speech on the humane aspects of euthanizing? Were you just lying to me?"

"Oh, my Lord, now the upstart is calling me a liar!" she cried out. "For your information, Miss Knight, I was on the debate team in college. I can argue an issue with the best of them. Kind of a sport to me, in fact, and quite useful in my line of work."

"If Bev was holding something over your head to force you to back her idea—"

Dayton came to a complete stop and waited for me to catch up to her. "Did I *say* Bev was holding something over my head?"

"You implied she was."

"You're impertinent." She started off again at a fast stride. "Convinced doesn't mean blackmailed."

"So are you saying Bev *convinced* you that changing the policy was just a matter of economics?"

"Stop putting words in my mouth."

"But it *is* cheaper to run a kill shelter, isn't it?"

"That was Bev's argument. As you said, other shelters manage."

"Here's what I don't understand," I said, nearly panting in my efforts to stay abreast. "You won't tell me how Bev convinced you to go along with her plan, so why tell me anything at all? Aren't you worried Marco and I will dig around to see what she was using to *convince* you?"

Dayton laughed loudly. "Don't waste your time investigating me, Miss Knight. You won't find anything. But please do understand that I absolutely abhor—got that?—*abhor* having to acknowledge that a person of Bev's competency got the better of me. Dayton Blaine never admits to mistakes. I told you about this *only* because it might somehow be useful in tracking down the real killer. And by the way, you forgot to ask where I was between five and seven o'clock Monday night, so here's your answer. I don't remember. Check with my secretary. She knows every move I make."

"Will she talk to me?"

"Her name is Joan and I'll make sure you have full access to her. I'll call her on my way to the meeting." Dayton came to a stop beside her car. "Cross me off your suspect list, Miss Knight. I didn't do it. And forget what I said about your lack of spunk. You've got loads. You can also tell your private investigator boyfriend that you didn't do too badly for a rookie."

"Thank you, Miss Blaine. If you have just another minute, can I tell you about this little dog named Seedy whose life is in jeopardy because she's considered unadoptable?"

"Please. I've heard all the sob stories I care to. You want something to cry about? What about dogs that spend their entire lives in cramped wire cages?"

"That's why the shelter has to make an effort to find homes for them."

"To do that, they'd need more staff, so again, we're talking money issues. Remember this, Miss Knight. It's always about money."

She got into her car and slammed the door. I stepped to one side as she backed out with a roar of the powerful engine and took off, her cell phone plastered against the side of her face.

"I'm still shaking, Marco."

"But you did it, Fireball. You got your interview."

"It's not very long, but I feel good about what I learned. I didn't have any luck changing her mind on the issue of euthanasia though."

"You worked that into the interview?"

"I snuck it in at the end. A lot of good it did me."

"Where are you now?"

"I'm still in the parking lot at Blaine Manufacturing."

"Want to give me a rundown?"

"Sure." I took a slow, deep breath, trying to calm my jumpy nerves. "First of all, Dayton can't remember where she was at the time of the murder, so she gave me full access to her secretary. She also told me something shocking. Bev was the one who was pushing for a policy change at the shelter, not Dayton or Stacy Shaw. Dayton said Bev convinced her and Stacy to go along with it, but when I asked how Bev convinced her, she wouldn't tell me. She said to stop wasting time on her and go after the real killer."

"Very common for a suspect to say, Abby."

"I know, but if her secretary can prove where Dayton was, I feel comfortable in crossing her off our list, Marco. I got really good vibes from Dayton. And if what she said about Bev is true, then Stacy lied to us when she said she was in favor of the policy change and Bev wasn't. If she lied about that, who knows what else she lied about?"

"Sounds like another visit with Stacy is in order."

"And Emma. Dayton said she learned about Emma taking PAR funds from Bev. Apparently Bev called Dayton on Friday and said she wanted to fire Emma, but Dayton advised her to give Emma a chance to defend herself first. She said it was SOP."

"I'll give the PAR fiscal director a call right now and check it out. If funds were moved, he had to know."

"Before I head back to Bloomers, I'm going to take Dayton up on her offer and stop in to see her secretary."

"Okay, babe. Let's reconnoiter at noon."

"One more thing. I was so flustered about everything yesterday evening that I forgot to tell you I saw Reilly, and he said the tox results came back negative for drugs and alcohol and the final autopsy results would be in later today."

"Where did you see Reilly?"

I was afraid he'd ask that. "On Concord Avenue."

"On Concord Avenue," Marco repeated, as though trying to understand. "Did he flag you down to talk to you?"

"You could say that."

"Abby, did you get pulled over?"

"Yes, but I just got a warning, and I'm being very careful now with the speed limit, so no lecture, please."

"Why would I lecture you?"

Clearly that was the wrong thing to say because Marco sounded peeved.

"Did Rafe say something about me lecturing him?" Marco asked.

Yikes. Didn't want to be in the middle of that. "I'm getting out of the car now and walking toward Blaine's main door."

"Abby."

"My phone's going to cut off. See you at lunchtime. Bye."

Ten minutes later, I left Blaine Manufacturing fully satisfied that Dayton Blaine should not be a suspect. Along with times and places, Joan had given me the names and phone numbers of the people with whom Dayton had met right up to the minute she appeared at the PAR meeting. She apparently hadn't even taken a break to eat dinner.

When I got back to Bloomers, Grace and Francesca had a parlor full of customers, and Lottie was behind the cash register taking payments for prewrapped packages of scones. Before jumping in to help, I slipped into the workroom to check the spindle, but there were only three slips of paper on it.

So much for the orders rolling in.

At noon, I met Marco in the Central Park Plaza one block west of the courthouse, where we sat on a bench to eat turkey and Swiss cheese sandwiches.

"It's still early," he said, after I'd complained about the lack of orders.

"The day is half over," I said.

"You're looking at the glass as half empty, Sunshine. You can't expect things to happen right away. The flyers just went out yesterday evening. Take a breather from worrying."

Easy for him to say.

"How did my mom do?" Marco asked. "Did she bug you about the wedding?"

"No, we were too busy."

"That's good news."

"She was still helping when I left. The parlor is doing great business because of Grace's scones, but unfortunately that's not where the money is."

Marco said nothing. His attention was on something across the park, so I followed the direction of his gaze. Was that Rafe walking along West Lincoln? With a girl?

Whomever or whatever Marco was watching, he didn't look happy about it, so I changed the subject. "Dayton Blaine's secretary gave me a list of the people Dayton met with Monday afternoon up until seven p.m., along with phone numbers. I'll bring them down after work tonight — which reminds me. Are we meeting for dinner?"

"I'll contact the people on the list tomorrow instead of at dinner."

"No, I asked if we were getting together for dinner."

Without turning his head, he asked, "Tonight?"

"No, next Saturday."

"Next Saturday is our wedding."

"Marco, who are you watching?"

He finally looked at me. "What?"

"Never mind. Did you talk to the fiscal director at PAR?"

"John Bradford. Yes, I did. He told me that Bev had been reviewing the PAR account ledgers when he left the office last Friday. He didn't think anything of it because Bev was in the habit of doing random bookkeeping checks, and he didn't think she'd found any problems because she didn't say anything to him on Monday. But when he got to work on Tuesday morning, he had an e-mail in his in-box from Bev saying that she wanted to meet with him at lunchtime regarding some funds that had been moved. I asked John if he had any idea what she'd meant, and he said he assumed Bev had shifted money around and just wanted to let him know. Apparently, she'd done it before."

"When had Bev sent the e-mail?" I asked.

"Monday at four twenty-seven p.m."

"Then our time line is that Bev reviewed the books during the day on Friday, then consulted with Dayton Blaine about firing Emma, sent an e-mail to John, then left the PAR building and went to the animal shelter."

"You can insert that Bev threatened to fire Emma on Monday afternoon, too. I phoned Bev's assistant, Holly, to double-check what she'd told us before, and she remembered very clearly that Emma ran out of Bev's office on Monday afternoon crying. And don't forget, Emma told us herself that Bev had threatened to fire her."

"Except Emma said that Bev had threatened to fire her because she was moonlighting, not because she took money."

"Which would you own up to?"

"Good point. So we now have two suspects who lied to us."

"After I spoke with John and Holly, I asked to talk to Emma, but Holly said Emma had called off today. I tried to reach her on her cell phone, but so far she hasn't returned my call."

"She's probably hoping to avoid us," I said.

"If she's smart, she'll realize that avoiding us will make her look guilty. I'm hoping she'll call me back so I can set up a meeting with her this evening, but not at the bar. I don't want Rafe interrupting again."

"If you do hear from Emma," I said, "try to schedule the meeting after seven o'clock. I have to go for my gown fitting at six thirty."

"Abby! Marco!"

I looked around and saw Jillian coming across the park from the direction of Bloomers. She wasn't pushing the baby stroller this time. Instead, she was cuddling something against her chest. When she got closer, I could see that she was wearing what looked like a black baby sling over her T-shirt.

"Here you are," she said breathlessly, plopping down beside me on the bench.

"What do you have on?" I asked.

She turned toward me so I could see the papooselike device that crisscrossed her front. Inside was a bundle wrapped in a familiar-looking pink baby blanket. "It's a baby wrap. It keeps the baby close so she can hear her mommy's heartbeat. Want to try it on?"

"No, thanks," I said.

"Oh, go ahead; try it." She removed the bundle inside and thrust it into Marco's unsuspecting arms. "You can hold the baby while I get Abby suited up."

"I'm not putting that thing on, Jillian," I said, hopping to my feet, drawing the attention of several women strolling past.

"Fine." Jillian turned to Marco, who was fumbling with the rolling sack of potatoes. "You look good, Uncle Marco."

Marco stood up and promptly handed the blanket-wrapped sack to me, mumbling, "I have to get back to the bar. See you at five." He nodded to Jillian and strode off.

"What's his hurry?" Jillian asked.

"Jillian, no guy wants to cradle a pink-wrapped sack of potatoes in his arms in the middle of a public park, and, yes, he's a non-supporter just like me. Get over it."

"You're cruel."

"Jillian, honestly, have you ever come across any other young women who are going to the same lengths as you are to prepare for an upcoming birth?"

"I'm not your average young woman, so don't even try to compare." She inserted the bundle in the sling, then sat down. "Is business still slow? Is that why you're out in the park today instead of at work?"

"Yes, business is still slow," I said, sitting down beside her, "but I came out here to have lunch with Marco. What about your business?"

"I have a new client," Jillian said excitedly. "I'm meeting with her at seven o'clock this evening. Tara said she'd babysit."

"You really asked Tara to sit with your—" I pointed to the bulge under her sling. I couldn't bring myself to call it a baby.

"Of course I did. I take this very seriously, Abs."

I couldn't imagine that Tara would take it seriously. But if Jillian was willing to pay, I had no doubt but that Tara would be willing to accept her money.

Jillian got up and adjusted her load. "Okay, I'm off to work out with my personal trainer. I do special pregnancy exercises with her. I'll give you her card so that someday you can . . . Hey, isn't that Rafe coming this way?"

I peered around Jillian for a look and saw Rafe strolling along the path toward me, holding hands with a familiar-looking young woman.

"Looks like Rafe has a new girlfriend," Jillian said.

She was new, all right. Emma Hardy. Just the person I needed to see, although I doubted she'd be thrilled to see me.

I ducked behind Jillian and waited.

CHAPTER SIXTEEN

"Hi, Rafe!" Jillian called, waving.

I waited until I could see their legs; then I stood up next to Jillian and pretended to be surprised. "Hey, you two."

"Hi, Abs!" Rafe said, smiling broadly, while Emma's eyes widened in surprise.

"Hello again, Emma," I said. Then at Jillian's elbow nudge in my side, I whispered to my cousin, "I was going to introduce you." I smiled at Emma and said, "Emma Hardy, this is my cousin Jillian Osborne." At the second elbowing, I said, "Jillian owns a personal shopping service called Chez Jillian."

"And just so you know," Jillian said, "I'm always willing to take on a new client. And you do look ready for a makeov—"

"Jillian," I said loudly, causing her to jump, "you're going to be late for your workout."

"You're right. Nice to meet you, Emma, and don't forget what I said. *Ciao*, Rafe. Okay, Abs, I'm off to exercise."

"I didn't know your cousin had a baby," Rafe said, as Jillian hurried away.

"She doesn't," I said. "She's rehearsing."

"Rehearsing for a baby?" Rafe asked.

"It's a long story," I said, "and not worth going into. You just missed your brother, by the way."

"That's okay," Rafe said with a roll of his eyes. "I see way too much of Marco. I don't know how you put up with him."

Emma was edging away, tugging Rafe along with her.

"Hey, Emma," I said, startling her, "I need to talk to you about Bev Powers."

"I don't know how I could be of any more help," she said. "I've told you everything I know."

I pretended to search my purse. "Darn, I left my notes at Bloomers. Tell you what. Why don't we sit down for a short chat this evening at the Daily Grind coffee shop?"

Emma glanced at Rafe. "We sort of made plans, right?"

"We did?" Rafe asked, clearly puzzled. "I'll be at the bar until midnight."

"Then it'll work," I said to Emma with a smile. "We'll meet you at seven thirty."

"You and Marco?" she asked, sounding hesitant. "I don't know . . ."

It was the first time I'd ever encountered a female who did not want to sit down with Marco. Then again, he had pulled the rug out from under Emma at our last meeting.

"Just you and me, then," I said. "We'll have some girl time. I'll buy the coffee."

Her eyes, which were not twinkling at that moment, searched my face, as though trying to deduce my true intentions. With an unhappy shrug, she said, "I guess so."

"Perfect. I have to run now. See you tonight. Bye, Rafe." I turned and started across the park at a quick stride so Emma wouldn't have time to change her mind.

Before I reached Bloomers, I phoned Marco and told him what had transpired. "I thought she'd feel more pressure to show up if she knew I'd be waiting there by myself."

"Good thinking."

"Let's go over the questions at dinner like we did last night. That worked well."

"Sure."

Dead silence followed.

"Marco?"

"Sorry. I was just going over some accounting. We can talk more later."

"That's fine. I'm back at Bloomers now and it looks like your mom is gone."

"Uh-huh."

He wasn't listening.

"So other than three little green men with horns sticking up out of the tops of their heads, Bloomers is back to normal."

"Good. I'll see you after five."

I slipped my cell phone into my purse and stepped into Bloomers. Marco was quite clearly distracted. Why wouldn't he talk to me about it?

"Hey, sweetie," Lottie said, "you've got orders on your spindle."

"Really?" Maybe those flyers were working after all. "How many?"

"Well, just two. But both customers asked for the discount we advertised, so at least people are paying attention to the flyers."

"Two is better than nothing," I said, trying to sound cheerful. "I'll get on them right away. How did Francesca do this morning?"

"She was fine, love," Grace said, gliding out of the parlor. "Francesca works well under pressure, and not everyone can do that. And you'll be happy to know we sold out of all the scones, so I thought I'd make a bigger batch to sell tomorrow."

"That's great, Grace, but please turn in your receipts so I can reimburse you for your expenses."

"Perhaps we can use the money we made on scones to put toward the plumbing bill," Grace said.

"It should also go to the printer to pay for the flyers," Lottie said, as she tidied up the cash counter.

"We have a credit at the printer for that," Grace said.

"Don't forget we still have to pay off that new back door," Lottie said.

"We may need to run a bake sale all week," Grace said.

Feeling more depressed than ever, I left them discussing the bills and went through the curtain to work on the orders. Surrounding myself with fresh, fragrant blossoms was always a mood booster. I just wished I had more than two arrangements to make. There were a lot of flowers to use up before they went bad.

At three fifteen, Tara came bouncing into the workroom and hopped up onto a stool to watch me prep a big delivery of roses that had just come in. "What's up?" she asked.

"Nothing much on my end, but you look like the cat that swallowed the canary."

"A cat ate a canary? *Ew*. That's gross."

"It's a saying, Tara. It means you've got a secret."

"A secret," she said, her eyes lighting up, "that I'm

going to share with *you*. Guess what Grandma and I are going to do in ten minutes. Okay, you'll never guess. We're going to the animal shelter. Yay!"

"This isn't your volunteer day."

"I know, but I told Grandma about Seedy and Seedling, and she totally got how much I want to visit them, so I asked if she would take me there after school today and she said yes! She even promised not to tell Dad and Mom until the time was right. Isn't Grandma amazing?"

"She's a cool grandmother," I said. I only hoped my brother and sister-in-law would be okay with it when they found out.

"Why don't you come, too? I really want you to meet Seedy and her puppy."

Hmm. My spindle was empty. There was no reason I couldn't go—and there was even a reason why I should. It would be the perfect opportunity to question Stacy Shaw about her lie.

"I have to be back at five," I said.

"No problem. I do, too. So you'll go?"

"Sure. I'd love to."

"Awesome! I'll text Grandma and tell her to pick us both up here."

Standing in their usual positions behind the reception counter at the animal shelter, the Friendly Sisters informed me that Stacy was on a conference call in her office and wouldn't be available for at least ten minutes, so I joined my mother and Tara in the dog ward. Tara was bouncing excitedly as Brian brought the puppy, Seedling, out to a small play area. I couldn't help but smile as Tara got down on her knees and cuddled the caramel brown furball against her body.

"Isn't Seedling amazing?" Tara asked, as the puppy galloped around her, yipping excitedly and wagging his little tail so hard, I thought it would fly off.

"He's darling, Tara," Mom said. "Abigail, you need to work on your brother."

"I will, but let's give Jordan time to get used to Tara working here first," I said.

"What if someone wants to adopt him?" Tara asked, as the pup chewed on her fingers. "I'd just die if that happened."

"Do you know if Tara can put a hold on Seedling?" I asked my mom.

"I'll have to ask," Mom said, then whispered to me, "But what will we do if Jordan and Kathy say no?"

Tara heard her anyway. "Aunt Abby won't let them say no. Right, Auntie A?"

"I'll go find out if it's possible to hold the puppy," Mom said.

"Where's Seedy?" Tara asked Brian.

"I wasn't sure you wanted me to bring her out since you have family here," Brian said. To me, he said quietly, "Seedy turns a lot of people off."

"Of course we want you to bring Seedy out," Tara said, clearly wounded by his comment.

Brian walked down the row of cages until he found the one he wanted. He opened the door and reached inside to bring out one of the dogs; then, holding what looked like a pile of twigs covered with scruffy fur, he walked toward us.

"Here she is," he said, and set Seedy down in the play area beside Tara, who immediately scooped her up and hugged her.

"Look at this face, Aunt Abby," Tara said, turning so I

could see the sad little dog staring back at me. "Isn't this a face to melt your heart?"

There was nothing cute about Seedy. She had large, pointed ears that stood straight up, with tufts of hair on top that fanned out at all angles, brown eyes that had seen a lifetime of misery, a foxlike face with bristly whiskers on her muzzle, and protruding lower teeth. Her coat was a mix of brown, black, and tan in fur of uneven heights, her tail was raggedy, and she was missing her left hind leg.

As I reached out to scratch her behind her ears, Seedy's eyes searched mine, as though looking for kindness. I couldn't help but smile at her, if only to reassure her that I meant no harm. At that she began to wiggle in Tara's arms until Tara had to set her down. Seedy immediately hobbled up to me, so I crouched down and put out my hand for her to sniff.

"Seedy likes you, Aunt Abby," Tara said, returning to the puppy. "She's usually afraid of people."

After a few sniffs, Seedy licked my fingers, then pushed her muzzle under my arm so I'd pet her. I ran my hand down her head and back and felt the sharp bones of her spine poking through. Clearly she'd been in a bad way for some time. Now at least she had food and a safe place to sleep, even if it was a wire cage. Surely that was better than being put to sleep.

Seedy sat down on her haunches and let me stroke her, gazing up at me with big adoring eyes as though she'd found an owner.

I fell backward onto my rear. "No, no. Not me," I said, as the dog hobbled closer to me. "I can't take you home."

"Of course you can't," Tara said. "I'm going to take her. Come here, Seedy."

But the dog sat down right in front of me and watched my face, wagging her tail as though to say, "I like you. Don't you like me?"

Geez. What was I supposed to say? I'd never seen an uglier dog, or a more pathetic one. I wasn't even a dog person; I'd always preferred cats. So why was this mutt calling to me?

The puppy came over to his mother's side, and Seedy turned to lick his little face. The two romped together for a while; then Seedling galloped back to Tara and leaped into her arms, licking her face and panting with his little tongue hanging out one side of his mouth.

"I see you've met Seedy," Mom said, coming to stand next to me. She reached down to stroke the dog's head. "Quite a sad little thing, isn't she?"

"She's really horrible looking," I said, rising.

"Why are you smiling?" Mom asked.

"I'm smiling? I guess I was thinking about something else." Because I definitely was *not* thinking about adopting that dog. Or any animal for that matter. Not now. The timing was all wrong.

"You can see why no one has adopted her." Mom crouched down and reached out a hand for Seedy to sniff. "Surely someone will take pity on this poor little girl, because if not . . ." She sighed sadly.

I had the strongest urge to scoop up that homely mutt and run out the door with her. But that was crazy thinking. Besides, I wasn't even sure that Marco liked dogs.

"What did you find out, Grandma?" Tara asked, cuddling both dogs.

"Mrs. Shaw said she'd hold Seedling for no more than a week."

"A week?" I asked. "That's all?"

"Looks like you've got your work cut out for you, honey," Mom said, putting her arm around me.

Like I needed more to do before my wedding.

"What about Seedy?" Tara asked.

"Mrs. Shaw said Seedy wouldn't be a problem," Mom said, giving me a knowing look.

"That reminds me," I said. "I need to go talk to Stacy. I'll be back shortly."

I left the dog ward and went up the hallway to Stacy's office. The door was closed, so I knocked. At her brisk, "Come in," I opened the door and stuck my head in.

"Hello, again," I said with a smile.

Although I hadn't thought it possible, Stacy's hair seemed more bouffant than the last time I'd seen her. She was seated at her desk, wearing a black blazer over a tight mint green blouse that showed plenty of cleavage, huge silver hoops on her ears, and stacks of silver bracelets on each wrist.

"What can I do for you?" she asked in her clipped manner. She wasn't smiling.

I stepped into the room and closed the door behind me. "I came across some information about your sister's case that I need to run past you." I indicated the chair in front of her desk. "May I?"

She checked her watch, her mouth pursing. "If you make it quick. I'm very busy."

Had there ever been a suspect who wasn't conveniently busy? "Perfect. So am I." Settling onto the chair, I dug through my purse and found a tattered notebook and a pen, just so I'd look official.

"You're going to take notes?" she snapped. "Exactly how long are you planning to be here?"

"Not long, I promise." I tapped the notebook. "I just

have a bad memory." She was on edge. What could I start
with to put her at ease?

"When you talked to your sister last weekend, did she
happen to mention that she had gone over the PAR ac-
counts on Friday and found a problem?"

Stacy thought for a moment. "No. Not that I remember. Why?"

"Because she sent her fiscal director an e-mail on
Monday before she left for the day stating that she
wanted to meet with him regarding some funds that had
been moved. She didn't explain anything more than that."

"Bev didn't say anything to me about it. Why is that a
concern?"

"Your sister phoned Dayton Blaine that same day
wanting to fire Emma Hardy for allegedly moving PAR
money into her own account."

"Really!" Stacy sat back and crossed one leg, a satisfied
smile on her face. "There's the outrageous audacity my sister mentioned. And now you have your murder suspect."

"So will you let us talk to your son?"

"What for?" she asked with obvious irritation. "What
do you think Kyle can tell you about Emma Hardy?"

"Nothing about Emma, but we have to cover all of
our bases, and we'd be remiss if we didn't talk to Kyle."

"I'm not going over this again, so read my lips. N. O. *No.*"

"Can I mention again, Stacy, that by not cooperating,
you look like you have something to hide?"

She held her arms open wide. "What could I be hiding? I've been an open book to you people."

"You haven't been open on everything."

She wrapped her jacket tightly over her blouse, as
though she were suddenly chilled. "I don't know what
you're talking about."

"For instance, today I learned that Dayton was never in favor of changing the animal shelter's no-kill policy."

"Of course she was. Dayton even convinced the board that it needed to change."

"No, your sister wanted the policy changed. *She* convinced Dayton to go along with it and then had Dayton convince the board."

"Bev convinced Dayton?" Stacy let out a forced laugh. "That's so outlandish, I don't even know where to begin. Bev was the only one *against* the policy change. She was fighting to keep this a no-kill shelter."

"Come on, Stacy, be honest. You weren't in favor of changing the shelter's policy either, but Bev somehow forced you to push for it."

"Why do you keep saying that? Bev would never have pushed for a change. She knew it would go against the voters' wishes."

"Exactly. But if Bev was outvoted by you and the board of directors, she'd be helpless to stop it. Wasn't that her plan?"

Stacy stared at me, obviously at a loss for words. It took her a moment to come up with a retort. "Did Dayton feed you this nonsense?"

"Dayton had no reason to make it up, Stacy."

"I beg to differ. She's trying to cover her ass. I know my sister's wishes, and it was to keep the shelter's policy as it is."

"Stacy, Bev is gone. You don't need to pretend any longer."

With an irritated huff, Stacy uncrossed her leg and sat forward. "This is utter garbage. Please leave. I have no more to say to you."

I pointed to the photos behind her. "I won't believe

that someone who obviously loves animals the way you do would meekly go along with Bev's plan."

"Meekly!" She picked up a blue pen and threw it across the room. "Do *not* refer to me as a meek person. You have no idea what I've gone through in my life."

"Then how did Bev get you to back the kill shelter? Threaten to fire you?"

Practically sneering, Stacy said, "I answer only to Dayton and the board!"

"Then what was Bev holding over your head?"

Stacy jumped to her feet and pointed at the door. "Get out! Now!"

At the door, I paused to say, "Just so you know, Stacy, Marco is a very good private investigator. If you don't want him to keep digging, you'd better talk to us. You have Marco's number, or you can reach me at Bloomers."

I heard the door slam behind me as I walked down the hallway.

I returned to the dog ward and found Tara saying good-bye to Seedy and Seedling. She had tears in her eyes as she hugged first the mother, then the puppy. I found my own eyes welling up.

"I'll come see you again as soon as I can," Tara promised them. She wiped away the tears rolling down her cheeks, watching morosely as Brian returned both dogs to their cages; then she turned to me with big sad eyes. "Please help me adopt them, Aunt Abby."

I put my arm around her, and we walked out of the ward together. "Tara, I promise to do everything I can. It would help if you worked on your parents, too."

"If I nag them, they'll just get mad and say no."

"How about dropping a few hints? You know, like

when a commercial for Dog Chow comes on, you could sigh longingly, or maybe you'll see an ad in a magazine that you can accidentally leave out. Oh, I've got it. You can post cute puppy photos on your Facebook page."

She looked at me askance. "I'm not *friends* with my parents, Aunt Abby."

"Well, you get the idea."

"I'll try," Tara said. "I still think you're the only one who can get them to say yes."

"There's always Grandma," I said, hooking my arm through my mom's.

"Leave me out of this," Mom said. "I've got enough on my mind."

"See?" Tara asked. "It's up to you, Aunt Amazing."

"Everything go okay with Stacy?" Mom asked quietly, as we left the building.

"Depends on whether you ask me or her," I said. "Let's just say Stacy's not a fan of mine right now."

"Do whatever you need to do," Mom said. "Just don't get us banned from the shelter."

CHAPTER SEVENTEEN

"Marco, I'm telling you, Stacy is going to be a tough nut to crack." I reached for a French fry and dipped it in ketchup. Marco was seated across from me at "our" booth at Down the Hatch, having an Italian beef sandwich, while I tucked into a new favorite—roasted turkey, sliced avocado, tomato, jalapeño peppers, and Monterey Jack cheese with brown mustard sauce on a whole-wheat bun. "There's no reason for Stacy to keep protecting her sister, yet she refuses to admit that Bev was behind the push to change the shelter's policy."

Marco looked doubtful. "Are you sure Dayton Blaine told you the truth about Bev?"

"Why would an influential woman like Dayton confess to being coerced into backing a policy she was against unless she had a compelling reason to do so? It's certainly not flattering to someone with her clout."

"And her compelling reason is that she wants us to find the killer?"

"I think it was more about us leaving her alone. She said you were being a nuisance."

"If Dayton was so up-front with you about being co-erced, why wouldn't she tell you how Bev was coercing her?"

"That woman is all about pride, Marco. Whatever the reason was, it must have been embarrassing—or scandalous—and she didn't feel it was necessary for me to know."

"Did you explain that our knowing would verify her claim?"

"Not in those words, but, yes, and then she nearly stopped talking to me because I insulted her." I pulled folded sheets of typing paper out of my purse and opened them up so Marco could read them. "Here's Dayton's schedule for Monday afternoon and evening, with names and phone numbers. Dayton promised me full access and she delivered. I'm telling you, Marco, the woman gave me nothing but positive vibes."

Marco glanced over the papers, then set them aside. "I'll make these calls tomorrow. Let's get back to Stacy. I'm puzzled about why she would keep insisting that her sister was against the policy change if she wasn't."

"Maybe she's trying to protect Bev's image."

"Or maybe Stacy's telling the truth."

"Then that would mean Dayton is lying, and I don't think she is."

"What if they're both telling the truth?"

I had a hard time wrapping my brain around that. Maybe I needed to eat my sandwich and let Marco do the talking. "I'm not following you."

"I'm tossing this out there as a possibility. What if Bev

told Dayton Blaine the truth about wanting to change the shelter's no-kill policy but lied to her sister?"

I swallowed a bite of sandwich. "What would be the point?"

"Dayton told you that Bev wanted voters to believe she opposed changing the shelter's no-kill policy, right? Maybe Bev wanted her own sister to believe it, too, for whatever reason. That's all I'm saying."

"I see your point," I said, "yet I have a really strong feeling that Stacy was opposed to changing the shelter's policy but had to go along with it because Bev forced her to. I think we need to investigate that further."

"I'm not disputing that, Sunshine. Stacy is still a big question mark. Our main problem right now is that she doesn't want us to talk to her son."

"Which could mean that the boy has some incriminating evidence or might simply be because Stacy is an overprotective mother."

"Right. But for tonight, you're going to focus on your meeting with Emma Hardy, and I'm going to see Justin Shaw's customer. I want the guy to look at Justin's photo and verify that it was actually Justin who came out to tow his car. Let's finish eating and come up with a strategy for Emma."

"I've already thought of two items she needs to address," I said. "The first is to explain the real reason why Bev called her into her office on Monday."

"Asking her to explain won't get you anywhere. You'll need to *tell* her that you know Bev called Dayton Blaine on Friday to get permission to fire her for stealing money. Otherwise she'll stick to her story that Bev was angry about her moonlighting."

"I can do that." In fact, I'd already planned to do just

that, but I decided not to say anything. Marco enjoyed being my teacher. No reason to burst his bubble.

"Good," he said. "What's the second item?"

"I figured Emma would deny taking money, so I'll insist that she offer us proof that she *didn't* move PAR funds into her own account."

"Scratch that second one, Abby. Emma will just say she doesn't have to prove anything to us. Innocent until proven guilty. A better tactic would be to claim to already have proof—maybe some accounting Bev showed or e-mailed to John Bradford. Emma will undoubtedly react by getting angry, but if you can make her believe you actually have a copy of what Bev showed John and are going to the cops with it, she might be frightened enough to talk."

"This is going to be fun, Marco."

"Don't get too cocky. That's when you make mistakes. Just keep stressing that we want to cross her off our suspect list. And if she does have proof, so much the better."

"Hey, you lovebirds," Gert said, stopping at the booth, "if you've got things to do tonight, you might want to get them done soon. We're supposed to get a nasty thunderstorm with high winds coming in around nine o'clock."

At six thirty, I went to the bridal salon for my fitting, and fortunately my rash had faded, so the owner didn't cringe even once as she helped me put on the dress.

"It fits well," she said, checking the strapless ivory bodice and waist and fluffing the full bell skirt with its layers of delicate lace. "How does it feel?"

I stood in front of the three-way mirror, squinting at my reflection. I always looked thinner that way. "I feel like a princess."

She put the fingertip veil on my head and held it in place so I could see it. "How are you going to do your hair?"

"To tell you the truth, I don't know. My cousin made an appointment with her hairdresser, Emily, for the morning of my wedding. All I know is that Emily promised I'd love it."

"And you have your shoes already?"

Oops. I'd forgotten to bring them with me. "My cousin took care of that, too."

"How wonderful to have such a helpful cousin. I'd love to meet her someday."

"Betty, just so you know, you already have. We're talking about Jillian Osborne."

Betty's smile stiffened. Just the year before, Jillian, who had been a true bridezilla, had bought her wedding gown from Betty's Bridal Shop. In addition, Jillian had all her bridesmaids—her spoiled college sorority sisters and me—purchase dresses through Betty's Bridal, too. I had a feeling the experience had scarred Betty and her staff for life. And now Betty had to deal with Jillian because she was my bridesmaid.

"Well," she said with forced cheerfulness, "how nice that Jillian can guide you through your nuptials."

That was putting a positive spin on things. "I'm assuming she's been in to pick up her dress."

"Yes, she has," Betty said, "after innumerable fittings."

"I'm so sorry," I whispered.

"I'll go pack up your dress."

By 7:25, I was seated at a table in a back corner of the Daily Grind with a cup of tropical green tea, waiting for Emma to show up. I went over my note card with the two items written on it, then, to kill time, amused myself by playing solitaire on my cell phone.

I checked my watch at 7:40, then again at 7:50, but still no Emma. I even looked outside to be sure she wasn't waiting there, but saw no sign of her. I finally texted Marco at eight o'clock to let him know that Emma had failed to show up.

Maybe she's on the run, I texted.

Just go home, he texted back. *Major storm coming soon.*

I stepped outside the coffee shop and scanned the starry sky. It didn't look at all threatening to me. In fact, it was a beautiful evening, so I headed to Down the Hatch. But as I walked along Lincoln, gusts of wind kept blowing my hair into my eyes, and I could feel the humidity level rising. I turned the corner onto Franklin and heard the distant rumble of thunder.

Marco was behind the bar but came out when he saw me. "Abby, you need to get home. The weather is supposed to get bad soon."

"I just wanted to stop by to find out if Rafe knows where Emma is."

"I haven't seen Emma since lunchtime," Rafe said, coming up behind Marco.

"Do you have plans to go out with her again?" I asked.

"She said she'd stop by the bar at noon tomorrow," he said. "We're going to do lunch in the park."

"Great. I'll try to be here too," I said.

"Just don't run her off," Rafe said, "like *someone* did last time." He tilted his head toward his brother, whose attention at that moment was on one of the televisions mounted over the bar.

Marco turned back to me. "The national weather service just issued a tornado watch for our area." He put his hands on my shoulders and steered me toward the door. "Go home."

"On my way," I said.

By the time I reached my apartment, thick gray clouds had obliterated the stars, lightning was zigzagging across the sky, and the rain was starting. I knew Simon would be hiding because he hated storms, but all it took was the buzzing of the can opener to bring him skittering around the corner into the kitchen, ready for his dinner. He'd eaten only a few bites, however, when a large clap of thunder shook the building, sending him scampering for safety.

I turned on the TV to get an updated weather report and saw that the tornado watch had turned into a warning. Nikki called from the hospital to see if I knew about the weather alert and urged me to take shelter in the basement.

"This is a solid building, Nikki. If it gets really bad, I can always go into the bathroom. It doesn't have any windows."

At that moment, the electricity went out, leaving me in the dark. "We just lost power," I told Nikki. "Hold on while I get the flashlight."

My cell phone beeped, so I put Nikki's call on hold to answer.

"Hey, babe," Marco said. "Are you okay?"

"I'm fine, Marco, just in the dark."

"In the dark generally, or actually *in* the dark?"

"Ha. Funny."

"I'm being serious now. There've been reports of a

tornado touching down west of New Chapel, so you'd better get to the basement."

"I'll wait it out the bathroom, Marco. Simon is hiding somewhere in the apartment and I can't leave him. I've got Nikki on the other line. Okay if I call you back?"

"Just put me on hold. I don't want to lose contact with you."

"Hey, Nikki, Marco's on the other line. I've got to go."

"Take care of my kitty, Abs," she said. "I've got to go, too. The hospital lost power and we're running on the generators."

I hung up with Nikki and clicked over to Marco as I grabbed a bottle of water and went to find a blanket to wrap around myself.

"Abby, do you have a candle and matches handy?"

"There's some around here somewhere. But I've got a flashlight in my hand."

"What if the batteries run down? Go find a candle."

Marco sure could get bossy at times. I tossed my big comforter into the tub with the water bottle and dashed back to the kitchen. Outside, the wind was howling, rattling the windowpanes and whipping branches against the glass.

"Okay, Marco, I have a box of kitchen matches and a fat candle. Now I need to find Simon."

"Don't worry about the cat. Get into the bathroom and wait out the storm."

"I'm in the tub wrapped in a blanket," I told him, as I got down on my hands and knees and looked under my bed.

Rats. No Simon.

"Our power just went out here, Abby, so I've got to go. I'll call you back in a short while. Stay put."

What else would I do?

I checked my closet for Simon, then looked under Nikki's bed and saw two shiny green eyes gazing at me. He blinked when the light hit his eyes. "Come on, Simon," I called. "Come with me."

Simon wasn't budging. I crawled around on the side closest to him, and he scooted to the middle. Realizing I'd have to drag him out by his tail, I gave up and returned to the bathroom, curling up in the bathtub to wait. Having nothing to do but listen to the howling wind, I dozed off.

An hour later, I was jolted awake by the light coming on in the hallway. Suddenly, the TV started playing, the air conditioner kicked back on, and the clock on the microwave beeped. I went to the living room and cautiously opened the drapes. Down below, I saw tree limbs strewn about the parking lot and lots of leaf debris in the wet street. It seemed that the worst of the storm had passed, but it was still raining.

My cell phone rang back in the bathroom, so I dashed up the hallway to get it.

"Abby, everything okay there?" Marco asked.

"A-okay. I was just looking out the window to see if there was any damage, but except for some big branches down, it looks fine."

"Not so fine on the north side of town. They're reporting a number of big trees uprooted from a tornado that touched down. We're okay here. We just got our power back."

"Here, too."

"Glad you're safe, babe. I've got to get back to the bar. We've got more business than we can handle. Seems like half the town came in seeking shelter. They're calling it a tornado party."

I sat down on the sofa, grabbed the remote, and tuned in to the local news just as Simon came creeping out of the hallway, jerking at every little sound.

"Come here, Simon," I said, patting the seat beside me.

His ears swiveling like twin radar towers, Simon crept up to the sofa and jumped onto my lap.

"Ouch, Simon. We need to trim those claws."

He sat down on his haunches facing me, as if to say, *I'm here. I'm nervous. Pet me!* So I scratched him behind his ears, trying to put him at ease.

"Damage on the north side was extensive," the newscaster was saying. "We're now getting reports of destruction in the Fairfield Park neighborhood—roofs ripped off, windows shattered, and two vehicles crushed after a large tree fell on them. A camera crew is on its way."

A pounding on the door sent Simon running for cover and left gouges in my thighs from his claws.

"Abby, are you there?" Jillian called.

"I'm coming," I called back. "Hold on."

I unlocked the door and opened it to find Jillian and her husband, Claymore, standing in the hallway. They hadn't come far; they lived in a three-bedroom apartment at the other end of the hallway. And both looked like they'd stepped out of a magazine ad for Neiman Marcus clothing—with the exception of the sack of potatoes in a pink blanket that Jillian was clutching to her bosom.

"We just wanted to be sure you were safe," Claymore said.

"I'm fine. Come on in. I was listening to the news."

Jillian passed off the bundle to Claymore and hurried inside to sit on the sofa directly in front of the TV. Clicking through the channels with the remote, she said, "I want to see if there are any more reports about the tornado that touched down in Fairfield Park."

"*In* the park? Are you serious?"

"That's what my mom told me," Jillian said. "You know how she listens to her emergency radio whenever there's a storm."

"I'll take Storm back to our apartment, darling," Claymore said, "so you girls can visit."

"Storm?" I said to Jillian. "What happened to Rain?"

"Live in the moment, Abs. Do you have any Vitamin Water? I'm parched."

"How about plain water?" I asked, heading into the kitchen.

"If that's all you have," she called.

I took two bottles from the fridge and grabbed a bag of Snikiddy baked fries, then sat down beside my cousin. "Any news?"

"Not until the camera crew gets there." She took a handful of the crispy fries and munched on them. "How did your fitting go?"

"The dress fits perfectly."

"Did you remember to take your high heels?"

"Jillian, how often do I forget important things?"

Jillian studied me, shaking her head sadly. "Of course you forgot. This is why you need me with you for your appointments and why I'll be there when Emily does your hair."

"Tell me how she's going to do it."

"No."

"She'd better not do anything weird."

"Would I *let* her do anything weird? This is my reputation as a fashion consultant at stake here, remem—"

With a gasp, Jillian pointed to the TV with one hand

and grabbed my wrist with the cheese-covered fingers of the other. "Oh, Abby, look! Look!"

"I'm looking." I searched the scene being shown on TV—several large trees toppled, their branches covering an expanse of green lawn—but judging by the way Jillian kept pointing to the screen, I obviously wasn't seeing what she wanted me to see.

"Look in the background," she cried.

"I don't see anything."

"Exactly my point, Abs. They're showing Fairfield Park. See that big tree lying across the grass? That's where your gazebo used to be."

CHAPTER EIGHTEEN

I stared at the TV screen in horror. Where my cute little gazebo had once stood, all I could see was part of a raised cement base sticking out from under the tree. As the camera panned the area, I spotted a few pieces of white lumber tossed haphazardly among the numerous large branches that littered the park.

"My gazebo is gone!" I cried in disbelief.

Jillian stared at me with big saucer eyes, as sickened as I was. "I know."

"I have nowhere to be married!"

I grabbed my cell phone and called Marco, who answered on the fourth ring. "Hey, babe," he called over loud voices talking and laughing, "I was just going to call you. How's everything there now?"

"The gazebo, Marco, the little white gazebo at Fairfield Park — it's gone. The tornado blew it down!"

There was only bar noise on the other end.

"Marco, did you hear what I said?"

"I don't know what to tell you, Abby. I know it's bad,

but these things happen. We'll have to find somewhere else to be married."

"Somewhere like *where*? We have a week, Marco."

"Maybe it's a sign," Jillian was saying in the background. "Maybe it means you're not supposed to get married."

"You're not helping," I hissed, covering the phone.

"Listen, Sunshine, we're mopping up water that got in the back door," Marco said. "We can talk about the gazebo later."

Sunshine? There wasn't any sunshine where I was sitting. Clearly, Marco wasn't as disturbed as I was.

I tossed the phone onto the coffee table and plopped down on the sofa, staring at the television, my chin in my hands. There went my dream of being married outdoors in a cute little white gazebo, surrounded by family and flowers. "What am I going to do now?"

Jillian put her arm around my shoulders. "There's always a solution, Abs."

"Really?" I snapped. "Then what is it? You know nothing is available this close to the date."

"I didn't say *I* had the solution." She took a swig of water, then jumped up. "Let me go ask Claymore."

"Jillian, forget it. Claymore isn't a magician. He isn't going to have an answer either."

Jillian sat back down with a sad sigh. "I wish I could help. You always help me and now there's nothing I can do for you."

I turned to look at her and saw her brush away a tear. "I'm sorry for snapping at you, Jill. I know you want to help. Marco and I will just have to work something out."

"You know I'm here for you, Abs."

"Thanks. I appreciate it. I think I'd like to be alone now."

*   *   *

My phone rang as I was closing the front door. It was Mom, wanting to know if I was okay and if I'd heard the news about Fairfield Park.

I couldn't help sighing miserably. "I heard."

"Honey, don't be sad. I know you wanted an outdoor wedding, but there's always the chapel at church."

"Thanks, Mom. I've got another call. I'll talk to you tomorrow."

Marco's mom was the next caller. She volunteered Marco's sister's backyard, which was a small space filled with a large playhouse and a swing set. After that, calls came in from both of my sisters-in-law, but I let the answering machine pick them up. I was tired of talking about my ruined wedding plans.

That mood lasted until Nikki came home at midnight, and then she had to listen to me whine for a good half hour before pleading exhaustion and escaping to her room.

Saturday

Marco wasn't the type to tolerate whining, so the next morning he tried to snap me out of my funk by telling me that where we got married wasn't as important as I was making it out to be. Sitting at my desk in my workroom before we opened for the day, I rested my chin on my hand and stared at the bare spindle in front of me, feeling about as low as a person, even one who'd flunked out of law school, could feel.

"I suppose," I said with a heavy sigh.

"With your access to flowers," he said, "we can make any place beautiful."

He obviously didn't get it. I had my heart set on having my wedding in a little white gazebo surrounded by a bounty of blossoms in the great outdoors and nothing, not even a grand cathedral, was going to measure up to the romantic vision in my head.

"Was there any damage to Bloomers?" he asked.

"No, fortunately."

"See? There's something to be thankful for. Now, are you ready to get on with the investigation, or would you rather sit and pout the rest of the day?"

Pouting sounded awfully good at that moment, but Marco was right. I'd wallowed in self-pity long enough to bore even myself. Mustering up about a microgram of enthusiasm, I said, "I'm ready to get on with the investigation."

"There's my fireball. It's almost nine o'clock, so I'll see you in about three hours. We can have lunch and wait for Emma to show up."

"Doing any better, love?" Grace asked as she came through the curtain. It was her Saturday to work. Lottie had the day off.

"On top of losing the gazebo"—I pointed to the computer screen—"a paltry two orders came in."

"I just took a call out front," she said, "so make that three."

That would keep me busy for all of ninety minutes. "I thought we'd be swamped with work after my flyer went out."

Grace cleared her throat. "As English theologian Thomas Fuller said, 'It is always darkest just before the day dawneth.' You just have to be patient, love." She put a cup of coffee in front of me. "This is my brand-new brew. I thought you'd find it invigorating."

"That'll help. Thanks." I picked up the cup, inhaled

the fragrant aroma, then took a slow drink to savor the taste. "This is wonderful, Grace. Hazelnut?"

"Not today. Have you thought about getting married right here at Bloomers? We could decorate the shop in a wedding theme."

I walked to the curtain and held it open, envisioning how I might turn the shop into an indoor gazebo. "I guess it's an option, but then I'd be getting married in a place of business. That's not exactly the romantic setting I'd imagined."

The phone rang, so I picked it up at my desk and forced some cheer into my voice. "Bloomers Flower Shop. How may I help you?"

"Abigail," Mom said, "I just read in the obituaries that Bev Powers's visitation and funeral service are today. Had you heard anything about it?"

"No, I hadn't. That's really short notice, especially for people wanting to send flowers."

"I hate to speak ill of the dead, honey, but I'd be willing to bet not many people will be sending flowers or even attending the service, for that matter, which may be why Stacy decided to rush it."

"What a sad statement that makes about Bev," I said.

"I'm assuming Stacy is the one who planned the funeral. I don't think Bev had any other family in the area. According to the obituary, the visitation will be at Happy Dreams Funeral Parlor this afternoon from three to five with a service at five. I hope the PAR group thinks to send something."

The other phone line starting blinking, so I signaled to Grace and she hurried into the shop to answer it there.

"I'm sure you're busy," Mom said, "so I'll let you get back to work. I just thought you'd want to know."

As soon as I'd hung up with Mom, the phone rang, but before I had a chance to answer, Grace picked it up in the other room. In a few minutes she came through the curtain holding two pink slips of paper.

"Two orders for funeral flowers," she said, waving the slips. "Did you know Bev Powers was being buried today?"

By the time noon rolled around, I'd done three funeral arrangements for Bev—one from PAR, one from Stacy and her son, and one from the town council—delivered them to my friends at Happy Dreams Funeral Parlor, gone online to change my driver's license, worked on my wedding vows, reconfirmed with the photographer and bakery, and was sitting with Marco in the last booth at Down the Hatch. It was the perfect spot from which to watch the door without being noticed.

After we gave Gert our orders, I brought up the subject of our ruined wedding plans. "I called the park department to see if they would rebuild the gazebo, but they couldn't tell me when—or even if—it was going to happen."

"I'm not surprised. Nothing happens fast when you have to go through layers of government."

"I guess we'll have to go back to the original plan," I said with a resigned sigh.

"Nothing wrong with the church chapel."

"It's nice but not romantic. I really wanted something romantic."

"Decorate it with lots of flowers."

"I wanted something romantic *and* outdoors."

"How about your mom's backyard?"

"Okay, romantic and outdoors and not on a patio in someone's fenced-in backyard."

Marco waited until Gert had delivered our iced teas, then said, "I've got nothing."

"Me, neither." I resumed my chin-in-hand position. "It's hopeless, Marco. I mean, we might as well get married here."

"You make Down the Hatch sound like the pits of hell."

Compared to my little white gazebo, almost. "Is it okay if I start bringing clothing over to your apartment?"

"Of course, babe. Half the closet is empty, and you've got almost the whole dresser to yourself." He stopped for a drink of iced tea. "I drove out to see Justin Shaw's customer this morning."

Clearly, that was the end of the wedding discussion.

"When I showed him Justin's photo," Marco said, "the man didn't recognize him. He did remember a lanky, long-haired guy in a red plaid shirt who had a wad of chewing tobacco in his cheek."

"Tobacco Man," I said.

"Right. Which means Justin lied about where he was Monday evening. That means another trip to Shaw's Towing."

"The falsehoods are piling up. That's the third suspect to lie to us." I paused to take a drink of my iced tea. "Did you call the people on the list Dayton's secretary gave me?"

"Yep, and everyone has verified she was where she claimed to be. We can cross her off the list."

I waited until Gert had delivered our orders; then I said, "Bloomers closes at three today. Do you want to go see Justin then?"

"He's not open on Saturday afternoons," Marco said, peppering his stew. "We'll have to wait until Monday."

"Speaking of Saturday afternoon," I said, "Bev Powers's funeral service is at five o'clock. Is there any reason for us to attend?"

"It's not going to tell us anything about our suspects, so no."

"Hey, guys," Rafe said dejectedly, holding his cell phone. "Emma just texted that she can't make it."

"Did she say why?" I asked.

"Only that she'd be in touch." Rafe put his phone in his pocket. "She must be busy."

Or maybe Emma hadn't wanted to chance running in to Marco or me. *Hmm.* I glanced through the big plate-glass window at the front of the bar. Maybe there'd been no *chance* about it.

"I'll be right back," I said, then slid out of the booth and hurried to the door. Outside, I scanned the sidewalk in both directions and then the people across the street on the courthouse lawn, but there was no sign of Emma. I was just about to go back inside when I caught sight of her halfway across the lawn. She was practically running and glanced over her shoulder twice, looking back in my direction. There was no way I could catch up with her.

"What is it?" Marco asked, coming to stand by me.

"Emma was here, Marco. I just caught sight of her hurrying away. She must have seen us through the window. She kept glancing back at me like she expected me to come after her. If that doesn't scream *guilty of something*, nothing does."

"Do we have her address?"

"I'm sure we can get it from Holly or John at PAR."

"Let's do it then and stake out her home. If Emma won't come to us, we'll go to her."

CHAPTER NINETEEN

S ome people go to the theater on Saturday evenings. Some go to dinner. Others spend a quiet evening at home. We do stakeouts, or at least we did that night, and that meant sitting in Marco's car in the dark until well after midnight, watching Emma's apartment and sipping bottled water. It was my least favorite part of being a private investigator.

Emma lived in an apartment building called the Jefferson just two blocks north of the town square. It was a three-story gray stone structure that occupied half of a city block. We'd pinpointed Emma's exact apartment by talking to one of the residents, who said that apartment number 201 was a second-floor corner unit on the southwest side. So Marco parked up the block on the opposite side of the street, where we could see all three windows in her unit.

It was dusk when we arrived, but no lights were on inside her apartment. Even when darkness fell, not a single bulb came on, leading us to conclude she was out.

By midnight, the apartment was still dark, and my bladder was near the bursting point.

"I'm going to have to call it a night, Marco. I'll just walk back to my car. It's not that far."

"Abby, there's no way I'm going to sit here while you're walking back to your car. I don't care how safe New Chapel is. I'll drive you there. I have a strong feeling Emma isn't coming back here tonight anyway. Whatever she did, she knows we're onto her. She may have even packed a bag and left town."

"What do we do then?"

"I'll work on an Internet search in the morning, find out where her parents live, where she likes to go on vacation, and any good friends she visits. For now, let's get you back to your car."

My 'Vette was parked around the corner from Bloomers, in off-street parking, so when Marco dropped me off, I hopped inside the car and started the engine. But then I thought of that twelve-minute drive home and decided to end my misery sooner by dashing back to Bloomers.

I entered the shop through the new fire door in the alley because it was closer to my car and to the bathroom. Afterward, I set the alarm and left the shop through the same door, grateful for the motion-detector light I'd had installed overhead.

I had just moved outside of the yellow circle of light when a dark figure stepped into my path about six yards ahead, blocking the mouth of the alley. At once my heart began to pound, and I felt a surge of energy that told me to flee. I backed up into the light and grabbed on to the strap of my shoulder bag so I could fling it and run.

"Abby Knight," a female voice cried.

"Who's there?" I called, doing my best impression of a brave person.

"Why are you stalking me?"

Shouldn't I have been the one to ask that question? I eased my hand into my purse and felt for my phone. "Who are you?"

The figure stepped forward just enough for me to see Emma's face. She looked as terrified as I felt. "Why are you stalking me?" she cried again. "What do you want from me?"

"Emma, you scared me." I slid the phone out of my purse and kept it at my side, just in case. "No one is stalking you, least of all me."

"Wrong. You were waiting for me today at Down the Hatch, and then this evening you and your boyfriend were watching my apartment. I saw you. Don't deny it."

"We were watching *for* you because you didn't show up last night at the coffee shop and then you didn't show up at noon to meet Rafe. We thought you might be in trouble."

"Like I believe *that* story. You want to accuse me of killing Bev."

"Our job isn't to accuse anyone, Emma. It's just to gather information."

"Leave me alone," she cried, backing away. "I didn't do it."

"Terrific. Then talk to me."

She stood there staring at me, opening and closing her fists. I could see now that she was wearing a gray tank top with a pair of jean cutoffs and black flip-flops. She shivered in the cool night air.

"Look at me." I held out my hands. "I can't hurt you. I don't want to hurt you. What I want to do is clear your name so you can stop hiding. If you're innocent, you shouldn't be afraid to sit down somewhere for a cup of coffee."

She said nothing.

"Listen, Emma, I don't particularly like standing in the alley. It creeps me out. Can we at least walk out onto the sidewalk and talk?"

"I didn't kill Bev," she insisted.

Somehow I needed to gain Emma's trust so I could get out of the dark passageway. "I didn't think you did kill her."

She studied me in silence. Then, in a little girl's voice, she said, "Really? You believe me?"

"Really. Now, I don't know about you, but I'm cold. And we shouldn't be standing around the alley this late at night anyway, so let's get out of here, okay?"

I waited another few seconds, then started forward. I tried not to let my imagination get the better of me as I detoured around her but couldn't suppress a shudder when I heard the crunch of gravel behind me. And then she was walking beside me as I left the alleyway and turned onto Indiana Avenue, just steps from my car.

"I can prove where I was when Bev was killed," she said.

"Great, but let's not worry about that right now. Just be honest with me about what you and Bev talked about Monday afternoon."

"I told you already."

"You told me a story, not the truth."

"I said Bev threatened to fire me."

I didn't want to correct her—she hadn't said that happened on Monday—so I let it go. "Tell me again why she made the threat, and please, don't use the moonlighting excuse."

"But it's true! She was furious with me for taking outside work. She said I was being disloyal."

"But that wasn't the issue on Monday, was it?" I stopped beside my car and turned to face her. "I know you took PAR money because Bev e-mailed John Bradford about it."

Emma covered her mouth with her hands, her eyes wide with fear.

"Look, Emma, I also know you have massive student loans to pay off and probably big credit card bills, too, along with your monthly rent, gas and electric, and food expenses. Right?"

Her chin began to tremble, and then tears rolled down her cheeks as she nodded. "And my car loan. Bev knew how bad off I was and she still wanted to fire me for moonlighting. How did she expect me to live?" Emma covered her face and cried.

"I'm sorry you're in a financial bind, but you took money that didn't belong to you. You can't hide from that."

"What am I going to do?" She wept. "I don't want to go to prison. What will I tell my parents? They think I'm handling everything just fine."

"Here's what you'll do. You'll hire a lawyer and work out a plea deal where hopefully you'll only have to pay restitution—and maybe do some hours of community service. That sounds doable, doesn't it?"

She dug a tissue from her purse to wipe her nose. "If you want to know the truth, I hated Bev, but I didn't kill her. I couldn't have sicced those dogs on her. I couldn't hurt anyone."

"That's what we want you to tell us the next time we meet with you. And don't be afraid of Marco. If you're straight with him, he's a good guy to have on your side. You already like his brother, don't you?"

She lifted one shoulder, smiling shyly. Even wet, her eyes sparkled. "Yes."

"Rafe was really disappointed when you didn't show up today."

"Really?"

"I'm not lying. So why don't we meet tomorrow at the bar? You can have lunch with Rafe afterward. Okay?"

She shook her head, sniffling. "Tomorrow's Sunday. I'm supposed to drive home to Indianapolis to see my parents."

"Monday then?"

She shrugged. "I might as well. I'll be out job hunting anyway."

"Great. Where did you park?"

She pointed to a beat-up Toyota Corolla on the other side of the street. Sheepishly, she said, "I followed you here." With a sly glint in her eye, she added, "Maybe I should look for a job working for a private investigator."

Sunday

I was out before my head hit the pillow and woke in the morning confused as to what day it was. Oh, right. Sunday. The day I'd planned to pack for the move to Marco's apartment. Luckily, I had only personal belongings to box up. Everything else in the apartment was Nikki's.

But what time was it? Had I missed church?

As I turned to see the clock on my nightstand, Simon leaped onto the bed and came up to my pillow to rub his wet little nose against my chin, tugging at my heartstrings. I was going to miss him a lot.

"Are you going to miss me, too, Simon?"

He was purring loudly, but when I tried to cuddle him,

he darted away, jumped off the bed, and went to stand by the door, rubbing the side of his face against the door-jamb and glancing back at me with a look that said, *I'm starving and adorable; please feed me.*

I checked the time—yep, I'd missed church—then trotted to the kitchen to start the coffee and nearly tripped over Simon when he tried to wind through my legs. He meowed his displeasure until I opened a fresh can of cat food, then purred as I spooned the chunks of meat into his dish.

I started the coffeemaker, then opened the door to get the morning newspaper and saw one of my Bloomers fly-ers lying on top of it with a yellow sticky note attached. I picked up one corner of the flyer and it fell apart, sliced by something razor sharp. I plucked off the sticky note and read the message printed in thick black letters: *Your evil!*

Your? Had it been written by a child?

"You can't assume that," Marco said, after I'd called to tell him about the note. "The only thing we can safely assume is that the writer knows where you live, and that concerns me. Are you keeping the door dead-bolted?"

"Nikki does, when she gets home at night."

"Please, Abby, lock it whenever you're at home. Who-ever left that message was able to enter the apartment building and come up to your door while you were sleep-ing."

I hadn't thought of that. "I'm not trying to be flip about the situation, Marco, but seriously, the note isn't a warning or a threat, just a statement of opinion."

"Right, and the opinion is that you've done something that makes you evil. What will this person do next? Try to punish you for it?"

I hadn't thought of that either.

"Besides," he said, "what children do you come into contact with, other than my niece and nephew, who are old enough to write? Do you see why I'm concerned?"

"I appreciate that, Marco, but I'll be fine."

"Why don't you consider moving in with me? It's only a week early."

"Because that would take part of the fun out of getting married. You know I'm old-fashioned about that. I want you to carry me over the threshold of your apartment as a new bride. I want us to start living together as a married couple, not as two adults frightened of a sticky note."

"Maybe you think I'm being overly cautious, Sunshine, but when it comes to your safety, you know I'd do anything to protect you."

"Thank you, Marco. I love you, and I promise to take precautions, okay?"

"Then make sure you tell Nikki to do the same."

"I will. Now, let me tell you about the shock I got last night in the alley behind Bloomers."

"You're trying to give me a heart attack today, aren't you?"

I told Marco about my encounter with Emma and got a lecture about how I should have run first and asked questions later.

"I was ready to run, trust me," I said. "But I never felt any direct threat, and I could tell Emma was just as frightened as I was. Anyway, it worked out, and now she's going to meet with both of us at noon on Monday. Didn't I do well?"

"The security issue not withstanding, I'm proud of you, babe. You kept your wits about you, and fortunately, it did work out. But please, Abby, from now on, safety first. If anything happened to you, I'd never forgive myself for letting you get involved in these investigations."

Like he could stop me. "You've got it, Salvare. I should get packing now. Nikki brought home enough boxes to move three people. What are you doing today?"

"I was working on tracking down Emma, but now I can move on to other things."

"Are we getting together later?"

After a momentary hesitation, Marco said, "I'm not sure how long my work will take, so we'll see how it goes. Might have to be tomorrow."

Okay, so maybe he wanted to do guy things on his day off. No reason for me to feel rejected, right?

Wrong. I was in Rejection Central. But I mustered a cheerful voice and said, "Okay. Talk to you later."

In the middle of the afternoon, as I sat on the bedroom floor surrounded by boxes full of winter clothing and accessories, the doorbell rang.

"I'll get it," Nikki called from the kitchen. She had gone there to make popcorn, which we were using to fortify ourselves for the work. It wasn't that there had been so much to pack; it was that we had spent most of the time reminiscing about all the fun we'd had together, going all the way back to third grade. We'd also done our share of crying. It wasn't going to be easy to leave my best friend.

A minute later Tara appeared in the doorway, looking like a waif in a pair of beat-up jeans and an old T-shirt with paint stains on it.

"What'cha doing?" she asked.

"Packing."

She flopped down on the bed. "Want some help?"

"Actually," I said, standing up to stretch, "I'm just about done. What's up?"

She sighed and gazed at me forlornly. "I screwed up."

"How?"

"You know how you said I should leave my parents hints about the dogs? Well, I might have overdone it."

My cell phone began to ring.

"Yeah, that's probably my dad," Tara said, making a face. "He's slightly annoyed."

I picked up the phone but paused before answering. "With you?"

"No, with you."

"I'll just let this go to voice mail, then." I tossed the phone onto the bed. "So how did you overdo it?"

She shrugged, picking at the fingernail polish on her thumb. "I left little hints around."

"That's all?"

"Well, a lot of little hints." She sighed. "Okay, tons of them. And I kinda covered one of my bedroom walls with dog photos I printed off the Internet . . . and I used up all the ink in the printer . . . and most of my dad's paper. But you should see how cool my bedroom looks."

"So besides plastering your bedroom wall with photos, where did you leave the rest of the hints?"

She held out her hand to study her fingernails. "Just around the house . . . on the counters . . . in drawers . . . in the refrigerator . . ."

"Oh, yeah. You overdid it. But why is your dad annoyed with *me*?"

She went back to working on her thumbnail. "I told him it was your idea."

"Tara!"

"I didn't know what else to do! You know my friend who told me about Seedy and Seedling? He thought it was a great plan. But you can fix it, can't you? My dad always listens to you."

"If he's not happy with me, I'm not sure how much good a call from me will do."

"You've got to convince him, Aunt Abby," she pleaded, holding my hands in hers. "I'll die if I can't have Seedling. Seedy, too, Auntie A. Please help me."

"Okay, Tara. Don't cry. I'll do my best. Come on. Let's get your mind off the dogs for a while. I'd like your opinion on something." I went to my dresser and picked up the sticky note. "Take a look at this and tell me what you think."

Tara read the note, then snickered. "Someone doesn't know grammar."

"I found it on my newspaper this morning, along with this." I showed her the pieces of my flyer.

"Creepy."

"What kind of person do you think would write this note?" I asked.

She studied it for a moment. "Maybe someone my age or younger."

"Not an adult?"

Tara plucked her lips with her fingers as she reread the note. "I don't see this as coming from an adult. But you know who says this a lot? My friend, the one who told me about the dogs. He's always sick with allergies and asthma and stuff, and he's kinda geeky-looking, too, so he gets picked on by the bigger guys. That's what he says when they bully him. *You're evil.* He writes it all over his notebooks misspelled like that. But this can't be from Kyle. He's never even met you."

"Kyle?"

"Yeah. Kyle Shaw. You know his mom. She runs the animal shelter."

CHAPTER TWENTY

I shoved a pile of socks out of the way and sat down on the bed beside Tara. "Kyle Shaw is your friend?"

"Yes. I told you about him."

"You didn't tell me his name! Tara, I've been trying to get Kyle's mom to let me talk to him for a week, but she keeps saying no."

"Why do you need to talk to him?"

"To see if he'll corroborate his mom's alibi. And now to ask him why he left the note."

"I don't know for sure if he's the one who left it, Aunt Abby. I'm just saying it's something he might do. He's very passive-aggressive."

"Does Kyle know where I live?"

"I've never told him, but you're in the phone book."

"He'd have to know my name first, Tara."

She lifted one shoulder. "I do kinda talk about you a lot. Still, why would he think you're evil?"

"Why don't you ask him?"

"Sure," she said, pulling her cell phone out of her

jeans pocket. "Want me to see if he'll talk to you while I'm at it?"

"Wait on that. Legally, it might not be allowed, so let me check with Marco first, and if he says okay, then we'll arrange something."

"Hey, Kyle," she said into her phone. "What's happening?" She listened a moment, then covered the phone to whisper to me, "He's on the computer playing some stupid war game.

"So," she said to him, "what's up with that creepy note you left at my aunt's apartment?" She listened, then covered the phone to whisper, "He's denying it."

Returning to the conversation, Tara said, "Calm down, Kyle. She's not going to call the cops." Again she covered the phone to whisper to me, "You're not, are you?"

I shook my head.

She listened to him and rolled her eyes. "Okay, fine, if you didn't do it, you didn't do it." She whispered to me, "He did it."

"Find out why," I whispered back.

"How about this?" Tara asked him. "I know you didn't leave the note, but just say you did. What would be the reason?"

Tara held the phone to my ear as Kyle said, "How about for upsetting my mom? That's evil."

"Ask him why his mom is upset," I whispered, as she took the phone back.

"Why is your mom upset?" Tara asked him. She listened, then said, "What crime?"

She waited as he answered, then rolled her eyes again. "Fine. I'll drop it. Yeah, I'm going to the shelter tomorrow. I'll call you afterward to let you know how they're doing."

She ended the call, put away her phone, and shook her head. "He's so guilty of writing that note. But he knows we're onto him, so I guarantee he won't do it again."

"Thanks, Tara. What did he say when you asked him why his mom was upset?"

"He said you were treating his mom like she was a criminal, but when I asked what the crime was, he said the conversation was stupid because he didn't write the damn note—his words, not mine."

"If Kyle believes I'm treating his mom like a criminal, then Stacy must have complained to him about the interviews I did with her. Interesting that she singled me out because Marco was with me for one of those interviews. But maybe she didn't feel threatened the first time. Still, why would she confide in her thirteen-year-old son?"

"Kyle and his mom are really tight, Aunt Abby. They talk about everything."

"Which is why I really need to interview him."

"Whatever." Tara picked at her pinkie fingernail, clearly bored with the subject. "So you'll talk to my dad about the dogs?"

"Yes, as long as you stop leaving hints around your house. In fact, here's an idea. Why don't you use your babysitting money to buy your dad a new ream of paper and an ink cartridge? Show him how responsible you are so he'll be more receptive to the idea of a pet in the house."

"Pets."

"Tara, don't get your hopes up. What if he says you can have only one?"

"Please don't let him say that! How could I leave Seedy behind? It would be cruel."

"We'd have to find her a home where she and her puppy could visit."

Tara put her chin in her hands and sighed miserably. "Like that could happen." Then she brightened. "Hey, how about Aunt Jillian? She definitely needs something to take care of. Do you know what I have to do for her *again* this evening? Babysit her stupid bag of potatoes."

I put my hand on her shoulder. "You don't have to take the job."

"Are you kidding? Do you know how much Uncle Claymore pays?"

"Then go for it. I mean, it's not like you have to do anything with the potatoes."

"I wish. Do you know what Aunt Jillian makes me do? Change *Snow's* diaper. I mean, really. Snow? But at least I'll be seeing Aunt Jillian tonight, so I can start working on her about Seedy."

Better Jillian than me. Yet oddly, at the thought of Seedy belonging to Jillian, I felt the tiniest frisson of jealousy. What was that about?

"Hey, Tara, I just thought of something. Kyle's mom told me he's allergic to dogs and cats, so how did he know about Seedy and her puppy?"

"Kyle found Seedy hiding in the bushes on his way home from school. She was all skin and bones except for her big belly, so he took her to the shelter, and she had her puppy there. That was like a month ago."

"Kyle's mom told me he wasn't allowed at the shelter."

"He's not allowed *inside*, so when he rescues one, he ties it up *outside,* then calls the shelter and tells them."

"So he's done this before?"

"A couple of times that I know of," Tara said. "It's too bad he's allergic, because he really loves animals."

My inner antennae shot up. The two red-zone dogs had been found tied up to the front door. "Has Kyle ever mentioned rescuing a pair of German shepherds?"

"Not that I remember."

It was one more thing I wanted to talk to Kyle about.

"Popcorn!" Nikki said, coming into the room with a big plastic bowl heaped full of fluffy white kernels.

"Awesome," Tara said, and stuck her hands deep into the bowl.

"Jordan," I said into the phone later that day, "why are you so opposed to Tara having a puppy to love?"

"Come on, Abby. You just got done browbeating me into letting Tara volunteer. Now you want to force me to let her adopt a dog?"

"Do you understand how good it is for a child to have an animal to take care of? It teaches responsibility."

"Yeah, right," he said. "Do you remember the hamster we got Tara? The one with the squeaky wheel in its cage that kept her awake all night so we had to move it into the kitchen? The hamster that kept getting out of his cage and stealing food? And then had a heart attack and died when I tried to catch it running across the kitchen floor? Guess who took care of it, Abs. News flash. It wasn't Tara."

"But, Jordan—"

"And then there were the hermit crabs. You know who had to clean their aquarium? I did. Not Tara and not Kathy, because she said letting Tara have those little creatures was my idea. Do you remember what happened to them? They all died. Tara said it was because

I used bleach to clean the bottom of the aquarium when it got infested with little bugs. I killed her pets, Abs. Can you understand why I'm reluctant to try this again?"

"Tara's much older now. And we're talking about a dog, Jordan. A cute little puppy that everyone will love. Don't you remember the little dog you had when I was born? Inky? You loved that dog."

"Yeah, and because you came along, Mom gave Inky away. Thanks a lot, Abby."

"See? You need a dog to make up for losing Inky. Come on, Jordan. You're doing this for Tara and the whole family. I'll bet after a week of having that little puppy around, you'll wonder why you ever worried."

There was silence on the other end. That meant Jordan was considering it.

"Remember," I said, "you can send the puppy to obedience school. Tara can go, too, and learn how to get the dog to obey commands. Think what a great experience this will be for her."

"You know who'll end up taking care of it."

"Make Tara sign an agreement then. Come on, Jord. She doesn't have any siblings. She needs a best friend."

Silence.

"Would you please talk it over with Kathy and see what she says?"

"That's not fair. Kathy loves dogs."

"So it's all up to you, Jordan. Be a hero in your daughter's eyes. Let Tara bring the puppy home."

He sighed.

In the Knight world, a sigh was as good as a yes. "You're a champ, bro. And listen, would you consider taking the puppy's mom, too? She's a real sweetheart."

"See, there you go, Abby, always pushing for more, and I'm still not totally sold on the idea of one dog."

Yes, he was. I knew my brother. I hung up and did a happy dance around the living room. I couldn't wait to hear the news from Tara.

Now to convince Jillian to take Seedy.

Monday

My favorite day of the week started off as usual with Lottie's scrambled-eggs-and-toast breakfast and several cups of Grace's delicious coffee. Happily, we'd had nine orders come in over the weekend, which was five more than we'd had the previous Monday, so I hoped we were coming out of our slump. And after we opened for the day, the future bride came in, so I spent an hour helping her select her wedding flowers. It reminded me that my own wedding was in five days and I hadn't firmed up the location.

As soon as I was free, I called the park department a second time to ask whether there was any chance of the gazebo being rebuilt. After being shuttled to three different people, I finally spoke with the department head's secretary, who said that because of their limited budget, the gazebo wasn't a priority. In other words, I shouldn't hold my breath. It was just as I'd feared.

I called the church next to make sure the chapel was still available. Fortunately, it was, so I reserved it.

Shortly before noon, I met Marco at our usual booth at the back of the bar to wait for Emma to arrive. "I reserved the chapel," I told him. "I hope that's okay with you. I don't know what else to do."

"Sure," he said, watching something going on over at the bar. I craned my neck for a look, but all I could see was Rafe whipping up a drink in the blender, talking to two women sitting on stools in front of him.

"Something wrong?" I asked.

He turned to look at me. "What? No. Nothing's wrong. So are you going to reserve the chapel?"

"I did," I said calmly, "which I just told you."

"Sorry. I was thinking about something else."

"Want to talk about it?"

"Not really. It's just boring bar business. Have you spoken with Tara?"

"No, because I wanted you to remind me again what you told me on the phone last night about Kyle."

"Aha! Someone else wasn't paying attention."

He had me there. "You're right, Marco. I was thinking about the dogs Tara wants to adopt. I've got my brother pretty much convinced to take the puppy, but that leaves the mother dog, and if the shelter's no-kill policy is changed, that dog could be put down." Unexpectedly, my eyes welled up with tears.

"Why would a mother dog be put down?"

"Because she's not one of those cute, cuddly dogs that everyone wants, and she's been at the shelter for more than a month, so she falls into the category of unadopt-able. I called Jillian last night to talk her into taking the dog, but she and Claymore were out for the evening. I left a message, but she hasn't phoned me back yet. You don't know of anyone who might want a three-legged dog, do you?"

"I could ask around at the bar."

"That'd be great, Marco. I've got to find her a home soon. I don't trust the PAR board or Dayton Blaine to keep the policy as it is. As Dayton told me, it's about money."

"Sweetheart, you're too tenderhearted. You don't even know this animal and you're ready to cry."

"I've met the dog, Marco. The staff at the shelter calls her Seedy because she's so pitiful-looking, but she has the most soulful eyes you've ever seen, like she desperately wants to be loved."

Marco reached across to cover my hands with his big warm ones. "You have to trust that your mom's protest will work, Abby, and keep your focus on the investigation. Our wedding is at the end of the week, babe, and then we leave for our honeymoon, so we've got to tie up this case before we go. We can't take off with it hanging over your mom's head."

"I know." I wiped away traces of tears with my thumbs.

"Let's get back to that meeting with Tara and Kyle. We can't legitimately meet without a parent present, but if you happened to drop by when Kyle was at her house, then you could claim it was a chance encounter that couldn't have been avoided. But this is another case where you'll have to do it alone, sweetheart. Otherwise it'll look too much like a setup."

"I should do it soon, then."

"That's what I'm saying. We've got five days. Put the dog out of your mind, call Tara, and arrange your meeting."

"She's in school," I said, taking out my phone. "I'll leave her a message."

Marco checked his watch. "It's twelve ten. Emma's late."

By twelve twenty, there was no sign of Emma, and it looked like I'd been stood up again. I felt like a fool for trusting her.

"We'll track her down," Marco said.

"But that'll take time, and we don't have much."

"Look at it this way," he said as he got out of the booth. "What choice do we have? In the meantime, what do you want for lunch? I'll go put in our orders."

"A Caesar salad." I was too tense to eat anything heavy.

Just after Marco left, my phone dinged to signal a message. Hoping it was Emma, I pulled out my phone to check, but it was a text from Mom asking me to call her.

I was in the process of punching in her phone number when I heard, "Sorry I'm late."

I looked up to find Emma sliding into the booth opposite me. I broke into a wide smile. "You made it!"

"Barely. My car broke down." She sighed in frustration. "I had to walk here."

"Where did you leave it?"

"On the west end of Lincoln. You know where that old cement-block building is? I went to the law firm there to apply for a secretarial position. I hated to leave my car in their lot, but I didn't know what else to do. I've had it fixed twice already and I can't afford to buy another one."

"I know a great mechanic. His aunt works for me. His auto shop is three blocks south of here on Washington Street. Tell him I sent you, and he'll go get your car with his tow truck. He'll be able to tell you what's wrong."

She sighed miserably. "The problem is, how will I'll pay for it?"

I had no answer for that one. "Would you like some lunch?"

"No, thanks. I'm too stressed out to eat."

"Let me buy you a cup of coffee, then."

"I don't want anything right now, thanks. Just ask whatever you have to so I can take care of my car."

Marco returned just then and slid in beside me, nodding hello to Emma as he placed his notebook and pen in front of me. "How are you?" he asked her.

"Not very good, to be honest."

"Her car broke down," I explained to Marco, "and she had to walk here. Let's do the interview so she can get to the repair shop."

"You already know why I took the money," Emma said to me glumly.

"Will you confirm that the money issue is why Bev called you into her office Monday?" I asked.

"It's true," she said with a sigh. "Bev found out I took the money—but I had every intention of paying it back once I'd caught up on my bills." She held up one hand to stop my reply. "I know. The road to hell is paved with good intentions. Don't think I haven't thought about that every day since then. I wasn't raised like that, believe me. I was—am—in a terrible financial bind, and I couldn't get Bev to care. She had absolutely no sympathy for me."

"I'm going to repeat the question I asked at our first meeting," Marco said. "What were you doing on Monday between five and seven p.m.?"

Emma looked down as though ashamed. "I went to a bar and had a couple of margaritas. I knew I shouldn't drink before the PAR meeting, but I was rattled and needed to get away for a while."

"What bar?" I asked, taking notes.

"It's a place called Luck o' the Irish, up north near the lake."

"I know it," I said, and at Marco's surprised look, I said, "Don't you remember when I went there to interview a suspect when one of Jillian's groomsmen was murdered at the Indiana Dunes?"

"Hey, Marco, can I see you for a minute?" Rafe asked, then smiled at Emma and said in a sexy voice, "How're you doing?"

"I'm so sorry I wasn't able to make it yesterday," Emma replied. "Can we try again?"

"Sure," Rafe said happily, then saw Marco's frown and said, "But not today."

Marco got up and started toward the bar, so Rafe said to her quickly, "Before you leave, stop at the counter and I'll give you my phone number." He gave her a wink and swaggered off.

"Okay," I said to Emma, readying my pen, "you went to Luck o' the Irish and had two margaritas. Will the bartender be able to verify that?"

"I hope so. He was flirting with me like crazy."

"Do you have any receipts?"

"I didn't keep them, and I paid in cash. I've maxed out my credit cards."

"What time did you leave there?"

"Later than I should have because I got to the meeting after it started."

I remembered seeing Emma rush up to her seat at the front. I noted it, then looked at her. "Why couldn't you have given us this information the first time we met?"

"Because I couldn't believe that you would accuse me of murder."

"We didn't accuse you of anything."

"It felt that way. Anyway, it made me angry."

"It also made you look suspicious."

"I kind of figured that, too."

I pulled out my cell phone and turned the camera feature on. "I'm going to take a photo of you to show to the bartender, okay?"

She tossed back her hair. "Go ahead."

I clicked the button and checked to make sure I had a good shot. So far I was getting nothing but good vibes from Emma.

Marco returned and looked over my notes, then asked, "Do you remember the name of the bartender?"

"It was like Dan—or Don," Emma said. "Wait. It was Dan because someone called him Dan the Man."

"Why did you drive so far for a drink when you knew you had to be back for the PAR meeting?" Marco asked.

"Because I didn't want to run into anyone I knew here in town," she said. "After Bev yelled at me, I was a mess."

Marco reviewed his notes again, then said, "I think that should take care of it. If we have any more questions, we'll get back to you."

I watched Emma stop at the bar and exchange phone numbers with Rafe. She glanced back at me and waved before she left.

"What do you think about Emma?" Marco asked.

"I hope her story checks out. I just don't see her as the murdering kind. I'd like to say she and Rafe would make a cute couple, but I still question her scruples. She did take someone else's money, whether she intended to pay it back or not."

"Rafe spends too much time thinking about women," Marco groused, as Gert delivered our sandwiches.

"He's a young single guy, Marco. What were you thinking about when you were his age?"

"I went into the military at his age. I didn't have time to think about women. I'm just saying he needs to focus on business right now."

"What did Rafe want earlier?"

Marco moved the notebook aside and picked up his sandwich. "He had a few questions for me. Nothing to worry about."

I was getting really, really sick of hearing that. Did I look worried? Annoyed was more like it. Should I be worried? Marco said that so often that I was starting to think I should.

I studied my husband-to-be as he dived into his sandwich. He was totally clueless about my feelings, and that wasn't like him. I had to speak up.

CHAPTER TWENTY-ONE

"Are you having problems with Rafe? Is that why you've been so distracted lately?"

"Rafe will be fine. Don't worry. He just needs more training."

There it was again. I sat back with a frustrated huff. "Every time I ask you what's going on, you blow me off."

"I would never blow you off, Abby. I'm just telling you there's nothing to worry about." He took another bite, clearly blowing me off.

"You're doing it right now." I pushed away my salad. "You're distracted, and it's affecting me, Marco. I feel like you're shutting me out."

"Sunshine, you need to eat. We can talk about this later."

"Talk to me first. Please trust me enough to be honest with me, Marco."

"You know I trust you."

"Then why won't you be straight with me and admit you're having problems with your brother?"

"Because you'll worry."

"So you think telling me not to worry is the answer?"

"Abby, if you told *me* not to worry, I wouldn't."

"Well, there's the difference between us. I'll worry if I think there's something to worry about. So be honest. Is there?"

Marco put down his sandwich. With irritation in his voice, he asked, "Why won't you trust me when I say there's nothing to worry about?"

"Why won't you let me decide that?" I retorted.

He sat back, placing his hands flat on the table, clearly exasperated. "You know what? I need to get back to work." He stood up and picked up his plate.

Just what we needed five days before our wedding, a rift.

Angry and hurt, I said, "Fine. I need to get back to Bloomers. I'll take my sandwich with me."

Before I could scoot off the bench, Marco had put down his plate and slid in beside me. He took my hands and looked me straight in the eye. "I don't want you to leave here angry, Abby. Yes, Rafe is giving me problems, and I'm having to spend a lot of time straightening him—and them—out. I haven't told you because you've had your own problems with your business slowing down. I'm trying to protect you, babe."

"But don't you see that by keeping these things from me, you're sending the message that you don't trust me? Whether you realize it or not, I pick up on your emotions, Marco, and when you're distracted or tense or worried, I can tell immediately. I'm going to be your life partner, Salvare. It's important that we share problems with each other, and if I worry, that's my problem."

He ran his thumbs over the tops of my hands. "I just don't like to see you worried, that's all."

"Marco, I love that you're trying to protect me, but you can't protect me from life, especially not from our life together. I want to be a part of it, and that means sharing the ups and downs. That's why I've told you about my business slump. But you haven't seemed to care."

"I care, Abby, too much. I was just having a hard time balancing your worries on top of mine."

"You don't have to balance anything or fix anything, Marco. You just have to listen and be there to give me hugs and advice when I need them."

Marco put his arm around my shoulders and pulled me against his side. "I can do that."

"So you *have* been worried about Rafe?"

Marco sighed. "On several fronts. I tried to teach him how to use my financial software so he could help with the bookkeeping and bills, and he screwed up big-time. I didn't want you to know, Sunshine, but I've been as worried about my business as you have about yours. It's obvious now that unless Rafe settles down and focuses, he's not going to be able to take over for me here, and that means I won't have as much time to spend with you as you'd hoped—I mean, as we'd hoped."

"I'm glad you added the *we* part."

"I got that. Anyway, I don't want you to worry. I'm getting the finances straightened out and digging out from under the debt."

"Marco, we've had enough ups and downs that you know a solid, trusting relationship doesn't come easily. We have to have open lines of communication, okay? That builds trust. Do you understand what I'm trying to say?"

"Of course. But you need to understand that I've

never had a partner before, in business or in life, and I'm not much of a talker, so sharing everything will take some getting used to."

I gazed into those sexy deep brown eyes and smiled. "Believe it or not, I do understand."

"Just, please, never think I don't love or trust you if I forget."

I loved Marco so much, my heart ached. "I'll keep that in mind." Then, to lighten the mood, I tilted my head coquettishly and said, "Want to prove how much you love me?"

He lifted one dark eyebrow. "This is either going to be expensive or something we'll have to do later."

"Neither," I said. "Get me a to-go container."

Before I left Down the Hatch, Marco and I made plans to visit Justin's towing shop at five o'clock and then head out to the Luck o' the Irish bar to check out Emma's story. My next task was to phone Jillian and talk to her about Seedy. As it turned out, however, Jillian came to see me first.

I walked into Bloomers to find the Monday Afternoon Ladies' Poetry Society in session in the parlor, with Grace scuttling about among tables refilling teacups and plates of scones and Lottie waiting on a customer who'd come in to buy a bouquet of fresh flowers from the glass display case.

"Abby," Lottie called as I walked through the shop, "you have a visitor." She lifted her eyebrows in what was clearly a warning, so I proceeded cautiously.

I lifted one side of the curtain and peered into the workroom. There was Jillian sitting in my desk chair, flipping through a magazine. Okay, innocent enough.

Then I saw what was strapped below the waistband of her short skirt.

"Are you going to stand there looking at me," Jillian said, closing the magazine, "or are you going to come in?"

"What are you wearing?" I asked, walking around her.

"This little device," she said, tapping the MP3 player fastened around her middle, "is teaching my daughter French. And these," she said, lifting a pair of thin black wires coming from the bottom of the player and tracing them around to earbuds pinned on each side of her abdomen, "is piping the sound in stereo. *Comprenez-vous?*"

"You're teaching Snow how to speak French *now*?"

"Storm, not Snow. I changed it back. And, yes, now. Today and all this week. Next week it's Chinese, the following week it's Greek, and then it's Gaelic. By the time Storm is born, she'll be multilingual. *C'est très bon, oui?*"

"Are you sure this will work?"

Jillian pulled a book out of her oversized snakeskin tote bag and handed it to me. I turned it over and read the cover. *Learning Languages in Utero: Guarantee That Your Child Will Be Admitted to Top Universities*, by Takashi Francoise Dimitri O'Malley.

Another of Jillian's crazy ideas. I handed the book back, then glanced around for the stroller. "Where's Sno—Storm?"

"In utero. Duh." She tapped her chin. "Snowstorm. *Hmm.*"

"What happened to the potatoes?"

Jillian wrinkled her nose. "They started to rot. One exploded last night while Tara was babysitting. She wasn't exactly thrilled."

"Speaking of Tara," I said, pulling up a stool, "did she tell you about the dogs she wants to adopt?"

Jillian huffed. "She tried to get me to say I'd adopt one of them, but I asked her, what would I do with a dog when I'm about to become a mother?"

"Jillian, you have seven months before the baby is born. That would give you plenty of time to get used to having a dog around. And you could baby the dog and get real practice being a mommy. Plus, think about what a good guardian a dog would be for Storm, like a built-in babysitter."

Jillian chewed her lower lip. "You really think it's a good idea?"

I leaned forward to gaze into her eyes. "Wouldn't you just love to give some homeless little dog a rich and happy life?"

Jillian got a faraway look on her face, as though imaging herself with a dog, and then she smiled. "Maybe."

"Here's the thing. Tara wants to adopt this puppy named Seedling, but she doesn't want the puppy separated from its mom, and Jordan won't adopt both of them, so if you took the mom, they could visit. And Tara could always watch the mother dog for you if you had to be away."

The smile disappeared. "What about Claymore's allergies?"

"He has hay fever, Jillian. That doesn't mean he's allergic to dogs."

"He might be."

"Then let's go visit Seedy and see if Claymore's affected."

"Seedy? What a horrid name! Does the dog look seedy?"

I couldn't lie, yet I didn't want to nix the deal before Jillian had had a chance to meet Seedy. "Let's just say she needs a good clipping and a few weeks of steady meals so she'll fill out, because she looks like she hasn't been cared for very well. But, Jillian, she's so loving and has the most beautiful eyes you've ever seen. They'll melt your heart."

She slipped the magazine in her bag and stood up. The MP3 player stayed in place. "Okay, when can we go see her?"

I glanced at the spindle and saw three slips of paper. After a quick calculation, I said, "How about four o'clock?"

"We'll pick you up out front." Jillian gave me a hug. "I'm excited, Abs. I'll be able to practice my mothering skills and get an adorable little pet, too."

I was about to correct her on the adorable part but clamped my mouth shut instead. I'd have to prepare her for Seedy on the way to the shelter.

CHAPTER TWENTY-TWO

"Abby," Lottie said, coming through the curtain, "Eve Taylor down at Icing on the Cake Bakery would like a centerpiece made using this antique cookie tin. She's having a private party at the bakery this evening and asked if we could do something up quickly. What do you think?"

She placed an eight-ounce, tall, round Barnum's Animals cookie tin on the table. It was decorated with red letters inside a yellow banner on a red background, with four small squares on the front depicting cages holding a camel, an elk, an elephant, and a rhinoceros in a sand color set against a pale blue background. The words *National Biscuit Company* ran along the bottom. As soon as I saw it, I knew exactly which flowers I'd use.

"I can do it right now."

"Great, sweetie. She'll be delighted."

Basing my design on the four colors of yellow, red, blue, and beige, I set to work pulling flowers. Ten minutes later, I had my blossoms spread out on the table in front of me: Crimson Glory red hybrid tea rose, Cosmic Yellow Cosmos, the beautiful blue *Delphinium belladonna*, and tall, straw-colored wheat stalks. I hummed as I cut the wet foam and placed it inside the tin. All my other cares were forgotten. When I was arranging, I was in a zone.

But I couldn't keep reality at bay for long. Sitting in the backseat of Claymore's BMW, my palms started to sweat as I tried to come up with words to describe Seedy.

"Jillian, I need to tell you a little something about this dog."

"First of all," she said, turning to look at me, "we're changing her name to something cute and fitting to her breed. What is she, by the way?"

I pictured the dog and tried to match her image up to the breeds I knew. "Well, I'd say she's part terrier."

"Yorkshire?" she asked expectantly.

That wasn't what I'd pictured, but Jillian seemed to like it. "Um . . . possibly."

"*Hmm.* A Yorkie name." She tapped on her chin. "Let me think. What would be a cute name? Lily? Lola?"

"I like Lily," Claymore said.

"And," I added, "considering her coloring, let's go with part beagle."

"Terrier and beagle mix. Okay . . . In that case, an English name would definitely be appropriate, like Molly or Sadie."

"I still like Lily," Claymore put in.

"And maybe some Chihuahua," I said, "or Pomeranian."

"Chihuahua *or* Pomeranian?"

"Or both," I said.

Jillian stopped tapping her chin and turned again to look at me. "What are you saying?"

"Seedy is a mixed breed, Jillian. I'm not that well versed in dog breeds, so I'm not sure what all she is."

"I'll need to know, Abs. How else will I find the right name?"

"Wait to see what she looks like, darling," Claymore said. "Some name will speak to you."

Yep. Probably Seedy.

My phone rang, so I checked the caller name and saw Tara on the screen.

"I set up a meeting with Kyle on Tuesday after school," my niece said. "I could use help with my algebra anyway, and he's smart in math. So stop at my house at four o'clock and pretend you want to discuss Seedy and Seedling."

"Got it, Tara. Thanks." I hung up with her and saw my mom's name appear on the screen. "What's up?" I asked quietly, as the name discussion continued in the front seat.

"I just left the police station."

"What?" I whispered. "They took you in for questioning? Why didn't you call me?"

"Is someone in trouble?" Jillian asked.

"It's nothing," I said, waving her away.

"Abigail, calm down," Mom said. "I'm fine. Dave Hammond met me there, so I was well protected. I answered all their questions, and they seemed satisfied with my answers. Dave doesn't think I'll be called back, but if they do ask to interview me again, he's going to say no, not unless they want to charge me with something. He told me not to worry and he said to tell you the same."

Dave knew me too well.

"Anyway, I'm on my way home to tell your father all about it. I thought I'd better phone you so you wouldn't wonder why I hadn't stopped by with a new art project."

Yikes. I'd forgotten all about Mom's Monday afternoon visit. "And I'm so glad you did, Mom! So you'll bring something over tomorrow?"

"Yes, I will. See you then, honey."

The car came to a stop as I slid my phone back into my purse. We had arrived.

The women at the front desk recognized me at once and were ready to call Stacy, but I stopped them in time. "We're here to see one of your dogs for a potential adoption. Is Brian in the back?"

"Yeah," one of the women said, punching two buttons on her phone. "Hey, Brian, some people are here to see a dog." She listened a moment, then hung up. "He says to come on in."

I led the way up the hallway to the door on the left side and knocked, setting off dozens of barking dogs. A minute later, Brian opened the door and waved us inside.

"We want to see Seedy," I said.

He took in Jillian's and Claymore's expensive clothing, then looked at me skeptically. "You're sure?" At my nod, he shrugged and ambled down the row of cages.

Jillian and Claymore had stopped at the second cage, and Jillian was letting a medium-sized shorthaired dog lick her fingers. "This one's a Boston terrier, Claymore. I had a dog like this when I was little."

Brian took Seedy out of her cage and set her on the tile floor, where she promptly sat on her haunches and looked around. I glanced over my shoulder and saw that my cousin was still engrossed in the terrier, so I crouched down and held out my hand, making a clicking noise with my tongue to catch the little dog's attention. She studied me for a moment, then at Brian's urging, started toward me with her awkward hobbling gate. She came up to me and sniffed my fingers, then looked into my eyes and wagged her tail as though she recognized me.

I ran my hands over her head and scratched her behind her big pointed ears. She stopped panting to lick my wrist, then gazed at me again as I smoothed down her fur, which had been brushed but still stuck up at different heights.

Behind me, I heard Jillian gasp. "Oh my God, Abs. Do not tell me this is the dog you want us to adopt!"

"It has three legs!" Claymore announced. "You didn't tell us it has three legs."

"*It* is a she, and so what if she has three legs? She gets around just fine." I pulled the dog into my arms and stood up. "Meet Seedy, the sweetest little dog ever."

"But the dog has three legs!" Claymore said. He clearly could not get over it.

Jillian just stood there with her hand over her mouth, her eyes wide.

"Jillian, pet her," I urged.

Scrunching up her face, as though she found the dog distasteful, she reached out and tentatively ran her hand down the dog's back, then drew it away as though she'd been burned. "*Ew.* Bones. I can feel her bones, Abby."

"I told you she needs to fill out."

"But you didn't tell me"—she waved her hand over the dog from nose to tail—"all this."

"You have to look beyond her appearance, Jill. Take a long look into her eyes and tell me your heart isn't melting."

Jillian stared at the dog, but Seedy was watching me. Jillian put her hands on the sides of Seedy's little face and turned her head, but the dog wouldn't look at her. She wanted to look at me.

"Why don't you hold her?" I said, and held her out.

Both of them took a step back. "No, that's okay," Jillian said.

"She seems to like you," Claymore told me. "Why don't you adopt her?"

"Me? I couldn't. I can't. I've never owned a dog. Besides, my wedding is coming up and then I'll be on my honeymoon, and Marco's apartment isn't that large, and I don't even know if he likes dogs." I looked around for more reasons but couldn't think of any.

Jillian wasn't paying attention. She had moved back to the Boston terrier's cage. "Now *this* dog I like. Look, Claymore. Isn't he cute?"

With a sigh, I knelt down and set Seedy on her feet. She immediately pressed her little body against my legs and gazed up at me with big hopeful eyes. "I'm sorry, Seedy. It looks like it won't work out this time. But I'll keep looking."

She raised her nose into the air and gave a little yip. It broke my heart to watch Brian take her back to her cage.

"We're going to adopt the terrier!" Jillian announced, pressing her hands together.

"Are you sure you won't consider taking Seedy instead?" I asked. "She really needs a home right away."

"Abs," Jillian said, "I can't take a dog that doesn't *speak* to me." She put air quotes around the word speak. "You wouldn't want me to take a dog I didn't want, would you? That would be so unfair to the animal and to us."

For once Jillian made perfect sense. Unfortunately, it didn't help Seedy's cause.

Maybe my mom would take Seedy. She liked unusual animals.

*   *   *

At five o'clock, Marco and I headed toward Shaw's Towing. On the way, I filled him in on my upcoming meeting with Kyle, my mom's interview with the police, and my failed attempt to get Jillian to take Seedy. "I'm going to work on Mom and Dad next. They haven't had a dog since I was born."

"They have a llama."

"You can't cuddle a llama. You can't toss a ball or take it out for a jog. And my dad could use a companion. He's there all day by himself. He'd have to love having a little furry friend around, right?"

"He's the one you need to convince, not me."

"How about if we stop there on the way home? You can help me talk to them."

Marco turned a corner before answering, almost as though he needed those few seconds to think. But then all he said was, "I can't tonight, Sunshine."

"Because of Rafe?"

"Yeah," he said. "Because of Rafe."

Why did I sense there was more to it than that?

We turned into the gravel lot in front of Justin's building and parked. As we passed by the fenced-in lot, the two Dobermans ran up to the wire and snarled, baring their sharp teeth. What a contrast to shy little Seedy.

When we entered the shop, Tobacco Man wasn't there to greet us. Marco pressed the buzzer on the counter, and a few minutes later a man we'd never seen before came through the doorway in the back.

He wore tan work pants and a matching work shirt with a patch on the pocket that said *Bob*. He had a shaved head and a large tattoo of an eagle on his neck. He looked at Marco, ignoring me, and said, "What can I do you for?"

"We'd like to talk to Justin," Marco said.

"He ain't here."

"Do you know when he'll be back?" I asked.

"Hard to say. He had some police business to take care of."

"Oh?" Marco pulled out his investigator's license and let the guy see it. "We're working with the police. Did Justin mention what his business was about?"

"He just said the cops asked him to come by. So he went by. That's all I know."

"How long ago did he leave?"

"Mebbe half an hour ago. He told me to close up the shop at six in case he wasn't back."

Marco pulled out a business card and placed it on the glass countertop. "Would you see that he gets this? Tell him I want to talk to him."

"Sure."

Back in the car, I said, "Sounds like the cops are finally catching up with our investigation."

Marco had his phone out and was dialing. He put the phone to his ear, saying to me, "I'll ask Reilly to find out what's going on."

"Hey, Sean. One of our suspects, guy by the name of Justin Shaw, was pulled in for questioning. Any info you can get on that would help." He put the phone in the cup holder. "Let's see what he comes up with."

Our next stop was at Luck o' the Irish bar, a half-hour drive north, near Lake Michigan. The bar was a low muddy gray cedar building with a yellow wooden sign over the door sporting the bar's name and a faded green shamrock.

We entered to the smells of stale cigarette smoke, sour beer, and the sounds of an old-fashioned jukebox playing "Satisfaction." The bar itself formed a wide U shape, with wooden stools all around it. On the stools sat half a dozen patrons who seemed to be in a daze, some with their chins propped on their hands, some slumped over. Behind the bar was a former football player type with a thick neck and a buzz haircut.

With his arms folded over his massive chest, he watched us approach. "What'll you have?"

"Two drafts," Marco said, taking a seat. I glanced at the slouched figure on the other side of me as I climbed onto a stool. He didn't even stir.

As the bartender placed cold mugs of beer in front of us, Marco took out his wallet. He put a twenty-dollar bill on the counter and slid it forward. "We've got a photo we want you to look at."

"Sure," he said, pocketing the money.

I held out my cell phone with Emma's photo pulled up. The bartender studied it, and then a smile of recognition lit his face. "I remember her. A real babe."

"Do you remember anything else about her?" Marco asked. "Was she looking for someone? In a bad mood or good mood? Chatty or silent?"

"She wasn't silent but not what I'd call chatty either. She said she really needed a strong drink, so I was ready to pour her a shot, but then she asked for a margarita. I thought that was kind of funny."

"You sure it's this woman?" Marco asked.

"Yeah, I'm sure. Pretty, big bright eyes, long, wavy hair, nice figure. We don't get many like her coming in here except in the summer, during tourist season. Rest of the year, it's these dummies." He gestured to the patrons on the stools.

The guy beside me looked up and said, "Hey!"

"Sorry, man," the bartender said. "I'm just telling it like it is."

"Did this woman give you her name?" I asked.

"Nope, and I didn't ask. All she said about herself was that she'd had a helluva day at work and it was only Monday. After that, we made small talk, you know, the weather, what the Cubs and Sox are doing, stuff like that."

"Anything else you remember about her?" Marco asked.

"Just that she downed that second margarita real fast after she saw what time it was. Said she had to get to a meeting. Then she took off."

"Sounds like Emma," I said to Marco.

"I'm satisfied," he said. He finished his beer and set the mug on the counter. "Ready?"

"Yep."

"Thanks, man," Marco said to the bartender as we got up.

Everything Emma had told us checked out, so I mentally crossed her off the suspect list.

Marco pulled into the public parking lot where I'd left the 'Vette and leaned over to give me a kiss. "It'll be a late night for me, so I'll talk to you tomorrow."

I opened the car door to get out, then hesitated. I was so tempted to say, *Are you telling me the truth about working with Rafe tonight?* But considering our earlier conversation on open communication and trust, I couldn't do it. I either trusted Marco or I didn't.

"Good luck with Rafe."

"Thanks. Good luck with your folks."

I slid into the car and locked the door, then pulled out my phone and called my parents. "Hi, Mom. Hey, is it okay if I drop by for a while?"

"Abigail, is everything all right? Are you in trouble?"

"No, I'm fine."

"No, you're not. I can tell by your voice that you're worried, plus you never call here in the evening unless it's bad news. Do you have bad news for me? Did you hear something from Sean Reilly about my interview? Are they going to make me go back for more questioning?"

My mom was starting to hyperventilate, so I said, "Mom, it's not that. We haven't heard anything at all. What I wanted to talk to you about is Seedy."

"Seedy!"

"Yes. I just took Jillian and Claymore to meet her to see if they would take her, but they won't. And Jordan is being stubborn. I don't hold out much hope there."

"You can cross him off altogether. He said absolutely not."

"Did you talk to him today?"

"I talked to Kathy. She said you were lucky you were able to convince him to take the puppy, so we shouldn't press our luck."

"What about you and Dad? Would you consider taking her?"

"Honey, we have Taz."

"But Taz is an outside animal and not one you can really play with. You need an inside pet, something to keep Dad company while you're at school. You had a dog once upon a time, right? Then I came along and ruined it."

"What? Where did you hear that?"

"From Jordan. He said you got rid of the dog when I was born because having both of us around was too much work."

Mom laughed. "I'll have to make sure I set him

straight on that. We got rid of the dog because we discovered your dad is allergic to dogs. So, no, we won't be able to take Seedy. Have *you* considered adopting her?"

"I can't, especially now."

"You're right. You've got too many changes coming up. It isn't easy to move from one home to another, and on top of it, to get used to living with someone new. Adding a dog to the mix would be quite a challenge."

"Exactly. In the meantime, I need to find Seedy a home in case your protest doesn't work."

Mom sighed. "I hate to be pessimistic, but it doesn't look good for our side, Abigail. One of my fellow protesters talked to a board member today, who told her they were not enthused about making the policy change, but that tough economic times were forcing them to. They aren't getting in the big donations they once were, so measures have to be taken in order to keep the shelter up and running."

"*Measures* meaning euthanizing the unwanted animals?"

"That's how they're looking at it, honey. We'll put up a good fight, but ultimately it'll boil down to money. So try your best to find Seedy a home, Abigail."

I hung up with my mom and sat in the car thinking. Who else could I approach about taking an ugly little lovable mutt? Lottie? Grace?

It was worth a try.

CHAPTER TWENTY-THREE

Tuesday

"Positively not."

"No way."

"But you don't understand," I said to Grace and Lottie. "This dog will be euthanized if the shelter's policy is changed, and that could happen in a week. If you'd just come meet her, I'll bet one of you would change your mind."

"Positively not," Grace maintained.

"No way," Lottie said. "My quads have one year of high school left before they're off to college, and then *finally* Herman and I can start traveling. We've been waiting seventeen years for that day, and I'm not gonna be tied down by a mutt, no matter how lovable she is. I know I sound heartless, sweetie, but you got to remember, we've had our share of pets over the years. We've been pet free for the past three, and I'm not gonna take on another animal now. Someone will adopt your little Seedy."

"Grace?"

"I shan't bore you with a long explanation," Grace said. "Leave it that at this time in my life I'm not ready to be tied down either. Perhaps in a few years, but not now. Besides, I'm a cat person. So when the day comes, it'll be a cat, or two perhaps. But most definitely feline."

I plodded back to my desk in the workroom, took a look at the spindle, then laid my head on my arms. Only five orders—and no home for Seedy. It was days before my wedding and I was sick with worry instead of excitedly awaiting my wedding day.

Okay, Abby, take stock. Who else do you know?

Nikki was out of the question. Jordan was out. My parents were out, as were Lottie and Grace. What about Jonathan and Portia?

I grabbed the phone and dialed my older brother's office. "Hey, this is Abby Knight. By any chance is my brother available?"

Jonathan was a heart surgeon who spent hours in surgery, while his wife, Portia, spent her days shopping, golfing, and gossiping at the country club. They'd never had children. Surely she was lonely.

"He's seeing patients?" I said to his receptionist. "Would you have him call me as soon as possible? Thanks."

Catching Jon in the office was a stroke of luck, so I took that as a good sign. The only problem was that Portia was the most spoiled woman I'd ever met. She'd grown up in the lap of luxury, and Jonathan saw to it that she stayed there. Would they be a good match for an ugly little dog?

At that point, I didn't care. If I could get them to agree to house Seedy even temporarily while I continued the hunt, I'd be happy.

The phone rang, and I heard Lottie answer it up front. In a moment, she stuck her head through the curtains. "Marco's on the line."

"Hey, Daisy Belle," he said when I picked up the phone, "how's it going? Are those flyers working?"

"Not so much. I've got five measly orders waiting for me."

"Glass half full, remember?"

"How's this? I've got five orders waiting *and* the morning is young. How was your session with Rafe last night?"

"Fine. Listen, I just got a call from Reilly. He said that Justin lawyered up at his interview yesterday and is refusing to cooperate with detectives. Let's go put some pressure on him at lunch today."

"Sure."

"You sound down, babe. Is it because of the orders?"

"That and I'm worried about Seedy."

"Abby."

"I know what you're going to say. I've got a lot on my plate. I just can't stop thinking about that little dog."

"Well, think about this instead. My brother Rico is coming into town on Thursday for the wedding and my mom is throwing a big Italian feast. So find something nice to wear and get ready to be dazzled by another Salvare male."

Lottie peered through the curtain again and whispered, "Abby, Jonathan is on the phone."

I gave her the thumbs-up sign. "Okay, Marco, I'll prepare to be dazzled by your brother, and meanwhile, *my* brother is on the other line, so I'll see you at noon."

I punched the second button. "Hey, Jon, how are you?"

"I have twenty patients to see before two p.m., so I'm

just a *little* rushed. What do you need?" Sarcasm ran rampant in our family.

"Love you, too, bro."

"Seriously, Abs, what do you need? I'm in a hurry."

"A favor."

"Okay," he said with a resigned sigh. "Who needs my expert opinion?"

"No one. This is about a little dog that needs a h—"

"I have patients whose lives are hanging in the balance, and you're asking me about heart surgery on a dog?"

"Jonathan, calm down. It's not surgery this dog needs. It's a home."

"A home!"

"Yes, a home. Don't you think Portia would love a little dog to dote on?"

"Sorry, Abby. A dog would never work. Portia can't stand loose hair in the house. It freaks her out."

"Dogs have fur."

"Fur—hair. Same difference. Nice talking to you. Gotta run."

Click.

I sat with my chin propped on my hand, staring at the spindle, my mind hard at work. Who else, who else, who else?

Marco's sister?

Tobacco Man was back at the counter, chewing his wad and watching TV, when we entered Shaw's Towing. He nodded in greeting, then went through the doorway to get Justin.

"Sorry, man," he said upon returning. "Boss is tied up right now."

"Tell him we'll wait," Marco said.

Tobacco Man shrugged, then disappeared through the doorway. He came back shaking his head. "Boss says he doesn't have time to see you today. Come back tomorrow."

"That won't work for us," Marco said. "Tell him we're prepared to wait all day."

I glanced at Marco in surprise. There was no way I could afford to be gone all afternoon.

As soon as Justin's assistant left the room, Marco said, "Don't worry. He won't make us wait long. Watch and learn, Sunshine."

Tobacco Man returned. "Boss said suit yourself." He indicated the folding chairs along the front window. "You can grab a seat if you like."

Marco gestured for me to sit down, but he stood by the window.

Ten minutes went by during which time I checked for messages and then played FreeCell on my phone. Marco continued to stare out the window.

After another ten boring minutes, I tapped Marco's arm and whispered, "Are you sure we should wait?"

He gave me a look that seemed to say, *Have a little faith.*

Two seconds later, the phone at the counter beeped. Tobacco Man picked up the receiver and held it to his ear, then looked over at us and said, "Yep." Then he hung up. I had the feeling it was Justin checking up on us.

Five minutes later, Marco nudged my shoulder and said, "Let's go."

He was out the door first and starting toward the sliding gates in the cyclone fence, with me trotting behind. As the gates slid back, a tow truck came roaring out, spewing gravel, tearing across the lot to the street.

"It's Justin," Marco called, jogging toward his Prius. "Let's go."

We jumped in the car and followed him across town, up to the main highway, through a shopping center's parking lots, and back to town again, finally catching him when both vehicles got stopped by a train.

Marco threw the Prius into park, then hopped out and ran to the driver's side of the tow truck. He came back a few minutes later and reported that Justin was still refusing to talk. "I told him I was prepared to stake out his house and follow him wherever he went," Marco said, "but all he said was, if I wanted to waste my gas and my time, go ahead."

"What do we do?"

"The only thing we can do—make life miserable for him until he agrees to talk."

So how did you spend the week before your wedding, Abby?

Well, other than making someone's life miserable . . .

"Maybe I'll have better luck when I meet with Tara and Kyle today," I said.

At four o'clock, I rang the doorbell at Jordan's house and waited. I knew neither Jordan nor Kathy would be home from work, so I wasn't surprised when Tara answered the door.

"Hey, Aunt Abby! What are you doing here?" She winked as she let me in. "I was just working on math homework with my friend Kyle."

Kyle was seated at the long cherry dining room table, now littered with school paper, laptop computers, and books. He looked a lot like his mother, except that his hair was a darker blond and very curly. He was rail thin and pale to the point of looking sickly, with eyes that seemed both weary and watery. I'd seen that look before on people with severe allergies.

"Kyle, this is Abby Knight, my aunt," Tara said.

Kyle muttered, "Hi," turning red in the face. He seemed unwilling to meet my gaze. I guessed it was due to embarrassment.

"Want something to drink?" Tara asked.

"No, thanks." I pulled out a chair across from Kyle as Tara took the seat next to him. "Nice to meet you at last," I said. "I've heard a lot about you."

He glanced at me with a wary, somewhat hostile expression, but said nothing, so I added, "I heard how you rescued Seedy. That was really kind of you. Not everyone will go out of their way to help an animal."

As though it pained him to say it, he uttered a quick, "Thanks," and turned his attention to his computer.

"I've been trying to find a home for Seedy," I said.

Hearing that, Kyle looked at Tara with obvious alarm. "I thought you said you were going to take her."

"My dad said no," Tara said sadly.

"We can't separate her from Seedling!" he said. "You promised, Tara."

"I'm trying to find Seedy a home with someone Tara knows," I told him, "so the dogs can visit back and forth."

"Kyle, that's the best we can do," Tara said, putting her hand on his arm as though to calm him. "I'm still taking the puppy. I was lucky to get my dad to agree to that."

He gazed at Tara with big, worried eyes but said nothing. The conversation wasn't off to a very good start. And now, somehow, I had to lead him to the subject of last Monday afternoon.

"I understand you've rescued a number of dogs," I said.

He shrugged, avoiding my gaze.

"Too bad about your allergies," I said. "I'm sure you'd like to keep some of the animals you've rescued."

Still no response. Tara looked at me and rolled her eyes. I didn't know what else to do except jump right into it.

"It's lucky that you're here, Kyle," I said. "I was going to come see you at your house this evening."

His head jerked up as though I'd sent a shock through his body. "What for?"

"I'm hoping you'll help me prove your mom's innocence."

"There's nothing to prove. Besides, I don't know anything."

"You know a few things, I'll bet."   •

He folded his arms across his chest in more of a protective rather than stubborn way. "Like what?"

"Like whether your mom called you after work on Monday to tell you her plans for the evening."

"She didn't have to call me. I already knew about the meeting. She had it on the calendar in the kitchen."

"Does she write everything on the calendar?"

"Yeah," he said guardedly, dropping his gaze.

"Did she write down that she was going to the mall?"

"No, she told me that morning. She said it was an important meeting and she wanted to look nice for it."

"Sounds like you and your mom are very close."

Slowly, he looked up at me, his eyes narrowing in suspicion. "I guess."

"Did your mom ever talk to you about the possible change in the shelter's no-kill policy?"

He shifted in his chair. "Yeah."

"As kindhearted as you are," I said, "that must have been very upsetting to hear."

He shrugged, his mouth set in a frown. "Doesn't matter anymore."

"Why not?"

"They won't change it now."

"Because?" I asked.

"Because it was *Bev's* idea, and she's gone," Kyle said, fairly spitting out his aunt's name. "*She* was the one who wanted it changed, not my mom, like you want to believe."

"How do you know what I want to believe?" I asked.

"Mom told me how you questioned her," he said, his eyes cold and accusing.

"Your mom told me she was for the change, Kyle," I said.

"You are so totally wrong. She just had to say that while Bev was around, but now she's going to see that it doesn't get changed. She promised me she'd take action as soon as the time was right."

"What kind of action?"

He picked at a corner of his notebook. "She didn't go into it."

"When did she tell you this?"

"I don't remember."

"Before your aunt died? After she died?"

"I. Don't. Remember," he ground out. He shoved his notebook away and folded his arms again. I knew he was furious, but that was the best time to fish for information.

"I don't understand why your mom lied to me," I said.

"She had to lie so you'd leave her alone."

Somewhere in his brain that made sense. "I hate to

say this, Kyle, but it backfired. Lying makes it look like she's hiding something, so now we have to investigate her further."

"She didn't *do* anything," he said, his voice rising. "Bev's the one who caused all the problems. Don't you get that? Doesn't *anyone* get that? Bev was *evil*." Kyle was so angry, he started to wheeze. "My mom—couldn't get her—out of our lives. So what—if Bev—died? So what if—she's gone? We're all—better off."

"Kyle, please calm down," I said, as he struggled for breath.

"Where's your inhaler?" Tara asked, grabbing his backpack.

Holding his chest, he pointed to the outside pocket, so Tara unzipped it and handed the device to him. I watched him inhale twice, his face even whiter than before, and I wondered if I should press him further or let it go.

I waited until his breathing had slowed and he'd sagged against the chair; then I said, "I'm sorry for upsetting you. I really do want to clear your mom."

He looked at me with pure loathing in his eyes and said in a trembling voice, "No, you don't."

"Kyle, this is my aunt Abby," Tara said. "She's awesome. I trust her. She's not like your aunt."

He turned on Tara angrily. "Don't you get it? She *wants* my mom to be guilty. Case closed and your grandma is off the hook. Oh yeah," he said to me. "My mom told me your real reason for this so-called investigation."

"What are you talking about?" Tara cried. "Aunt Abby, is Grandma *on* the hook?"

"She might be, Tara. And, Kyle, whether you want to believe me or not, I would like nothing better than to verify that my mom *and* your mom are innocent, but you have to understand that as long as your mom can't prove where she was at the time of your aunt's death, she *is* a suspect, not just to us but also to the police."

"She was at the mall!" he rasped.

"Is Grandma a suspect because she found the body?" Tara asked in alarm.

"Tara, let's talk about it later, okay? Kyle, what about your dad? Did you hear from him on Monday afternoon or evening?"

Looking down at his lap, he shook his head, then abruptly nodded.

"You did? What time?"

"After I got home from school."

"Why did he call?"

"I called *him*," Kyle said. "I told him Mom was going to be gone at dinnertime and did he want to get a burger with me, and he said he had something to take care of, just like that."

Kyle's story felt contrived. "We'll have to see if it matches what your dad tells us," I said.

"He'll lie about it," Kyle muttered.

"Why would he lie about a phone conversation with you?" I asked.

"He knows Mom hates it when I call him. He'll lie to keep Mom from being angry. That's why I never tell her when I talk to him."

"He'll have to tell the truth if he's under oath," I said.

"He'll still lie." Kyle was trying to sound very offhand about it, but I could tell by his body language that he was tense. "My dad doesn't care if he has to swear an oath. He lies to me all the time. He keeps telling me he's not seeing anyone, but I saw them together."

"Your dad has a girlfriend?" I asked, just to be sure I understood.

Kyle nodded, his gaze still downcast.

"Why doesn't he want you to know?" I asked.

"She's married," he said with a careless shrug. "I go to school with her son."

That could explain why Justin wouldn't tell us where he really was on Monday.

I glanced at Tara to see if she was buying any of Kyle's story, and she said, "Mr. Shaw does lie, Aunt Abby. He told Kyle he was going to find homes for the two big German shepherds he used to keep at his business, but he was really going to have them put to sleep. Kyle rescued them and took them to the shelter."

"You weren't supposed to tell anyone!" Kyle snapped.

Tara gave him a fierce glare. "I was trying to help you."

My inner antennae began to rise. The red-zone dogs had been found tied to the front door. If these were the same animals, Kyle had just established a connection between the dogs and Justin. "Were they black shepherds?"

Tara looked at Kyle, and when he said nothing, she nodded.

"So the dogs that attacked your aunt were your dad's German shepherds?" I asked Kyle.

Refusing to answer or even look at me, Kyle closed the math book beside him and shut his laptop. "I have to go," he said to Tara. "Mom will be home soon."

"Oh!" Tara said, jumping up. "Grandma will be coming in a little bit to pick me up."

"You're going to the shelter?" Kyle asked.

Tara nodded. "I'll make sure Seedy and Seedling are all right."

"Kyle?" I asked. "Did your dad know you took his dogs to the shelter?"

He packed up his backpack, stubbornly silent.

"Kyle, stop it," Tara said. "My aunt is trying to help."

"Yeah, right," he mumbled, causing Tara to roll her eyes.

"I'm sorry, Aunt Abby. Kyle usually isn't this way. His dad must have figured out that he took the dogs, because he questioned Kyle about it twice. Right, Kyle?"

At his quick nod, I said, "Was your dad angry?"

Kyle shrugged. "He didn't care. All he cares about is himself. He was just glad they were gone."

That sounded like a line that came straight from Stacy's mouth. "Has your dad ever asked you for the key to the shelter?"

"No."

"So there's no way he could get inside?" I asked.

Kyle stood up and shoved in his chair. "His girlfriend, I guess."

"How would she let him in?" I asked.

"She's a volunteer."

Now we were getting somewhere. "Do you know her name?"

"Mrs. O'Day."

"Susan O'Day?" I asked.

"Do you know her?" Tara asked.

"She works at the shelter with Grandma."

Susan O'Day had called in sick on the evening Bev was killed. Was that by design?

CHAPTER TWENTY-FOUR

"**I**f you think of anything that will help your mom," I called to Kyle as he headed toward the front door, "will you get in touch with me? I know she'd appreciate it."

He didn't reply.

While Tara showed him out, I sat there trying to put my thoughts in order so I could relay the information to Marco. I reached for Tara's notebook and pen and began to write.

1. Kyle would do anything to protect his mom but still couldn't come up with any information to clear her.
2. Kyle firmly believed his mom was against the no-kill policy change.
3. Kyle held a lot of anger toward his aunt Bev for persecuting his mom and to a lesser degree toward his dad for lying to him.

4. Kyle was responsible for the red-zone dogs being at the shelter.
5. Justin had owned the red-zone dogs.
6. Justin's (married) girlfriend was a volunteer who had a key to the shelter and who worked with my mom.
7. Justin's girlfriend called off sick on the day Bev died.

As I dropped the piece of paper in my purse, Tara came back to the dining room to put away her homework. "That didn't go very well, did it? I'm sorry Kyle wasn't more cooperative, but you weren't serious when you said Grandma might be a suspect, right?"

"She'll be a suspect until the police find the real killer," I said, "but I don't think the police really believe she did it. It's just that she was the only volunteer working at the shelter when Bev was killed, so on the outside, it looks suspicious."

"That's stupid. Grandma wouldn't hurt anyone."

"I know that and you know that, but the police don't know it. That's why Marco and I are investigating, Tara."

"Do you think Kyle's mom or dad did it?"

"I wish I had an answer for that. Do you think Kyle was being truthful?"

"I thought so," Tara said. "He's really upset about me not taking Seedy. I promised him we'd find her a home."

"I'm working on it, Tara, but so far Jillian said no, and so did Grandma and Grandpa and Uncle Jonathan. I'm going to try Marco's sister next."

Tara wrinkled her nose. "The sister with the two crybabies?"

"They're little kids, Tara. Little kids cry."

"Seedy won't like that."

I put my arm around my niece's shoulders and gave her a hug. "I think Seedy would like it anywhere he had a good home."

"Okay, then *I* wouldn't like it because I'd have to take Seedling to their house to visit." She looked up at me with her big green eyes. "Can't you take Seedy?"

"No way. Not at this point."

"Come on, Aunt Awesome! You know you want her." She nudged me in the side. "I'll bet Uncle Marco would love her."

"Do you happen to remember that we're getting married at the end of the week?"

"So? You've had that planned for months. What's left to do?"

"Solve this case, for one thing. And then we'll be on our honeymoon. Seriously, Tara, I can't even think about taking on a pet now. Besides, I'm almost positive Marco's landlady doesn't allow pets."

"Someone has to take Seedy," she whined. "What if that crazy PAR board changes the policy before we find her a home?"

That was a "what if" I was trying not to think about.

Since it was almost five o'clock, I drove back to the square and stopped in at the shop to check in. Lottie reported that they'd had a handful of customers and that three orders had come in while I was out. She'd made up the arrangement that had to be done right away; the others would wait until tomorrow.

I gave both women a rundown on my interview with Kyle; then we locked up and headed our separate ways. I made straight for Down the Hatch, but unfortunately Marco wasn't there.

"He said to tell you he's working on a PI case," Rafe said in between customers at the counter.

"He must have a new case, then," I said.

"You got me," Rafe said. "Want a beer?"

"Not now. Did Marco say when he'd be back?"

Rafe wiped the counter in front of me. "He didn't know. He said he'd call when he could and you should go ahead and eat because he thinks it'll be a late night." Rafe turned to the person who'd just stepped up beside me. "What can I get you?"

Well, damn. Not only had I lost my dinner date, but I'd wanted us to go see Justin before six o'clock and confront him with my new information. Now it would have to wait until Marco and I had time tomorrow, and meanwhile, the clock was ticking on our wedding.

Hmm. I could always go alone.

On one hand, I told myself as I drove out to Shaw's Towing, Justin didn't know my yellow 'Vette, so I had the element of surprise on my side.

On the other hand, I had no Marco *at* my side. If Justin was the killer, I'd have to be careful.

No one was at the front counter when I walked in. I hit the buzzer and waited, but not a soul came forth. After waiting a few more minutes, I walked around behind the counter and headed for the door in the back wall. "Hello?" I called, peering around the door frame. The hallway was empty.

Then I heard angry voices, a woman's and a man's, coming from behind the closed door of Justin's office. I moved closer until I could make out Justin's voice. Was the other one Stacy Shaw's?

"Hello?" I called again, but much softer because I really didn't want them to hear me. I crept up to the door and listened.

"You said everything would be fine," the woman said angrily, "and now you tell me they've pulled you in for questioning again!"

"They're fishing," Justin cried. "They don't have anything on me."

"What if they find out about us?" she hissed. "If they show up at my house, what will I tell my husband?"

Nope. It wasn't Stacy Shaw. Could it be Susan O'Day? But wasn't she supposed to be doing her volunteer work at the shelter now?

"Stay calm, baby," Justin said in a soothing voice. "The cops aren't going to show up on my account. If they did come to see you, they'd probably just want to know why you weren't at the shelter on Monday. That's an easy answer, right? You always get migraines. Why wouldn't they believe you?"

"It's not them I worry about," she said. "It's my husband. He's starting to question everything I do, and I'm beginning to think my son said something to him."

"You're worrying for nothing, Sue. What could Peter know?"

"He's friends with Kyle. Boys talk."

"So? Kyle doesn't know my business, or care for that matter. The kid's head is always in the clouds. He's not paying any attention to me, believe me. All he can think about are animals."

"I know," she said with a sigh. "Kyle was trying so hard to get Peter to adopt a dog, it nearly broke up their friendship."

"See, that's what I mean. I've told his mom to get him a pet, but she's so worried he'll have an asthma attack that she refuses to even consider it. As if that were anything new. Look, baby, it's been a week and a half. We can't let the cops rattle us now. Trust me, everything will be fine, okay?"

A board under me creaked. They stopped talking.

With a pounding heart, I immediately tiptoed backward until I was in the front office; then I stood on the other side of the counter and waited to see if they'd heard me. A minute later Justin appeared.

"Can I help—" His eyes widened in recognition; then he pressed his mouth into a tight line. "What are you doing here?"

Eavesdropping?

Thinking fast, I said, "I've got some new information that I know you'll want to hear."

"I don't care about your damned information. Get out right now or I'll call the cops and tell them you're trespassing." He marched to the door and held it open, then glared at me until I walked through it.

Fine. I'd leave, but not until I verified who the woman was.

I drove the Corvette to a real estate office on the opposite side of the street about half a block east, then turned off the motor and waited, my cell phone camera ready. Within five minutes, a blond woman in jeans and a T-shirt came out of Shaw's and practically trotted to a blue Camry parked at the curb. Glancing around as though to make sure she hadn't been spotted, she slid into the car and put sunglasses on, but not before I caught her on camera. *Gotcha!*

Now to ID her.

I phoned Marco on my way to the shelter and was relieved when he picked up.

"Hey, babe. I'm kind of busy. Everything all right?"

"I won't keep you long. I just wanted to let you know what's going on. Got a minute?"

"For you, always."

I started with my interview with Kyle, quickly reading the bullet points off my list and moving on to what I'd overheard Justin and the unknown woman say. "I'm on my way to the animal shelter now to see if my mom can identify her from a photo. Mom and Tara are there now. Whoever this person is, Marco, we need to talk to her."

"Absolutely. As soon as possible. This certainly puts Justin in a new light."

"Especially since the dogs were his. He'd know exactly what they were capable of."

In the background, I heard an electric saw start up. "Where are you, Marco?"

"In . . . a construction area."

"You don't sound too sure about it."

"There's a lot going on here, Sunshine. I really need to get back to my surveillance."

"Okay. I'll let you know later this evening what my mom says."

"How about if we talk tomorrow? It'll be a late night for me."

"That's fine. Love you." I hung up, feeling unsettled and unhappy. Despite our talk, I had a strong suspicion Marco was still keeping something from me.

At the shelter, I had to phone my mom so she could let me in. She came to the front door with a worry line between her eyebrows. "Did something happen?"

"I need you to check out a photo," I said, stepping inside.

"You frightened the bejeepers out of me to show me

a photo?" She locked the door behind me, then looked at my phone. "What are you doing with a picture of Susan?"

"This is Susan O'Day, the woman you work with?"

"*Used* to work with. She gave her notice on Friday. That's another reason why I'm so glad Jordan and Kathy are letting Tara help. I could never count on Susan because of her migraines."

"Do you have her address?"

"At home. I'll call you with it this evening." Mom smiled at me for a moment, as though she wanted to say more, but then turned and started toward the hallway. "Come back and see the dogs."

"I really don't want—"

She was already at the dog ward, holding the door open for me. With a sigh, I followed.

Tara had Seedy and Seedling in the small play area, where Seedling was romping with a ball and Seedy was watching contentedly as Tara scratched behind her ears. At my entrance, Seedy turned and looked; then with a small *yip,* she came hobbling across the floor toward me. I crouched down and held out my hand, but Seedy didn't need to sniff it to know who I was. She came up and put her head on my knee, gazing at me with a longing expression that tore at my heart.

"She recognized you, Aunt Abby," Tara said. "See? You really need to take her home."

"We've been over this," I said, giving her a scowl.

"I've got to get back to the cats," Mom said. "Tara, you need to take the other puppies out now for some exercise."

And I had to leave before I did something stupid, like follow Tara's suggestion.

CHAPTER TWENTY-FIVE

"Hey, Gina," I said, the phone pressed to my ear as I sat on the sofa in front of the TV, "have you ever considered a pet for your children?"

There was a pause on the other end of the phone—was that a Salvare trait?—and then she said, "Oh, I get it. Ha-ha. Marco put you up to this, didn't he?"

"No, Marco isn't even here. I was just wondering if you'd ever considered it because there's this little dog that really needs—"

Her baby began to cry, drowning out the rest of my sentence. This was followed by Gina's three-year-old son, Christopher, shouting, "Mommy, I have to potty!"

"You're kidding me, right?" Gina asked me.

"No, I'm serious. There's this little dog that really needs a home, Gina. She's in danger of being put down if someone doesn't—"

"Mommy, huwwy!"

"I'd love to help you out, Abby," Gina said, "but I

can't keep up with the kids, let alone a dog. If I think of someone, though, I'll let you know."

"Okay. Thanks for listening," I said above the noise on her end. "I'll see you on Thursday at the dinner for your brother."

"Actually, Rico can't make it into town until Saturday morning, so the dinner is canceled. I'm surprised Marco hasn't told you."

No, Marco hadn't told me. Obviously he wasn't telling me much these days.

"Mommy!" Christopher screeched.

"Have to run, Abby. Bye!"

I'd barely hung up when there was a knock at the door, and then Jillian called out, "Abby, are you home?"

"Coming." I hurried up the hallway and opened the door. Jillian stood outside wearing her bridesmaid dress and high heels.

"Wedding's on Saturday," I said.

"Take a look at this." She proceeded at full steam into the living room, where she twirled around, making the skirt of the lacy pale yellow strapless dress bell out. She ended the show by presenting herself with a curtsy. "Well?"

"If I were the queen, I'd be damned impressed."

"Of course you would, silly," she said, standing tall. "That isn't the question. Didn't you notice anything?"

"Your heels match nicely."

She huffed in exasperation. "What about my baby bump?"

I studied the front of the dress below her waist. "You look trim to me."

She turned a quarter of the way around. "Now look." She smoothed out the front panel of the skirt.

"Nothing, Jill. No baby bump."

"Are you sure?" She smoothed the panel again.

"Positive."

"Claymore saw it. Maybe you should have your eyes checked."

"Maybe you're engaging in wishful thinking."

"Maybe you're no fun." She sat on the sofa with a flounce and a pout, then began tapping her fingernails on the cushion, a gesture I knew well. She was cooking up something.

"Don't even thinking about using that baby ball under your dress, Jillian."

"Actually, I was thinking about the wedding. Has Nikki tried on her dress yet?"

"Yes, and it fits fine. You'll both be beautiful."

"You picked up your gown, right?"

"Yep, and Marco will pick up the three rental tuxes on Saturday morning."

"Flowers?"

"I'll make the bouquet, the boutonnieres, and the floral arrangements for the chapel on Friday. Rehearsal is Friday evening, and Francesca is taking care of the dinner afterward. I've confirmed the restaurant reservations for Saturday evening. You're taking me to get my hair done Saturday morning. Photographer and videographer are confirmed as of yesterday morning, and other than moving my boxes to Marco's apartment, I think that's it."

"You know what we didn't do?" She jumped up and started toward the door, calling over her shoulder, "Throw you a personal shower."

"Jillian, I already had a big shower. There's no need for another one. Besides, it's too late to plan one now."

"That's what you think." She opened the door, then turned back to me with a grin. "Gotcha!"

Laughing at my perplexed expression, Nikki came running in to give me a hug, leading the way for Lottie and Grace, my mom, my aunt, my sisters-in-law, Marco's mom, Gina, who must have been on her cell phone and close by earlier, and my three closest high school friends. They brought food and beverages and presents, some of them too embarrassing to have opened in front of my mom and future mother-in-law, but all accomplished with a lot of fun and laughter, thanks to Jillian and Nikki. What amazed me most was that Jillian had managed to keep it a surprise.

To top off what turned out to be the perfect small bridal shower, I got a phone call from Marco at the end of the evening asking how it went.

"How did you know about it?" I asked.

"My mom told me and swore me to secrecy."

"So that's why you said you had to do surveillance work this evening?"

"No, I really was busy this evening. Still am. I just wanted to give you a quick call to see how it turned out."

"I had a blast."

"Good."

"You know what you forgot to tell me, Marco?"

"What's that?"

"That the dinner for your brother tomorrow night was canceled."

"Oops."

"Yeah, oops."

"Sorry, babe. Too much on my mind. I'll make it up to you. I promise."

That was one plus. I loved those paybacks.

"So tomorrow it's back to the case," he said.

"That reminds me: My mom brought over Susan O'Day's address. Mom said Susan's usually home during the day, so want to make it a date at noon?"

"You bet. See you then, beautiful."

And with that one word, all was forgiven. Anyone who thought a shorty, busty, freckled redhead was beautiful deserved it.

Thursday

Two more days until my wedding. *Two more days* until I married the man of my dreams! I'd taken care of all the wedding details that could be taken care of ahead of time, but I had yet to clear my mom or find a home for an unwanted dog. Those were the thoughts in my head as I put together a floral arrangement for a birthday celebration that morning. The good news was that eleven orders had come in overnight and four more had arrived after nine o'clock.

I glanced at the clock. I had ten minutes to finish the ninth order before I had to be down at Marco's bar, so I adjusted the greenery and tore off a big sheet of clear wrap.

"Anything I can help you with, sweetie?" Lottie asked.

"Mrs. Lampert will be here within the hour to pick up this arrangement. I'll have plenty of time to work on the rest of these orders later."

"If we're lucky, there'll be more waiting," she said. "I can just feel that ol' pendulum starting to swing the other way."

"I hope you're right." I stowed the arrangement in the

cooler, grabbed a bouquet of yellow and orange daisies, and picked up my purse. "I'll be back as close to one o'clock as I can."

"No problem," she said. "I'm in no rush. I brown-bagged it today."

I trotted up the sidewalk to Down the Hatch and found Marco waiting outside. We walked to his car, then made the eight-minute trip north to the O'Day house and found Susan pulling weeds in the front yard of her ranch home.

She stood up, brushing her hands together, as we came up her walk. Susan was an attractive fortysome-thing woman with short blond hair, blue eyes, and a trim figure. She had on a blue tank top with the PAR logo on it and tan capris that were smudged with dirt. "Can I help you?"

Giving her a big smile, I said, "I don't know if you remember me, but I'm Abby Knight, Maureen's daughter, and this is my fiancé, Marco Salvare, a private investigator." Then I held out the bouquet. "These are for you."

"Thank you." She took the flowers, clearly bewildered. "What are they for?"

"Hopefully for answering a few questions for us," I said.

"About what?" she asked, giving us both wary looks.

"About the animal shelter," Marco said. "I understand you're a volunteer there."

"I was," she said. "I had to quit recently because of my migraines."

"You normally volunteered on Mondays; is that right?" Marco asked.

"Yes," she said slowly, as though she suspected a trap.

"Was Bev Powers ever at the shelter during the time period that you and Maureen were there?" he asked.

"Once or twice that I remember."

"What about Stacy Shaw?" he asked.

"She usually left at five, about the time we would arrive."

"I understand you weren't at the shelter on the night Bev died," he said.

"That's right. I had a migraine that day."

"You have a key to the shelter?" Marco asked.

"Yes," she said hesitantly.

"Are you aware of Justin Shaw's connection with the shelter?" Marco asked.

I could see by the way she stiffened that the question surprised her. "Justin Shaw?" The way she said his name, it was as though she'd never heard of him before.

"We know you have a relationship with him," I said. "We interviewed Kyle Shaw, and he told us about you and his dad."

For a moment, she stared at us, obviously stunned; then she brushed off the front of her capris in short, angry motions. "I wouldn't believe everything Kyle says."

"It's okay, Susan," I said. "We're not here to judge you. We just need to know whether you let Justin into the shelter on Monday afternoon."

"I'm not talking to you," she said in a brittle voice, walking away.

"I'll bet Justin would be grateful for your help," Marco called. "He's the number one suspect in Beverly Powers's death right now."

She did an about-face and stalked back toward us. "You don't understand," she said in a furious whisper. "I *can't* talk to you."

"Why is that?" Marco asked.

"Because it would be extremely harmful to my family," she ground out.

"How about to Justin?" Marco asked. "Would it be harmful to him—or would it clear his name?"

She stared at Marco as though taking in the import of his words; then she looked away, rubbing her forehead as though she was conflicted, leaving a smear of dirt above her eyebrows.

Marco gave me a look that said, *She's weakening*.

"I sense that you care about Justin, Susan," Marco said, "and that you'd like to see him removed from the suspect list, so is there anything you can do to help with that process? And keep in mind that anything you tell us will remain confidential unless you give us permission to use it. I promise you. All we need are a few brief answers."

I glanced at him in surprise. How would we use her information to help my mom if it had to remain confidential? He replied with a slight shake of his head, as though to say, *Don't worry about it*.

Susan continued to rub her forehead, so Marco said, "Did you let Justin into the shelter on Monday afternoon? Just a simple yes or no will do."

"No! Of course I didn't let him in!" she said.

"Has he ever asked for your key?" Marco asked.

"Never," she said adamantly. She glanced around as though afraid the neighbors were listening, then said in a low, angry voice, "Listen, I don't know what you've heard about Justin, but he's a good person. If Kyle told you I let his dad in with my key, I'd question Kyle again, because that just didn't happen."

"The problem is," Marco said, "that Justin lied about

his whereabouts on Monday between the crucial times of five and seven p.m., which makes him look guilty."

"Justin lied about where he was," she hissed, "because he was with me. He's trying to protect me."

"Did you make it up about the migraine, then?" I asked.

"I *did* have a migraine," she said.

"But that didn't stop you from seeing him," I said.

Lowering her gaze, she shook her head.

"Would you be willing to sign a sworn statement that he was with you?" Marco asked.

She put her hand to her heart, her eyes wide with alarm. "I can't do that! Don't you understand? If my husband were to find out—" She shook her head, unable to finish the sentence. "I have to go now."

"There may be a way you can still help Justin," Marco said before she could walk away. "While you were with him Monday, do you remember whether he received a call from Kyle?"

She rubbed her forehead again, clearly frazzled. "He got a call, but it was from his ex-wife. In fact, she was looking for Kyle. He wasn't at home or answering his cell phone."

"Do you remember what time that was?" Marco asked, as I quickly dug out my little notebook.

"It was around five o'clock because we'd just gotten to the hote—" Her face reddened as she realized what she'd been about to say. Covering her embarrassment, she hurried to say, "Justin tried to call Kyle, too, several times, and finally just left him a voice mail."

"Are you certain no other calls came in while you were with Justin?" Marco asked.

"I'm certain."

"Do you know whether Justin turned off his phone while you were together?" I asked.

"Justin never turns off his phone," she said, "for business reasons."

Marco glanced at me to see if I had any other questions. When I shook my head, he said to Susan, "I know this has been difficult, but thank you for talking to us."

She gripped his wrist, looking him straight in the eye. "You promise this won't go any farther?"

"I never go back on my word," Marco said.

"At least we know now why Justin lied about his whereabouts at the time of the murder," I said, as we drove back to town.

"We need to see Stacy Shaw again," Marco said. "Can you be available at four forty-five today?"

"Sure. What are you thinking?"

Marco checked the rearview mirror, then moved into the other lane. "Neither of Kyle's parents knew where he was at five o'clock last Monday, and that concerned Stacy enough to call the man she despises. I don't want to speculate what it means at this point, but that kid is the key to solving this case, Abby. I can feel it."

"Shouldn't we confront Kyle before we see his mom?"

"It'll take too long to set up another meeting with Tara." He made a turn onto Franklin and headed toward the public parking lot. "Is that your stomach growling?"

"I haven't had lunch."

"Want to grab a sandwich to go at the bar?"

"Sure. Speaking of food, do we have plans for dinner tonight, now that your mom's meal got canceled?"

Marco turned into the lot and drove slowly up the

aisle, which was jammed with cars. "I may have to drop you off at the shop and drive around the block."

"Marco? Dinner?"

"Here's a spot." He pulled in and turned off the motor, then gave me a sheepish look. "I have to work again tonight, Sunshine. I'm sorry. I'll have this job wrapped up by Saturday, though, and then I promise I'll cut back, okay?"

Did I have a choice?

"Here's my strategy," Marco said, on our way to the animal shelter late that afternoon. He was wearing a gray sport coat, black T-shirt, and jeans, making him look professional and so yummily masculine. "I want to make Stacy believe that we're looking at Kyle as a serious suspect. If she's any kind of mother at all, and as protective as she's come across in her past interviews, she'll do whatever she can to change our minds." He put on his signal and changed lanes. "How she'll do it is the question."

"What do you mean? That things could get dangerous? Should we have Reilly on alert for backup?"

"I doubt there'll be any danger, Sunshine. Remember how the murder was committed."

"But we don't know how Bev was forced into the exercise pen, Marco. There could have been a weapon involved."

"Abby," he said, taking my hand, "I wouldn't bring you into any situation where there was a possibility of danger without being prepared for it."

I glanced at him in surprise. He was armed! "Beneath your sport coat?" I asked.

"Do you really want to know?"

Good point. I had a bad habit of staring where I shouldn't. "So we make Stacy believe that we think Kyle killed his aunt, and she tries to convince us otherwise. Does that include offering herself up as the killer?"

"Exactly."

"But what if she *is* the killer?"

Marco lifted one eyebrow. "Exactly."

We walked into the shelter at five minutes before five p.m., producing scowls from the Friendly Sisters. "It's closing time," one of them stated, arms folded across her bosom.

"We'd like to see Stacy," I said.

"It's *closing* time," the other one said, as if we hadn't heard correctly.

At a rapid clicking of heels on tile, I glanced around just as Stacy walked out of the hallway. "You two go home," she said to the women in a no-nonsense voice. "I'll handle this. Would one of you call my son and tell him I've been delayed?"

She was wearing a skintight bright pink pencil skirt and a black blouse, with black heels and humongous black-and-gold earrings that dangled to her shoulders. She turned sharply and started back the way she'd come, snapping out, "Follow me."

Once in her office, she took a seat behind her desk and crossed one leg, sitting upright and tense. I sat down opposite her as Marco started to close the door.

"Leave it open," she said curtly.

Marco opened it all the way, then sat down in the chair next to mine. "I know our timing is bad," he said, "but we've come across some new information that we need to run past you."

"And what would that be?" Her tone was heavily sarcastic.

"For one thing," Marco said, "we learned that your son was responsible for bringing the red-zone dogs to this shelter."

She threw a pen into her desk drawer and slammed it shut. "That's ludicrous. A boy who's highly allergic to dogs isn't going to go near two large, dangerous animals, let alone bring them here."

"It's not ludicrous at all," Marco said. "They were his dad's dogs and about to be put down. Knowing how softhearted your son is, I'm sure he was extremely upset when he learned of their fate."

Obviously caught off guard, she asked in surprise, "They were Justin's dogs?"

Finally, something I could answer! "Yes, they were."

It took her a few seconds to compose herself; then she asked angrily, "How do you know my son is softhearted?"

Obviously, Kyle hadn't told Stacy of our interview. "My niece, Tara, is a friend of Kyle's."

"And she claims Kyle rescued those dogs?" Stacy asked.

"She has no reason to make something like that up," I said.

"Well, so what?" she said, swinging her foot furiously. "I don't see why you had to come all the way down here to tell me my son rescued two dogs."

"The same dogs that attacked your sister," Marco reminded her. "That says to me that your son wasn't afraid of them."

Folding her arms tightly over her black blouse, she said, "Where is this conversation going?"

"You know where it's going," Marco said. "And *we*

know that neither you nor Justin could reach Kyle by phone on Monday afternoon after five p.m."

"Not true!" she cried. "He was in the backyard. He sits out there after school with his laptop doing homework. He just didn't return his dad's call, that's all."

"Did he return your call?" Marco asked.

"Yes, of course he did."

"The detectives will want to see your cell phone to verify that," Marco said.

"Then why haven't they asked for it?" she retorted, rising. "It's time for you to leave."

Marco made no move to get up. Instead, he said calmly, "Why are you being so defensive?"

"Because I know what you're trying to do." Stacy picked up her purse and put the strap on her shoulder. "You're trying to make it look like my son was responsible for those dogs attacking my sister."

"Can you prove he didn't?" Marco asked.

"He was at home!" she shouted, turning red in the face.

"Give us some proof and we'll go away," Marco said. "Otherwise, we'll contact the detectives with this new information and let them take over the questioning. I promise you, it won't go easy for Kyle."

Stacy turned her back on us, her arms folded so tightly across her chest it looked like she was giving herself a hug. "I came home and found him in the yard. *That's* how I know where he was."

"What time?" Marco asked, as I slid out the notebook and pen.

"Six thirty, six forty."

"You told us previously that you went to the mall between leaving work and going to the meeting," I said.

She turned to face us, her features set defiantly. "I *did* go to the mall. I just stopped at home afterward to make sure Kyle was all right. He's been having a lot of asthma attacks lately." She shrugged. "I worry about him, that's all."

"Wouldn't he know to call you if he was having trouble?" I asked.

"You obviously don't know how teens are," she said. "They think they can handle everything."

Redheads were known for that, too. "What condition was he in?" I asked.

"He was wheezing. His allergies were bad that day."

"What was his excuse for not calling you back?" Marco asked.

"He didn't have his phone with him. He left it in the house."

"The way teens are connected to their phones," I said, "that's a little hard to swallow."

"Suit yourself," she said, giving me a glare.

"We'll need to verify all this with Kyle," Marco said, "without you present."

"I've already told you that's not going to happen."

"Stacy," Marco said, "we know you're covering for him."

"I'm not *covering* for my son. There's nothing to cover. He's a kid, for God's sake. Leave him alone."

"I'm not going to debate it with you," Marco said, "so here's what you need to know. Of everyone who had the means, motive, and opportunity to kill your sister, only you and Kyle have yet to offer proof of your alibis. Give me that proof, and I'll be more than happy to take you off the suspect list."

"What about Maureen Knight?" Stacy demanded. "How

can she prove she had nothing to do with my sister's death?"

"Simply put, she had no motive," Marco said.

"Neither do I," Stacy cried. "And absolutely neither does Kyle. How dare you accuse either one of us! I told you I loved my sister. I was devastated by her death. And Kyle didn't even know Bev very well. What on earth would make you think a young boy could be capable of something that horrendous?"

"Stacy," I said, "I made it clear the last time we spoke that Marco and I know Bev forced you to be her spokeswoman for changing the shelter's no-kill policy. We also know that Kyle was aware that his aunt was behind it and hated her for that."

"How do you know that?" she cried. "From your niece? Is she your expert witness?"

"Stacy, you have to know that Tara and Kyle are close friends," I said. "She's been working with Kyle to find a home for another dog he rescued."

"Kyle can't even come inside the shelter because of his allergies," she retorted. "Besides, he couldn't have gotten in even if he'd wanted to. I have the key."

"Stacy," Marco said, leaning back, "you're too organized not to keep a spare set of keys at the house."

She pressed her hands to the sides of her head, as though it might explode. "I don't believe this is happening."

"Then make it go away," Marco said. "Let's talk to Kyle and get some understanding of how it happened."

"You still think my son—?" She paced behind her desk, still holding her head.

"I think your son came down to the shelter to change his aunt's mind," I said.

"Things went badly," Marco said. "He reacted as a

young teen might—with anger and without a clear understanding of what he was doing."

"This is my sister's fault," Stacy muttered, still pacing. "She brought this upon me. She's the one who's responsible, hateful, hateful bitch that she was. You want to know what happened? I'll tell you what happened. *I* was the one who tried to change her mind. And you're right. She *made* me go along with her idea to change the shelter's no-kill policy. And then she forced me to promote it as my idea!

"Do you see how hateful she was?" Stacy asked, tears rolling down her cheeks faster than she could wipe them away. "Can you blame me for wanting to stop her? *I* released those dogs. Me! I couldn't take her bullying any longer. But I never wanted her to die. I only wanted to scare her." She collapsed onto her chair and put her face in her hands, crying hard.

"We're going to have to notify the police," Marco said, "so you can give them a statement."

"Fine!" she shouted. "Just do it. I can't take this any longer."

"Just one question," Marco said. "How did Bev end up inside the fence?"

"What does it matter?" she cried. "I did it, okay? I. Did. It!"

"No, Mom, stop it!" came a distraught cry from behind us.

"Kyle!" Stacy cried, looking toward the door.

I swiveled in my chair and saw him standing in the doorway with a gun in his hands. Visibly shaking, he pointed it at Marco. "Leave my mom alone!"

"Kyle," Stacy said, her voice shaking, "put the gun down! You don't know what you're doing."

"Where did you get the weapon, son?" Marco asked, easing out of the chair.

"It's mine," Stacy said, also rising. "He took it from my closet." She held out her hand as she approached him slowly. "Kyle, please give it to me."

Kyle took a step back but kept the gun pointed at Marco. "She didn't do anything wrong!"

"Kyle!" Stacy shouted. "Listen to me. Stop talking and put the gun down. Everything's going to be fine if you do what I say."

"Shut up!" he bellowed, his voice cracking, making Stacy draw back. "You're not going to talk to the police, Mom. You know you didn't do anything wrong."

"Son," Marco said, raising his hands in the air as he took a slight step toward the boy's left, "your mom explained everything. It's okay. We know what happened."

"No, you don't!" he shrieked, tears rolling down his face. "Stop saying she did it or I'll shoot this. I swear I will!"

"Kyle," Stacy said, trying to hold back sobs, "you can't protect me. Let me handle this, please."

He looked at Marco, as though appealing to him man-to-man. "You have to believe me. It's my fault Bev is dead. She was going to kill Seedy. I found her memo."

"Kyle!" Stacy said.

Marco gestured for me to get up and move off to the right, but I was too close to the boy. I feared drawing his attention. I gave my head a little shake and Marco responded by inching farther to the left, so Kyle had to turn his head to look at him. But Kyle's attention was still on his mother, who was a few feet in front of him now.

"I saw it on your desk, Mom. Seedy was going to be

the first to be put down after the policy change. Bev didn't even care that I loved Seedy. Don't you understand why I had to stop her? Don't you?"

"Don't listen to him," Stacy said to Marco. "He's making this up to protect me."

"How did it happen, son?" Marco asked, slowly lowering his hands.

"Shut up, Kyle," his mom ground out. "Don't say another word."

"No, Mom, I want him to understand." Kyle used the side of his arm to wipe his tear-streaked face. "I've been coming here to see Seedy and Seedling after the shelter closes and the volunteers leave, but last Monday Bev caught me. She wasn't supposed to be here. I watched her leave before I went inside, but she came back and found me and the dogs in the exercise pen."

"How did she know you were in the pen?" Marco asked.

"I left the door to the ward open," he said unhappily.

"Did you use the spare key from home to get inside the shelter?" Marco asked.

He shook his head. "I had my own key."

"He's lying," Stacy said in a desperate voice.

"I got it copied at the hardware store, Mom," he argued.

"He wouldn't do that," Stacy cried. "He gets sick when he comes to the shelter."

Marco ignored her. "What happened after your aunt found you with the dogs?"

"Bev threatened to tell Mom, so I told her I knew what she was planning and that I was going to tell everyone that changing the policy was *her* idea. And you know what she said? That hideous beasts like Seedy deserved to be put down! That's what she said, Mom. I swear to God she did. I begged her not to kill Seedy, and she said I was pathetic. That I've been nothing but a pathetic weakling right from birth. She said"—he choked back a sob—"she said that's why she gave me up for adoption."

"Kyle, no," Stacy said, in tears. "That's a lie."

"I know the truth, Mom. I know she had an affair with Dad and got pregnant with me. I know she forced you to adopt me and I'm the reason why all of you moved here. I know you and Dad divorced because of me. She told me everything."

"Please stop, baby!" Stacy begged, her hands clasped together. "You don't—"

"I'm not a baby!" Kyle screamed, making Stacy cry harder. "Shut up, Mom. Just shut up!"

"This is insane!" Stacy cried, and turned away, as though she couldn't stand to watch.

"Does your dad know what happened, Kyle?" Marco asked.

"No one knows," he said, casting a guilty glance at his mom. It made me suspect that Stacy had figured it out at some point, which was why she wouldn't let us talk to him.

"How did you get out of the pen and your aunt didn't, Kyle?" Marco asked.

"I pushed her down," Kyle said, starting to wheeze, "and then I ran out—and shut the door behind me and locked it. She was—so angry, she started—beating on the door and saying she was going to—enjoy killing Seedy."

"Where were Seedy and her pup at that time?" I asked.

"I'd already shoved them through the doggy door so she couldn't hurt them. She tried to kick Seedling, Mom! I—hated her so much! Do you understand—how evil she was? Do you see why—I had to punish her—by letting—the shepherds out?"

Kyle was sobbing now and wheezing heavily. As he labored to breathe, the gun wavered in his hand. "She said—I almost ruined her life—and you never wanted me either—"

"That's not true!" Stacy cried. "Honey, I wanted you from the first moment I saw you. Please believe me!"

Kyle doubled over, gasping for air, and Marco moved fast, grabbing the wrist that held the gun with one hand and clamping his other hand around the barrel, snapping it out of Kyle's grasp before the boy could react.

At that, Stacy ran forward and wrapped her arms around Kyle, who seemed ready to buckle. Marco jerked his chair back and Stacy got the boy into it, where he continued to gasp for breath. "Where's your inhaler?" she cried.

"Back—pack," he managed, pointing toward the hallway.

Stacy ran out of the office and returned moments later with the inhaler. She put it into his hands and he shot it twice into his mouth, drawing in breaths until his airways began to relax.

"You have to stop questioning him," Stacy said to us, her eyes swollen and red-rimmed. "He can't take it."

"We'll let him calm down awhile," Marco said, "but we're going to need to call the detectives so he can give a statement."

"Don't you get it yet?" she said in a furious whisper. "He's lying. He made up this whole ridiculous story to protect me. *I* killed my sister. I pushed her into that yard and locked the door. And then I raised those dog doors and let the shepherds attack her. Kyle was nowhere near here. Do you see what just happened to him? If he'd been inside the shelter, he wouldn't have been able to function."

"Stop it!" Kyle cried. "Just stop it!" Turning to Marco, he said, "Call the police. I'll tell them how it happened."

"So will I," Stacy said. "I'll give them the exact details of how it all went down. I won't let them arrest Kyle for what I did." She wrapped her arms around her son's shoulders and rocked him as they cried together.

Marco pulled out his phone and pressed 911.

An hour later, Marco and I drove back downtown so I could pick up my 'Vette. I sat in the car in silence, still stunned by the turn of events. Stacy had called a lawyer, who had instructed her and Kyle to say nothing more. The only other information Kyle had given us was that he'd always been careful to not be seen when he'd gone to play with the dogs and that his visits had stopped with his aunt's death, which was when he got Tara involved. The police had come and taken both Stacy and Kyle to the police station, where they had planned to meet their attorney along with the detectives on the case.

"What will happen if they continue to give contradictory stories?" I asked Marco.

"It'll be up to the detectives to find out which one is telling the truth. I can tell you now that no prosecutor is going to want to try a young teen for murder, so they'll be looking extra hard at Stacy's story."

"And if they can't prove for sure which one did it?"

"You remember from working with Dave Hammond, don't you? The prosecutor will have to decide whether he has enough circumstantial evidence against either one of them to bring an indictment."

"And if he doesn't, they'll be home free."

"I've seen it happen," Marco said. "Kyle will still be in trouble for wielding a weapon, but more than likely he'll be tried as a juvenile for that."

I shook my head. "Wow. I'm still in shock. That kid was serious about protecting his mom. I think he would have shot you if you'd tried to call the police earlier."

"Which one do you think caused Bev's death?" Marco asked.

"Kyle, for sure."

"Because?"

"Because of how protective he is and how much he cares about Seedy, although I'm sure the horrible things his aunt said to him contributed to it, too. How about you?"

"I agree with you. Remember that Stacy originally told us Kyle had been having a lot of asthma attacks lately, and sneaking down to see the dogs could explain that. I can tell you right now, Sunshine, with the only witness who could verify that Kyle had been at the shelter dead, the prosecutor will have a devil of a time proving he was there."

"In a way, I'm glad, Marco. He's a kid yet, and kids have poor judgment. I don't think he meant for his aunt to die, but he'll still have to live with the results of his actions for the rest of his life, and that's severe punishment."

"On the other hand," Marco said, "if it was Stacy and no indictments come out of this, she'll never have to pay the price."

"Either way, she and Kyle will always know the truth, and that will haunt both of them."

Marco pulled up behind my Corvette in the public

parking lot and put his Prius in park. "Well, at least your mom can rest easy now, and we can get on with our wedding plans."

"But I won't see you tonight, right?"

"It doesn't make me happy to say this, Sunshine, but, no, not tonight."

I leaned over and gave him a kiss. "See you tomorrow, Salvare."

"See *you* tomorrow, Mrs. Salvare-to-be."

I got into my car smiling. Abby Knight Salvare. What a wonderful ring it had.

My cell phone rang. Still smiling, I pulled my phone out of my purse and checked the screen.

Grace Bingham?

My smile dissolved. Grace would never call after work unless something was wrong.

CHAPTER TWENTY-SIX

M y heart was in my throat as I answered Grace's call. "What happened?"

"Abby, love, do not panic. Where are you?"

"I'm sitting in my car in the parking lot, getting ready to drive home. Why?"

"Had you been at Down the Hatch, I would have suggested that you stop by the shop and take a look at the spindle, but it can wait till morning."

"Grace, you scared me to death. The least you can do is tell me why."

"Because the spindle is full, dear. Eighteen orders came in after you left. The flyers are working."

"Really?"

"Really." There was a big smile in her voice. "I wanted to share the joy with you. I know how worried you've been."

"That's great news, Grace! I'll have to come in early tomorrow to get started—it's my last day at the shop for more than a week. Or maybe I'll go back tonight and work on the orders since Marco is busy all evening anyway—or I can do both."

"Abby, love, take a breath. We'll manage it all tomorrow."

I was already out of the car and walking toward Franklin Street. "Thanks for calling, Grace. This is the second-best news of the day."

"What's the first?"

"We solved the case! Well, most of it anyway. I'll tell you and Lottie all about it in the morning. Right now, I need to call Mom and tell her she can stop worrying."

After assuring Grace I wouldn't stay at the shop until all hours of the night, I phoned my parents and got my mom at first ring. "Mom! You're off the hook. Marco and I solved the case."

"Oh, my goodness! Oh, honey, I'm so relieved, I have to sit down. You solved the case. How wonderful. I can't wait to tell your father. Who did it?"

"I'm ninety-nine percent sure it was Kyle, but his mom confessed to it, too, so the police will have to sort it out. Anyway, you don't need to worry about being called in for another interview. You can go back to creating your works of art."

"I can't tell you how much better I feel, honey—a huge weight has lifted off my shoulders—but I certainly do feel sorry for the Shaws."

"Me too, Mom. Whichever one of them is responsible acted in anger, never expecting that Bev would fall and break her neck. But what a terrible thing to live with."

I stopped outside of my shop and dug for my keys. "I'm at Bloomers now. I have to work on some orders that came in."

"Thanks for calling, Abigail. I already feel the creative

juices flowing again. Ideas are practically spilling out of my head. I can't wait to get back to my craft room and make something new for your shop."

Yay?

"Oh, before you go, honey, I have some good news for *you*. Tara told me she found a nice young couple who want to adopt Seedy. She said she knows these people well, so she'll be able to take the puppy to visit his mother. Isn't that terrific? I know how worried you've been. See you tomorrow at the rehearsal, honey."

I hung up the phone with a sigh, a not-altogether-happy sigh either. Seedy was safe, and I was free to go on my honeymoon without worrying about her life hanging in the balance. Why didn't that feel terrific?

Friday

I climbed out of bed bright and early and got to the shop by seven a.m., only to find that Lottie had beat me to it. She was humming along to a country-and-western song playing on the radio in the workroom while she de-thorned rose stems for an arrangement.

"Isn't it a glorious day?" she sang out as I dropped my purse on my desk. "Glor-i-ous! I saw that you were here last night working, but look at that spindle, sweetie. A new passel of orders came in overnight."

Grace sailed in with a tray in her hands. "Coffee is ready!"

I took a cup off the tray. "You came in early, too?"

"We've got a lot to do today," she said. "Don't forget we have to prepare your wedding flowers, too."

Eep. There *was* a lot to do. But I was so happy about all the orders that I dug right in, filling in Lottie and

Grace about solving the case as we worked. We were so busy that we continued straight through the morning. Unbelievably, I even found myself having to cancel lunch with Marco.

"That's okay, babe," he said over the phone. "I knew those flyers would do the trick. Anyway, I was going to have to take a rain check myself. I've got to wrap up my case today, so I'll see you at the chapel at six."

Marco had checkmated my rain check. Feeling slightly miffed, I sat for a moment with the phone in my hand, staring at a photo of us in Key West that I'd pinned to the bulletin board. I sure hoped he made more time for me after we were married.

By midafternoon we'd finished all but the last fourteen orders. I hadn't worked that hard in a long time and, although I was tired, I felt good.

"Abby," Lottie said, "take a look at this address."

I went around the table and read the slip of paper she'd placed beside the arrangement she'd just started. On the *Delivery Address* line, it said *6004 North Concord Avenue.* "What's wrong with it?"

"Look at the last one I did."

I checked the slip attached to the arrangement waiting to go into the cooler: *6004 North Concord Avenue.*

"Same address, right?" Lottie asked. "How about the next one?"

I took the top slip off the spindle and read it. "Six thousand four North Concord Avenue." I checked the slip of paper I'd set beside the stems I'd just pulled and it, too, had the same address.

Mystified now, I took off the rest of the orders and fanned them out on the table. They all had the same address. I said to Lottie in bewilderment, "What's going on?"

"Could it be a joke?" Lottie asked.

I sat down at the computer and did a search for the address. It came up: *Blaine Manufacturing*. That didn't sound like a joke to me. Still, for a woman who claimed to hate flowers, there sure were a lot of them going to Dayton's company's address.

Determined to find out who was behind it, we loaded all fifteen arrangements in our rental van and I drove them over to the Blaine complex myself.

"I have a large floral delivery for this address," I told the woman at the reception desk, "but I'm not sure who ordered them."

"I'll take care of that, Abby," she said with a smile. "Here's your check, and I'll have someone meet you outside."

I glanced at the signature on the check. There it was, in precise handwriting: Dayton Blaine. "Forgive me for saying so," I said to the receptionist, "but Miss Blaine hates flowers. Why would she order so many?"

Instead of replying, the receptionist pulled a small brown paper–wrapped package from beneath the counter and handed it to me. "This is for you, too."

Clearly she wasn't going to give me any answers. "Can I speak to Miss Blaine?"

"She's in a meeting," the receptionist said, reaching for the ringing phone. "Have a nice day."

I looked at the check in my hand. I certainly would.

Once all the flowers were out of my van, I shut the door and started the motor, then glanced over at the package on the passenger seat and turned the motor off again. I had to know what was inside. Maybe that's where I'd find some answers.

I tore off the brown paper and found a hardback book

inside. It was entitled *How to Be an Effective Business-woman* by Dayton Blaine.

I opened the cover to see if she'd written anything and found one of my flyers with a note attached. In Dayton's precise handwriting, it said:

> *Dear rookie:*
> *The no-kill policy issue will be tabled indefinitely.*
> *It's not always about the money.*
> *Good luck.*
>
> *D.B.*

I didn't stop smiling for hours.

We finished up the wedding flowers at closing time, after which I ran home and changed into a pair of cream-colored pants and a turquoise blouse and then rode to the church with Nikki. There we found the minister and wedding party gathered in the chapel—everyone, that was, except for Marco, Rafe, and their brother, Rico. It wasn't until we were all standing in our places at the front of the chapel that Marco strode in alone, looking handsome in a light blue shirt and dark jeans.

"Sorry," he said to me as he took his place at the altar. "We were left without two bartenders this evening, so Rafe and Rico had to fill in."

"How will they know what to do tomorrow?" I asked, feeling miffed again. I so wanted everything to be perfect.

"I will coach my sons. It won't be a problem," Francesca Salvare said. "Please don't worry, Bella."

"It'll be fine," Nikki whispered, standing to my left.

Jillian didn't seem to be concerned either, nor my parents. Marco gave my hand a reassuring squeeze.

Okay, then.

After we rehearsed, we went downstairs to the church hall for a feast of Francesca's homemade lasagna, garlic bread, Italian green beans, and tiramisu. I sat beside Marco at the long banquet table, listening to Francesca entertaining my parents with her funny stories about raising a large family and Nikki and Jillian discussing the latest fall fashions, and I felt bad that Marco's brothers were missing the dinner. I'd also hoped to meet Rico before the wedding.

"What are you thinking about?" Marco asked, his hand draped casually across my shoulder.

"How great it is to see everyone enjoying themselves," I replied, "and how much I love being here with you. How about you?"

"What am I thinking?" he mused, looking up at the ceiling. "I'm thinking that my life is about to change for-ever—and I'm a little nervous about that."

"Me too!"

He turned his head to gaze into my eyes. "But mostly I'm thinking about how much I love the gorgeous red-head seated to my left."

I glanced over my left shoulder. "Where is she? I want to meet her."

He smiled a full-on smile. "You *are* the prettiest woman in the room, you know."

I wasn't—Jillian had me beat by a mile—but as long as Marco thought so, I didn't care. He made me feel pretty.

Marco put the tip of his finger between my eyebrows. "Your worry line is gone."

It was! What a relief it wouldn't be messing up my wedding photos. I leaned in to look down the row of people. My mom's was gone, too.

We all pitched in to clean up, and then Marco and I went back to my apartment to load up my boxes. After unloading them at Marco's place, he walked me to my car, where he didn't linger long. "It won't always be this way, sweetheart. Trust me."

"It better not be."

He hugged me close, his cheek against my head. "Tomorrow's our big day, Abby. Are you sure you want to go through with it?"

"Are you?"

"I asked you first." He leaned back and smiled into my eyes. "Of course I do, Sunshine. I've never been more certain of anything."

"Me too, Marco." I laid my head against his shoulder and breathed in his essence, basking in the warmth of his embrace. I wanted to stay there forever.

After one last kiss, he said softly, "Get a good night's sleep and I'll see you tomorrow."

Saturday

What can any bride say about her wedding day besides *Aaaaaack!*

Hovering mother, photo-snapping father, annoying cousin, giggling niece, overconcerned best friend, breakfast you have no appetite for . . . make that lunch, as well, makeup application by annoying cousin and overconcerned best friend, and hair appointment. *Yes, I like the updo, I swear.* This was followed by the wedding gown squeeze — *French fries, I hate you* — assistants wielding flowers, Mom supplying her pearl necklace and drop earrings as the "something borrowed," a quote from Grace about love, a last photo with Nikki as my roommate, tears and tissues and makeup repairs, final gown adjustments, and—finally!—a nervous ride to the church in hovering mother's car.

Except we were headed in the wrong direction.

"Mom?" Nikki and I were in the backseat of her car, a mélange of white lace and pale yellow satin. "You're going south."

"We have to go back to our house to get the van," Mom said. "Your dad wants to ride with us."

They had just decided that now? *Deep breath, Abby. That'a girl.*

Nikki patted my arm. "Don't worry. They can't start without you."

Good thing.

I held out my left hand and took a long look at my diamond engagement ring. Soon it would be joined by a wedding band, just a simple band, but a circle of gold that held so much promise.

I looked through the window and sighed wistfully. The sun was shining, the sky was blue with a few puffs of white clouds, the trees were still full and green, the temperature was seventy-five degrees . . . the perfect setting for an outdoor wedding, if only that little gazebo hadn't blown down.

At my sigh, Nikki said, "Doing okay?"

"Just thinking." Thinking about how my life was going to change. About how fun it would be to sign my name Abby Salvare . . . make that Abby Knight Salvare. About how safe and secure I would feel lying in Marco's arms every night.

And wondering. About how Marco was doing right now. About how my parents were handling their little girl getting married. About how good it would be to have Marco come home to me every day. About how uncomfortable it would feel to use his bachelor apartment as my new residence. About how I wished I could tell him that but didn't want to hurt his feelings.

Nikki gave my hand a squeeze. "I'm so excited. The wedding will be amazing."

We pulled up in the driveway of my parents' house, and Mom hurried inside. A moment later, she waved us in from the front door.

"What's wrong?" I called.

"Your dad wants a photo of you in the living room," she called back.

I glanced down at my full, flouncy skirt, which had taken forever to stuff inside the backseat, and sighed. "Couldn't we have done this earlier?" I said to Nikki.

"Go on," she urged, pushing against my arm. "Your dad is probably sad about giving away his little girl."

I grabbed handfuls of lacy white material and climbed as gracefully as possible out of the car, with Nikki making sure my fingertip veil stayed in place. I had no bouquet to carry. Grace and Lottie had taken everything over to the chapel.

Mom held the door open while I stepped inside. My dad was nowhere to be seen.

"In the backyard," Mom said. "Your dad changed his mind."

I wanted to say, *We have no time for this,* but I knew it was important to my parents, so I held my tongue. To help calm me down, Nikki kept up a constant stream of conversation as we walked through the living room and into the kitchen, where platters of hors d'oeuvres were laid out on the kitchen table.

"What's all the food for?" I asked, tempted to take a nibble.

"Some people might stop by here afterward," Mom said. "I like to be prepared."

Nikki took my arm and pulled me toward the back door. "Move it, lady. There's no time to waste."

Mom stepped out ahead of us, and I started to follow, but Nikki pulled me back and gave me a big hug. Since she was taller than me, I left a lipstick smudge on her neck.

"Sorry," I said, using my thumb to wipe it off.

"You look beautiful, best friend," she said, smiling. "Count to five and then follow me."

"Why count to five?" But she was already gone.

Somewhere outside, Pachelbel's Canon in D began playing. The music swelled as I walked out the door. I stopped and blinked in surprise. Ahead I saw a sea of beaming faces—my parents, my aunt and uncle, Tara, Nikki, Francesca Salvare, Rafe, the mystery brother, Rico, who looked like an older version of Marco, his sister, Gina, and her family, my brothers and sisters-in-law, Jillian and Claymore, my minister, and Grace and Lottie.

Before I could express my surprise, they parted down the middle so I could see Marco waiting at the end of a path that had been strewn with rose petals. With his gleaming dark hair and deep brown eyes, his black tux and white shirt, he looked more handsome than ever a James Bond had looked at his tip-top best. My heart swelled with love. That man was going to be my husband!

Then I noticed what was behind him and gasped. It

was a little white gazebo surrounded by vases of white, yellow, and pink roses. More flowers lined the two steps up into the small structure. And even though we were in a fenced-in yard, everything was *perfect*.

"Marco was determined to give you an outdoor wedding," Mom said.

"He and his brothers have been laboring back here for days," Dad said, wheeling up to take his place beside me. "Rico came to town early just to help."

"Lottie and Grace worked all evening yesterday to make the arrangements," Mom added.

Tears filled my eyes as I took in the scene before me. Now I understood everything.

Across the distance between us, I smiled at Marco with all the love in my heart, and he smiled back. Nikki and Jillian, escorted by Marco's brothers, walked up the aisle and slid into their places. Our minister went up the two stairs to stand inside the gazebo, facing me, Bible in hand. Lottie stepped forward to hand me my bouquet of pale yellow roses. Grace gave me her serene smile and a queenly nod, while a photographer snapped photos and a videographer began filming.

"Well, Abracadabra, shall we?" Dad asked. He had tears in his eyes, too.

I took a deep breath and let it out. "Let's go, Dad."

As we moved up the aisle at a slow, stately pace, I had to subdue the urge to pick up my skirts and dash straight for Marco, whooping with joy. But that was the old Abby. The new Abby was going to be much calmer and way more dignified.

Yeah, right.

We halted in front of the gazebo, and Dad gave me away, placing my hand in Marco's. The music stopped,

Dad wheeled back to his spot beside my mom, and Marco and I faced the minister.

"Dearly beloved," Reverend Williams began.

"Wait," Marco said, looking around. "The ring bearer isn't here."

"Marco," I whispered, "we don't have a ring bearer."

He took my shoulders and aimed me toward the house. As if on cue, Tara came out the back door carrying a bundle wrapped in a pink blanket. I glanced over at Jillian with a scowl and whispered, "If you brought a sack of potatoes—"

"Look," Marco said to me, pointing toward Tara.

She put the bundle on the ground and removed the blanket. There stood Seedy, wearing a yellow collar with a big yellow bow on top, looking around at all the people, clearly as bewildered as I was.

"She's our ring bearer?" I asked.

"That's right." Marco took my hand in his. "She's ours, Abby."

My heartbeat quickened. "What?"

"Ours. You know, as in *yours* and *mine.*"

"But"—I took a breath to still my racing heart—"Tara said a nice young couple was adopting her."

"We're the nice young couple."

Marco had done all this for me? I wanted to tug on my ears to make sure I was hearing correctly. "I thought you couldn't have pets at your apartment building."

He smiled into my eyes, his own shimmering with love. "Then I guess we'll be house hunting when we get back from our honeymoon."

"Really?"

"If you can stay away from murder investigations that long."

Was there any reason we couldn't do both?

"Aunt Abby," Tara called, "Seedy hasn't spotted you yet. Call her."

I bent over and held out my hand. "Seedy! Come here."

The little dog stared at me for a second; then, shaggy tail wagging fiercely, she hobbled up the aisle as fast as her three legs would carry her. When she got close, I saw that our wedding rings were tied to her collar.

I scooped Seedy up in my arms, and she licked my face, making me and everyone else laugh—except for Jillian, who gasped in horror, probably at the thought of the makeup she had so carefully applied being ruined. Seedy wiggled with happiness and gave me another lick. Her patchy fur was downy soft and smelled like strawberries. Someone had given her a bath.

"Hey, Seedy," Marco said, scratching her under the chin. "Are you happy you've got a family?"

The dog responded by licking his wrist.

Marco nodded to the minister. "*Now* we're ready."

"Abs," Jillian whispered, "put the dog down."

I shook my head. So what if I got a few paw prints on my dress? What did that matter when this loving little dog was mine?

Make that ours.

Abby and Marco return from their honeymoon and discover a dead body in the basement.

Read on for a sneak peek at the next Flower Shop Mystery,

Throw in the Trowel

Available in February 2014 from Obsidian in paperback and as an e-book.

Prologue

June 1975

Look at him sitting there in the bowels of the old building, propped against a sawhorse, drunk out of his mind. Don't turn away in disgust. Isn't this the opportunity you've wished for? No one's around. You've got an hour before dark. Do it!

Tears ran down my face as I stood behind him, scalding, bitter tears of anger and betrayal and confusion. What I was contemplating was wrong, terribly, terribly wrong. I loved the bastard. How could I even think of ending his life?

And if you don't? How long will you let him continue to wound you? How much more of his neglect and duplicity can you bear?

But this wasn't just about me anymore or I might have been able to endure his deceit. I might have been able to step back and wait for him to slowly self-destruct. But I'd never know that now.

My grip tightened on the handle of the trowel, slick with sweat. My stomach roiled.

Do it! What are you waiting for?

CHAPTER ONE

Present day

Hey! You there. Abby Christine Knight! Snap to it, girl. You've got to get to work. The honeymoon is over.

Correction. Let's make that Abby Christine Knight Salvare.

Pep talk over, I yawned, scratched my head, and squinted at my reflection in the bathroom mirror. A short, sleepy, freckle-faced redhead squinted back, a bit bleary-eyed but generally happy. No, make that extremely happy, because I was a married woman now. Me. A married woman. Hitched to my dream guy in a fantastic wedding ceremony, followed by an incredible honeymoon in Key West, Florida. Wow.

I sighed wistfully at the thought of those stunning sunsets over the Gulf of Mexico, primrose pink, golden-rod yellow, pansy purple — a florist's dream — as I'd stood arm in arm with Marco watching the sun melt into the ocean. I remembered holding his hand as we parasailed high over the island and neighboring Sunset Key, pointing out the places we knew. I sighed again, recalling how we'd biked along the Atlantic side of the island as pelicans dove for fish, and strolled along Duval Street licking gelato cones, and toured the coral reef in a glass-bottom boat, and Jet-Skied across turquoise wat—

I leaned closer to the mirror. Could those be bags under my eyes? Did people get bags at the age of twenty-seven?

Confession time. I was extremely happy and also extremely tired and, if truth be told, just a little bit— minuscule even, hardly worth mentioning but yes, I'd have to say it—annoyed. Marco had rolled to the middle of the bed during the night, taking up more than half of the mattress, forcing me to squeeze onto one edge and sleep fitfully. Plus his bedroom had too much morning light coming in behind the old window shades, waking me at the crack of dawn. And forget about prying my clothes from his small bedroom closet, where I hardly had room for two shirts and a pair of jeans.

I splashed my face with water, hoping that would rev me up.

Okay, then, maybe coffee would do the trick. Marco would probably have a pot already brewed and a cup waiting for me on the kitchen counter. I just needed to look presentable for my gorgeous groom. Unlike him, I didn't roll out of bed looking camera ready. I didn't even roll out of bed. It was more like a tumble.

I balanced my hairbrush on the edge of the sink, shoved the hand soap dispenser as far back into the corner of the narrow countertop as possible, zipped open my flower-print makeup kit, and laid out my blush, eye shadow, mascara, and lip gloss. They barely fit in the small space.

"Good morning, Sunshine," Marco said, standing in the doorway, looking indecently hot in his pajama bottoms. "Coffee's made. Want to join me for a bowl of oatmeal?"

"Do you have toast?"

He shook his head. "Oatmeal is it. You like oatmeal, don't you?"

Had he ever seen me eat oatmeal? At my apartment I had kept a box of oatmeal for him. Why didn't he have toast for me? But, hey, this was Day One of our brand-spanking-new life together (honeymoons didn't count), so I forgave him and gazed at him with tired but adoring eyes. "I'd love to join you. And maybe we can shop for groceries after Bloomers closes today."

Marco stepped in behind me for what I thought was going to be a hug. Instead, he opened the medicine cabinet in front of me with one hand and began to rummage through it with the other.

"Let me get out of your way," I said, trying to duck under his arm.

"No, you're fine. I'm making room for your things."

How considerate was that? "Thank you, Marco."

He removed a box of bandages and a bottle of ibuprofen. "There you go."

If he thought that would do it, my helpful hubby had a whole lot to learn.

My hairbrush slid into the sink. I grabbed for it and knocked over the tube of lip gloss, sending it plummeting to the floor. "You know what we need in here?" I pointed to empty wall space above the toilet tank. "A cabinet."

"We need a house, Abby. A cabinet isn't going to give us the kind of space we want."

"In the short run, it will. We're not going to find a house overnight."

A wet tongue licked my ankle. I glanced down and saw Seedy gazing up at me as if to say, "Hey, don't leave me out!"

And doggy makes three.

Marco had adopted Seedy the day before we got married as a surprise wedding gift. She was the homeliest dog I'd ever seen, with patchy brown-and-white fur, large, pointed ears with tufts of hair that fanned out at the top, a small, pointed muzzle, protruding lower teeth, and the kicker—pardon the pun—only three legs. I'd first seen the dog while investigating a murder at the animal shelter. My niece, Tara, had wanted to adopt both Seedy and her adorable pup, Seedling, to keep them from being separated, but her parents had said an emphatic no. They'd let her have the puppy but not his mom.

Abused, malnourished, and timid around most people, Seedy had instantly bonded with me, even though I'm more of a cat person. From that moment on, I wasn't able to get the little mutt out of my mind, especially after I'd learned that she was in danger of being put down, due to her unadoptable status. Because I hadn't thought Marco would want to start off our new life with a dog, and because I'd known that his landlady wouldn't accept pets, I'd tried my best to find her a home. But eventually I'd run out of options. That was when my hero had come to Seedy's rescue.

Fortunately, Marco's landlady was allowing the dog to

stay, with the understanding that we would find a new dwelling as soon as possible. And now that we were back from our honeymoon, the house hunt could begin.

While I was spooning oatmeal into a bowl from the pot on the stove, Marco's cell phone rang. He took the call in the living room, where I could hear the floor planks creak as he paced. His apartment occupied the second floor of an old two-story house, and while it had high ceilings, decent-sized rooms, and sturdy plaster walls, it also had noisy floors, drafty windows, and scant counter space in both the kitchen and bathroom.

I heard Marco grumbling to the person on the other end. Whatever the call was about, it couldn't be good.

"That was Rafe," he told me a few minutes later, pouring himself a cup of coffee.

I knew two things instantly. First, Rafe, Marco's younger brother, called only when something at Marco's bar, Down the Hatch Bar and Grill, had gone wrong. Second, Rafe was not the most reliable person you'd ever want to meet. Which was why Marco's next statement was alarming.

"He said there's a plumbing problem in the basement, but he's been handling it."

"So the problem is ongoing?"

"Apparently it's in the process of being repaired. Rafe wanted to prepare me because the old cement floor had to be torn up to locate the problem. I'm heading down to the bar now to see what they found."

A hard shudder ran through my body. That happened when I was cold or when my sixth sense vibrated a warning. Since I wasn't cold, I said, "Marco, be careful."

"Abby, it's an old basement. No boogeymen down there, I promise."

"I've just got a bad feeling about it."

He gave me a kiss and then hugged me close. "You worry too much."

Seedy let out a little yip and leaned against my legs. As Marco headed for the door, I scooped her up, felt her trembling, and wondered if she had picked up something bad, too.